an open door

a novel

by

anne leigh parrish

an open door
Copyright © 2022 Anne Leigh Parrish
All Rights Reserved.
Published by Unsolicited Press.
Printed in the United States of America.
First Edition.

No part of this book may be used or reproduced in any manner whatsoever without written permission except in the case of brief quotations embodied in critical articles or reviews.

Attention schools and businesses: for discounted copies on large orders, please contact the publisher directly.

For information contact:
Unsolicited Press
Portland, Oregon
www.unsolicitedpress.com
orders@unsolicitedpress.com
619-354-8005

Cover Design: Kathryn Gerhardt
Editor: Kristen Marckmann
ISBN: 978-1-956692-34-1

To John, Bob, Lauren, Lacey and Sam

contents

an open door

chapter one

On Friday afternoons the mood in the typing pool was a gathering storm. Heads bent tensely over keyboards. Machines clacked. High on the wall hung a big clock like a cold sun above the room. As the hour hand moved toward five the atmosphere became electric. Edith's supervisor, Miss Grett, running the show from behind her desk felt it, too, though all she ever did was take a quick, furtive glance at herself in the small mirror she kept in her plain, sensible handbag.

Edith returned to the page she was working on.

> *August 20, 1948*
>
> *My Dear Mr. Undersecretary,*
>
> *As you know, in my capacity as Ambassador, I can only refer your request to the Belgian Counsel for Immigrant Affairs. It will be my pleasure to make such a referral. You may expect a response at the Counsel's earliest convenience.*

Dull, dull, dull! Week after week of typing requests for a conference room; or a list of those invited to a reception; or a summary of the latest report from the Belgian Board of Trade. The interesting subjects were off-limits to her, and to all the other girls in the room.

Edith didn't know much about their backgrounds other than they were all college-educated, but she thought her work as a mapmaker during the war would have allowed her to obtain the necessary security clearance to see more sensitive discourse. Perhaps the others had done their share of secret stuff, too, and were similarly denied. Who knew? Walter would say that wasn't the kind of thing you could discuss.

She'd made no friends in the two months she'd worked there, probably because she didn't want to talk about herself. There was always that phase of polite inquiry when you got to know someone, wasn't there? She didn't like answering personal questions and could easily avoid them—except at that inane luncheon last month. One of the typists had gotten engaged. Dora, it was. How did Edith end up sitting next to her? On her other side was Lillian, plain as a post, who looked cross every time she glanced at Edith because Edith was pretty, with dark hair and skin so pale Walter sometimes called her Snow White.

Lillian asked Edith if she had a fella. The reply stuck in her throat like a piece of stale bread. All Edith could do was shake her head. Lillian seemed pleased by her response and by the big plate of spaghetti in front of her. After that, Edith steered clear. She assumed they thought her a snob, or neurotic, or in the grip of some devastating sorrow that made socializing too painful to bear. Who cared?

The hour came, and the storm broke. Typewriters fell silent; excited voices rose. Chairs were pushed out and then back in. Drawers opened and closed. Shoes smacked across the tile floor. There were no coats or jackets to pull on, no umbrellas to pluck from the many stands positioned near the door. The weather was hot, sticky, and horrible, as only late summer in New York City can be, or so said Miss Grett, who didn't complain much as a rule.

Edith removed her document and put it in the wooden box on her desk. You weren't allowed to leave anything in your typewriter when you left for the day. She wished she'd had time to finish it because it was overdue. She'd been too distracted by the coming weekend and the thing that always cast it down—another letter from Walter, which she was sure to find when she got home. She'd traveled quite a distance in herself because of those letters. First, she dreaded getting them. Then if one didn't come on the usual days, which were Tuesday and Friday, she worried. When his tone was neutral and pleasant, she was glad. Lately, he sounded unhappy.

From several rows away came a chorus of female squeals. A blonde typist in a pale blue suit extended her left hand to display an engagement ring. She must have just slipped it on because if it had been on her finger all day the fuss being made now would have happened before. The girl looked happy. The girls around her looked happy too, or was there some thin veil of jealousy in their eyes? Dora had gotten her share of hungry looks. Everyone wanted to get married. When it happened to someone you knew, and not to you, weren't you a little frustrated? Edith didn't know. She'd never felt that way.

On her way out she said, "Congratulations," and got warm smiles from those who heard. In the hall, she passed the Belgian Ambassador's office. The door was closed, and spirited classical music played on a phonograph inside—Beethoven's third symphony, if she had to guess. She'd only laid eyes on the ambassador once or twice. She assumed being assigned to his department meant she'd see him daily, but the only one who did was Miss Grett. Monsieur Parthon was pretty much what one would expect—middle-aged, plump, balding, and with a splendid handlebar mustache. He'd called her "Mademoiselle" and nodded as he went by. That was over a month ago.

She stepped onto the sidewalk. The heat rose from the asphalt. Sweat collected on the back of her neck, just above the collar of her dress. The walk from the United Nations to the public library took her along East 42nd Street. In cool weather, the walk took about fifteen minutes. Today it would be longer. At the intersection of Park Avenue and 42nd Street cars were stopped in all directions. The traffic light was broken; the sidewalk was thick with people waiting to cross. A policeman blew his whistle and waved his arms. Some said it was a city's noise that made you crazy and want to bolt for the quiet countryside; or the maddening nudge of the crowds; or the dirt that drove you into the washroom to rinse your hands the first chance you got, then, at home, to put your stockings right into the sink; even your handkerchief seemed to pick up soot, tucked away in your purse. Despite all that, Edith loved New York, though she hadn't at first. After Cambridge, it was like watching horses stampede, and thinking all the time you'd be crushed, or caught up in a frenzy you couldn't stop.

She crossed the street and kept going until she climbed the stone steps of the library. She went to the holds desk where her two titles were waiting. Both *The Heart is a Lonely Hunter* and *A Tree Grows in Brooklyn* had received rave reviews. Walter said reviews shouldn't be the reason one read a particular book, but how else could she know if it were worth her time?

She stood with her books and waited for the uptown bus in the shade of an office building. The bus was late. Every bus in New York City was always late. The subway was no better, but who'd take the subway this time of year? Finally, the bus lurched into view, and of course, it was packed. She boarded and found a seat near the back vacated by a man who remembered at the last minute he wanted to get off. He yelled to the driver and the driver yelled back, "Take it easy, Mac! How far can I go in this jam?"

Why hadn't everyone left town for vacation? Walter wrote Cambridge was still full of people because the summer term hadn't let out yet. She supposed Boston might be empty. Walter hadn't said. He didn't venture across the Charles.

As the bus rolled up Central Park West, traffic thinned. Edith got off on 86th Street and walked west, toward Riverside Drive and the apartment building where she lived with Walter's Aunt Margaret.

Sure enough, there was a new letter from Walter in the box. Once read, it would join the others in her dresser drawer. At the end of the month, she would tie the bundle with a blue silk ribbon. After a while, if they piled up, she'd move them into an empty shoebox.

Edith walked up the two flights of stairs. The elevator had been out of order for three days. The concierge was on vacation, and his nephew was hard to reach, so the tenants complained to each other. Mrs. Braddock declared she simply could not manage the climb to her third-story apartment with her arthritis, though Edith had observed her doing it, with good energy and effort. Mr. Pole said it was the fault of the Russians. They were out to destroy the infrastructure of American cities. Edith found this laughable. The Russians had enough problems of their own. They'd come out of the war badly, much worse than the Americans had. People just needed something to be unhappy about, which was so silly given unhappiness came to us all, unbidden and cruel.

Aunt Margaret was out. She had a bridge club. She would return woozy from gin and full of good cheer. Her disposition was sunny unless her thoughts turned to her late husband, dead now eleven years. He'd keeled over at his desk, working late one night, and wasn't found until the morning. Aunt Margaret thought he was stepping out on her—she'd had her suspicions for some time. She hated thinking about all the hours she spent wishing him ill when he was already dead. She hoped his soul forgave her. She still tried to forgive herself.

Edith stood before the tall picture window in the living room and watched the summer light dance on the Hudson. Growing up in a land-locked state made her fascinated by large bodies of water. She longed to travel abroad, sail for days on a huge, luxurious ocean liner, walk along cobblestone streets, hear violin music pour from open windows, drink rich wine, devour sweet cakes—these were her dreams and fantasies of Europe.

She went into the kitchen and removed two pork chops wrapped in brown paper from the refrigerator. It was her turn to cook. Aunt Margaret was scrupulous about doing her share in the kitchen. She'd had a full-time cook before the war, but since then good help had been so hard to find. She'd managed as best she could on her own, dining out a lot with friends, or in their homes, and later, when Edith moved in, she tried her hand at some simple dishes she'd made when she was first married. Edith wished she wouldn't. Her meat was always tough, vegetables boiled to mush, and everything had too much salt. Edith suspected Aunt Margaret's heavy smoking made her taste buds crave the stimulation salt provided. She put the chops on a plate to bring them to room temperature. Some butter, flour, and chicken broth would make a nice gravy. There were peas she would shell. There were also two plump russet potatoes. She couldn't decide if they should be mashed or baked and decided to bake them. She lit the oven.

She poured herself a glass of scotch from the bottle in the cabinet. She learned the habit of a nightly drink from Walter, who allowed himself two, sometimes more, depending on his day. He was often tense. Harvard Law School was demanding, and his admission through the GI Bill made him question his ability and wonder if they'd made a mistake in letting him in. Edith wished he had more confidence in himself. He was a bright, capable guy. Would he have been able to break so many Japanese codes, otherwise? And what of all those medals on his chest? They didn't give those out to idiots.

She washed the potatoes and put them in the oven. Aunt Margaret would be home any minute. She probably wouldn't be hungry with all that liquor in her.

The telephone rang. It sat on a small table in the hall. Edith didn't get up. She didn't want to talk to anyone. It couldn't be important, in any case. Bad news would have come in a telegram. The ringing stopped, then resumed.

Edith went to the phone and lifted the receiver.

"Is that you, dear?" Aunt Margaret asked as if anyone else would answer that number.

"Yes."

"I'm running late. An old friend of Laura's dropped in, and we're going to play a few more hands."

"All right."

"What's the matter? You sound funny."

"I'm fine."

The sound of ice rattled in a glass.

"Well, I better get back. Don't hold dinner for me," Aunt Margaret said.

"I won't. I'll see you later."

After she hung up, Edith turned off the stove, removed the potatoes, and put the pork chops back in the refrigerator. She wasn't hungry. The heat flattened her appetite. She'd lost almost ten pounds over the summer. She didn't mind. She liked having a good waistline. She finished her drink, went into the living room, and turned on the radio. She sat down on the sofa and slipped off her shoes. Energetic swing flowed from the speaker, and she was with Walter and their classmates at graduation, dancing to the rhythm of the band on the makeshift stage, rejoicing in being young, alive, whole, all the while knowing these conditions were transient.

Since VJ day, everyone had been looking for a way back to the feelings of those days, but those days were gone forever, replaced with the grim reality that peace was itself a tricky business and awfully hard to maintain, especially in a world where Little Boy and Fat Man could fall from the sky and set the world on fire.

She was low for days afterward. Newspaper photos were relentless. The world hadn't been truly altered until that moment. She cried and begged to understand. Walter cited necessity.

"Necessity? Are you *insane*?" She'd come close to screaming.

He used his familiar tack—she spoke in ignorance—it was he who really knew the score. Seeing her color rise, he then said he admired her compassion. It was a beautiful trait in a woman and suggested the loving mother she would eventually become.

How could he talk of children, at a time like that? Who would bring children into this world?

He was dumbfounded.

"Every woman wants to be a mother," he said.

He'd always sought to guide her, to instruct her. They fought bitterly once about this, and he admitted she knew her own mind.

Another time, he said he wished she didn't read so much. He wasn't sure it was good for her. This, from a man who loved literature! She thought of the two titles she'd brought home from the library, and how she would read late into the night and for most of the weekend. Then she remembered Aunt Margaret had invited friends for tea on Saturday afternoon, a woman and her adult son. Oh, drat! Entertaining strangers was the last thing Edith wanted to do. Poor Aunt Margaret thought herself an excellent judge of character and was certain Edith would enjoy this young man's company. Aunt Margaret had assured her he was quite charming. His mother and Aunt Margaret went way back. They served on relief committees together in the thirties and later turned their energies to the war effort. Edith wondered if she could invent a good excuse, perhaps fake a blinding headache? She used to do that with Walter until her sense of duty got the better of her.

The music changed. She envied it. To become something else in an instant—poof!

She was a bit tipsy.

"Too bad about that," she said.

The light dropped, and she turned her head to take in the river. Its surface undulated so beautifully she was filled with sorrow. Or was it remorse?

What was Walter doing right now? Researching some esoteric rule of property, no doubt—zoning, easements, and rights-of-way. He was interning for a law professor. He'd jumped at the chance. The professor's recommendation could very well land him his first job out of school.

Walter's nose was too big, and his front teeth too crooked for braces to correct. But they saved him, those teeth. He wanted to join the Air Force and the oxygen mask wouldn't fit easily over his mouth. He was sensitive about his appearance, though he was a handsome man. It was his manner he should worry about, Edith thought. Sometimes at a party, he drank too much and dropped his "g"s. His laugh was more like a bark. The oversized nose turned red. Someone once called him Rudolph, but he hadn't heard. Once, he dropped a cracker on the carpet and she crushed it to crumbs with her shoe. Then she stood there to keep it covered until the room thinned.

The telephone rang again, then stopped.

Edith made herself a piece of toast and a fried egg. Walter loved her fried eggs but fretted about the amount of butter she used. He'd had bad skin as a teenager and was leery of food he believed would clog his pores. Edith told him to wash his face twice a day and to shower regularly. She said he smelled bad, so bad she urged him to shave his underarms. It wasn't something men did, he said. Well, perhaps a serious swimmer. Someone who competed, won medals.

Medal shmedal, she'd said. But he shaved them. Then he complained of how bad the itch was a few days afterward. She didn't urge him to improve himself after that, though there were many times she might have, like when he didn't have a handkerchief during a bad spell of hay fever. She caught him wiping his nose on his sleeve and wanted to box his ears. Later, she thought her response overly hostile. She bought him a set of handkerchiefs, washed, and ironed them. Yes, just as well as his mother would have.

Aunt Margaret came through the door calling "Yoo-hoo!"

"In here."

"Laura's daughter ran off with a Chinaman. Can you believe that?"

"A Communist?"

"I'd assume so."

Aunt Margaret dropped down on the other end of the sofa and patted her face with a lace handkerchief.

"It's murder out there," she said.

"Yes."

"Have you eaten?"

"Yes. I don't think there are any Red Chinese in New York. Unless they're with the UN," Edith said.

"Oh, it's probably all some nonsense. Laura had had a few."

Aunt Margaret's diamond bracelet caught the light. Her brooch, in the shape of a peacock, was made of diamonds, too. Edith didn't know why she wore such expensive things just to play bridge, but that was her way. One morning, just after Edith arrived, she threw an elegant satin coat over her nightgown to go down to the lobby to get the paper before the bellman brought it up. Aunt Margaret liked to be noticed. Edith did, too. She was just no good at it.

She remembered the woman and son who were due tomorrow.

"I don't think we have any fresh cream for your friends," she said. Aunt Margaret looked blank. "The ones you invited to tea," Edith added.

"Oh, that stupid milkman!"

"You didn't write it on the order."

"What did he deliver, then?"

"Eggs."

"Well, we'll break an egg in our tea and be very . . . oh, I don't know. There must be some dreary country where that's a cherished custom."

"Where eggs are in short supply, sadly."

Aunt Margaret removed a gold case from her beaded clutch. She plucked out a cigarette from it, patted it against her opposite forearm, then lit it with a charming silver lighter decorated with the head of a dragon. Edith loved that lighter. Every time she saw it, she wanted to start smoking again. Aunt Margaret inhaled deeply, gratefully, mindlessly. Her gloved hand (gloves in this heat!) reached carelessly for the heavy crystal ashtray on the marble-topped coffee table by her chair. She put the ashtray in her lap and kicked off her high heels.

"You're a clever girl," she told Edith.

"Yes, I am."

"But not modest."

"What good is modesty?"

"What good indeed?"

Edith loved bantering with Aunt Margaret. Her gaiety and frivolity made Cambridge seem like a dream. Sometimes it felt as if she'd never lived there, never had things go wrong, and would never want anything more than what she had just then.

Late that night, alone in her room, Edith read Walter's letter. It closed differently from the others. Rather than *All Best* he wrote *Darling, I implore you. The time has come for you to return to the marriage.*

chapter two

Edith pretended she was surprised, though she'd known for weeks what Walter was going to say. Her roommate, Mary Jane, was dating Walter's roommate, Tom, and Tom let it slip Walter was looking for a ring. When Edith heard, she was flooded with mixed feelings, among them an absurd prick of jealousy at the idea he might have another girl in mind. She mentioned this to Mary Jane and Mary Jane said, "Golly, Edith, how long have you two been dating?"

"Since high school."

"Well, I'd say he's good and hooked."

It made sense to think about getting married because the war was winding down. Then, in November 1944, when Walter popped the question, hearts were lighter than they had been in years, though Walter liked to remind everyone dark days still lay ahead. Edith said she needed time to think about his proposal because it didn't do to look too eager. But she wasn't eager, just aware another expected piece of her life's puzzle was falling into place.

Both Edith and Mary Jane were mapmakers. Housing in Washington was so scarce, everyone had to double up. For a while, they had a third girl in with them, Harriet, who also made maps. But then Harriet learned her fiancé had died in the South Pacific, and she went home to Oklahoma. Mary Jane said they could look for another roommate and keep their rent nice and low, but Edith didn't want to. She felt squeezed enough.

Tom and Walter were in Naval Intelligence and studied codes. This exhausted Walter, but never seemed to pull Tom down, almost as if it were a game to him, and real lives didn't attach to the outcome of the strange figures they scrutinized. Maybe that was healthy, Edith thought. When the world was falling apart, keeping an emotional distance was the only way to go about anything. She used those very words to Walter once, and he said, "But we're trying to keep the world from falling apart, don't you see?" In truth, Edith couldn't keep any distance at all. The maps she made from aerial photographs were of real places, occupied by real people, who bled real blood.

She accepted Walter's proposal the first week of December, and a few weeks later, traveled home to Urbana to visit her parents over Christmas. Walter's family lived in Urbana, too; both their fathers were at the University of Illinois, hers taught Math; Walter's father taught Philosophy. Walter couldn't get away just then and asked Edith to convey his regards to everyone.

The train was slow, and she couldn't afford a sleeper, so she dozed as much as possible, which was hard to do. Walter could sleep anywhere, lying or sitting. As fatigue closed her eyes, and nerves made them snap open, she found it an enviable talent. She fell asleep and woke up when a soldier with his arm in a sling entered the compartment. He sat across from Edith. He took out a cigarette and asked her if she could light it for him. She said she didn't have a match. He handed her a book of matches, which he kept in his shoe, for some reason. Edith thought that was a stupid place to put them, especially if it rained. He offered her a cigarette, and she declined. She returned to her book, Somerset Maugham's *The Razor's Edge*. She'd started reading it the week before, then became distracted by the thought of going home. Now the journey of Larry Darrell made her yearn. How nice it would be to have no responsibilities and to roam at will. Her mind wandered as her eyes dutifully passed over the words. What if she got off the train in Chicago and disappeared into the city? The idea of a new life somewhere else had great appeal. She could get a job somewhere, maybe as a waitress, but no, she was already on her feet all day at her drafting table. She could work on a switchboard and use a different name. She'd always thought she looked more like a Mable than an Edith. Her documents could have all been lost in a fire. Her parents were long dead. She would supply information about made-up people and get a new birth certificate. She'd forget about Walter and meet an exciting man whose greatest ambition was to devote himself to her happiness.

She closed her book and watched the world glide by the window.

She had to admit Walter had his merits. He was a good athlete and played a dynamite game of tennis. They understood each other, she thought, in a way other people didn't. She admired him because he was quick to figure things out. And he was funny. He made her laugh. She loved that he didn't take himself too seriously. Sometimes, when they were together, he would stop talking and just sit, watching her. She asked him why. He said looking at her face made him feel peaceful and strong at the same time. She said it was a lovely sentiment, but she wanted him to feel something else—passion. He felt it, clearly, but he always stopped himself. He refused to be carried away. Getting carried away was all she wanted in the moment. She wasn't so lustful she didn't plan ahead, reckon her cycle, determine when it would be safe to make love and when it would be more dangerous. But they never got to that point. He said it was important she come to the marriage bed a virgin. She tried not to laugh. She couldn't tell him the truth, which was she hadn't been a virgin for years.

During her first year at the University of Illinois, a graduate student in the English department caught her eye one day in the library. He'd taught a class she'd taken on American novelists the semester before. He'd thought of her ever since, he later confessed. His name was Reynolds. She was drawn to him because he was witty and different from other people she knew. He was from California and had been places—Europe, Asia, even parts of Africa—because his father was in the Foreign Service. His attitudes toward women were more democratic than she was used to, and their affair was riotous and hard to conceal. Edith lived at home and coming in late caused her mother, who feared she would end in ruin, to ask probing questions. She was dating Walter at the time, which was another issue that made seeing Reynolds maddeningly difficult. They managed, though, for several months. She wasn't in love with him, but she could see a life with him, so she asked him idly one day what he thought of that idea. He said it sounded lovely, but he was already married.

He hadn't brought his wife from California because they were having problems. That is, he was having problems.

"Like what?" Edith asked, in shock.

"I don't love her."

"Divorce her, then."

He couldn't. He believed in duty, and marriage was a duty if nothing else. Edith said one also had a duty to one's own happiness. And besides, how was he fulfilling his duty to his wife with all those miles between them?

"She doesn't have the embarrassment of divorce to contend with," he said.

Just a husband who cheated on her, Edith thought, as the soldier across from her got to his feet, announced he was mighty hungry and thought he might take himself down to the restaurant car for a spell.

Say, did Edith fancy joining him? She held up the flattened ham sandwich she'd been carrying in her purse for the last ten hours. He nodded and left the car.

The sandwich upset her stomach. Her head hurt, and so did her neck. She used the restroom and splashed water on her face. As she washed her hands, her engagement ring slipped over her knuckle and dropped into the metal sink. She'd thought to pull up the stopper, so it had no chance to disappear down the drain. She put the ring on the fourth finger of her right hand, where it fit better and didn't slip. When the wedding band went on, it would hold it in place, but until then it would stay where it was.

The train made its scheduled stop in Chicago. She thought again of getting off, never to be seen by anyone she knew. But Walter had contacts with the sort of government people who were probably very good at finding a missing person. She'd spend years always looking over her shoulder. People filed off the train; people filed on. She didn't want to marry Walter. She'd known that all along. She didn't want to marry anyone, but given she had to, Walter was as good a choice as any and probably better than most.

A couple of hours later, they pulled into the station at Urbana. She removed her suitcase from the overhead rack and joined the line of passengers waiting to exit. She'd told her parents she would find her own way from the station, and as she went toward the taxi stand someone behind her called her name. It was her father. There was no mistaking his loud, clipped, angry voice. She kept going, then knew it would be absurd to pretend she hadn't heard. He was a strong man and would overtake her easily in another moment, so she stopped, turned, and forced a look of cheerful surprise. He didn't smile back.

"Papa, how nice," she said and kissed his cheek. He took her arm but didn't offer to carry her suitcase.

"Walter couldn't come?" he asked as they wove through the crowd.

"No."

"His mother will be disappointed."

"I'm sure she wasn't expecting him. They know he's tied up."

In the car, driving those familiar streets past her elementary school, the church her father refused to attend so she and her mother stopped going, and the golf course where she and Walter played nine holes every chance they got, a growing sense of panic descended. She couldn't wait to get to the house and the protective layer of her mother's company. She remarked on the absence of snow on the ground, and her father said the winter had been mild. She asked how his semester had been and if the students were up to snuff. He said the proportion of idiots to agile minds was unusually high. He asked her nothing. Maybe he realized she couldn't talk about her work. But she had a life outside of work, one which clearly held no interest for him.

Her mother, though, wanted to know everything to the point her questions soon became tiresome.

Edith answered. She embellished dull details; spoke lovingly of Walter; and then as the soup was being served, announced her engagement.

Her mother lowered her spoon and stared. The color drained from her face. Like Edith, she was naturally pale, an effect enhanced by the string of fake pearls she wore at her throat.

"I know all about it," Edith's father said. "Ran into Walt's father on campus. He was about to burst."

"You didn't say a word," Edith's mother said to him.

Edith's father glared at her.

Edith tasted her soup. It was her favorite—tomato with a dollop of cream.

"But, where's your ring?" her mother asked.

Edith held up her right hand. Her father said it was supposed to go on her left hand. How could she possibly not know that?

"It's too big. I'll have it sized before the wedding," Edith said.

"And when is that to be?" her mother asked.

"Not sure yet. February, maybe."

"That's so soon!"

"Oh, for heaven's sake. They've been dating since high school," Edith's father said.

Edith said it would be held before a justice of the peace. They were welcome to take the train out if they wanted, but really, there was no need. The whole thing would be over in less than ten minutes. Her father grumbled about the vulgarity of wartime weddings, and Edith's mother gave him an imploring look then stood to clear the soup bowls. She returned with two plates of thinly sliced roast beef, boiled potatoes, and green peas. She put the first plate in front of Edith's father and the second one in front of Edith. Edith's father lifted his knife and fork and went to work on the beef while Edith's mother was still in the kitchen getting her own plate.

When they were all together, they ate in silence. Edith had no appetite yet kept putting the food into her mouth. She'd seen a lovely lemon cake in the kitchen, which her mother would offer for dessert. Cakes were a tricky business in that house. Sometimes her mother put an especially good one on the table after dinner and waited in silence while Edith's father decided whether he'd like a slice. A small nod had her on her feet, with the cake knife in hand. No motion from him meant the cake went back into the kitchen where she and Edith could help themselves after the dishes had been cleared and washed.

Edith's father leaned back in his chair and lit his pipe. He said it was clear things were coming to an end soon and the future was up for grabs.

"Isn't it always?" Edith asked.

"The future of the world, not of silly young women."

"I'm not silly."

"Of course you're not, dear," Edith's mother said.

"I wasn't referring to you. You always assume I am," Edith's father said.

The conversation stalled. Edith's mother cleared the table and brought out the cake and three plates. Edith's father said he was full. Edith said she'd like a slice. Would her mother like one, too?

"Yes, dear, I would!"

Edith cut the cake and put a large slice on the plate she handed to her mother, then a smaller piece on the one she kept for herself. She dug in. The cake was delicious.

Her father set his pipe in the ashtray and nudged it forward until it just touched the edge of Edith's plate.

"No, thank you, I haven't taken up smoking," Edith said. Her father stared. Her mother chuckled quietly.

Edith finished her cake and considered a second slice. She decided against it.

"And, speaking of the future," Edith said. The room stilled. She said Walter was applying to law school at Harvard when the war ended. She would apply to school, too.

"What kind of school?" Edith's mother asked.

"Graduate school."

"Also at Harvard?"

"Yes."

"What will you study?"

"American poetry."

"What?" Edith's father asked.

"I'm sorry, Papa. I know you think it's frivolous, and I should have become a mathematician like you."

"Are you mad? You're going to be married."

"Yes, I know. And then I'm going to graduate school. If they'll have me."

"Oh, I'm sure they'll be happy to have you," Edith's mother said.

Edith's father told her mother to shut up. Edith then told him to shut up. Someone in the room gasped; Edith thought it was probably her mother. Her father got to his feet and stood over her. He raised his hand in a gesture that lived in Edith's earliest memories. She stood up.

"Go ahead, and you'll see what you get," Edith said. She clutched her fork and pointed the tines at him. Edith's father stared at her, then at the fork.

"You're an ungrateful, disrespectful little bitch," he said, quietly.

"And you're a first-class bastard."

He sat down and asked Edith's mother if there were any cognac in the house. When she took a moment to answer, he asked again.

"Yes, I think so. I'll just go and see," Edith's mother said.

"Sit. I'll go," Edith said.

Edith went into the kitchen and stood, looking at nothing, seeing nothing. She put the fork in the sink. She was slow, taking herself in. She'd said what had been in her heart for years, yet the scene which had just taken place was nothing like the ones she'd imagined over and over. In those, her father was livid and slapped her face, or better, packed his things and left forever. Now, with the future altered, he sat and spoke in a low voice. She couldn't make out the words. Was he begging her mother to side with him? No, he never begged. Was he explaining himself? Again, he never did that, either. Then he was silent, perhaps wondering what kept her.

Her mother said, "No." Her voice was clear and calm.

Edith opened the top cabinet where her mother kept the good liquor. Ordinary liquor was kept in the sideboard where a great show could be made of sliding open the door to display what was inside, making guests think they were about to get the very best. Only, there were seldom guests. She couldn't remember the last time anyone came to that house. Walter, of course, before the war, and his sister, Kathleen, once or twice. The night they graduated from college, Walter's mother made dinner for both families at her home, though Edith's mother very much wanted the honor of doing so. Her father told her to be quiet and accept the invitation. He looked up to Walter's father because he'd become a full professor two years sooner; had served as acting chairman of his department—a position not yet awarded Edith's father—and because he had a son to carry on the family name, while he only had her.

Edith returned with the cognac and three glasses. She poured them each a drink. She drank hers quickly, helped her mother with the dishes, and then called a taxi to take her back to the train station. She would sit up all night and wait for the morning run back to Washington where, with luck, she would arrive exactly on Christmas Day. Her mother didn't object, though her grief at Edith's change of plan was palpable. Her father retreated to the living room with his pipe, another glass of cognac, and the radio.

Walter met her early return with mild disapproval. He had plans to spend the holiday with Mary Jane and Tom. He didn't like the idea of calling them up to cancel. He asked her what happened.

"I had an argument with my father," she said.

"About what?"

"Getting married."

"Oh?"

"He thinks I'm too young."

"You're twenty-two."

"I know."

Walter worried her father had never really approved of him and wanted someone better for her. Though she didn't disabuse him of this, she told him it didn't matter what her father thought. The man was a fool and seldom knew what he was talking about. Walter chided her and said she shouldn't speak of him that way. He was her father, after all.

They married. The first time they had sex they fell off the bed, which Edith found hilarious, and Walter found mortifying. The sex was terrible, and Edith told herself it would get better with practice. It didn't.

The war ended. He applied to law school, and she applied for a master's. Reviewing her paperwork made him wistful. He'd once wanted to be a scholar, but the war realigned something in him, driving him toward a more practical end. Both of their applications for the fall of 1946 were approved, and they celebrated with a glass of champagne. A month before school started, they moved to Cambridge, Massachusetts.

In school together, Edith felt as she had when they first went out to Washington, bound by a common goal. They went off to class, sometimes met for lunch, came home to their shabby apartment, and ate what she cooked. She quickly settled on Walt Whitman and his passion for the working man as a subject for her thesis. Professor Gray, her advisor, suggested she include Carl Sandburg and compare the two. The research was both grueling and beautiful. She saw true American voices with a uniquely American focus on nature, war, common people, and the passion for new places. She spoke of this with Walter, wading through his casebooks on Constitutional Law, Torts, and Property. He was polite, but not curious, and she realized he was jealous and longing again to study literature. He'd majored in English in college and yearned for Romantic poetry. She told him he could always read it when he wanted.

"And when will I have time for that?" he asked.

"I'm sorry."

During her second year, she felt more and more that she wanted to continue her studies by applying to the doctoral program. She raised it with Walter, and he called it a fine idea. After he got his degree, he'd look for a firm right there in Boston. He'd already assumed they'd stay. Really, where else would they want to live? And with all the colleges around, she could get a teaching job—if that sounded good to her. It did! She wanted it more than anything. She applied and was accepted for the following fall.

When she told Walter she had good news for him, he took her hand and said it would be a struggle, but they'd manage. He was happy for her, happy for them both. Within only a few minutes it became clear he was talking about a baby. His face fell when she set him straight.

He had to be honest. He didn't like the idea. She reminded him he'd encouraged her. Had he done so because he doubted she'd be accepted and so had nothing to lose by expressing support? Was that it?

"No, of course not. It's just that things have changed," he said.

"What things?"

He said it was complicated. She pressed him. It had been suggested a man with his talents and drive had a bright future, one a certain kind of wife could help bring about. She didn't have to ask what kind that was. While Walter was just getting started, it didn't matter what she did. Now that he'd been spotted, as it were, someone to keep an eye on, she had to stick to her assigned role and make a comfortable, nurturing home so he could thrive.

She begged him to be broadminded, to widen his understanding of what marriage could mean.

"Next you'll be asking to step out on me," he said.

She contacted the dean of graduate studies and said she would not be entering the program after all. A few days later she said she was going to New York. Walter forbade her. Her place was with him. He would not allow her to desert him. She wasn't deserting him. She was taking time for herself.

"But how will it look?" he asked.

"Is that what you're worried about? Appearances?"

He hadn't meant to put it that way. He just didn't want her to go. He needed her. He loved her.

"I love you, too."

He told her she'd feel better in the morning. She assured him she wouldn't. She needed time away, that was all. She knew it was inconvenient, but he'd get used to it. After all, husbands and wives were apart all the time during the war.

"They didn't have a choice," he said.

"Try to understand."

He asked what she would do, and where she would live.

She'd get a job. And Aunt Margaret had offered her a room. Walter didn't care much for his Aunt Margaret. He thought her silly and frivolous.

"She escaped from Illinois, didn't she? Went to New York, married a man with money, made a good life for herself. Doesn't sound so silly to me."

Walter ignored her, which told her on some level, he agreed.

They talked in circles most of the night, then watched the late spring dawn rise through the trees. She got up to close the living room drapes, and he asked her not to.

When she turned around, she saw tears on his face.

He held out his hand, and she went to him. She sat in his lap. He put his arms around her and rocked her the way he sometimes did. He buried his face in her neck.

"Oh, Edie. Who will wake you from your nightmares?" he whispered.

"I don't have nightmares."

"You do."

"Do not."

He pulled away and looked at her.

"You really don't remember them?" he asked.

"No."

All she remembered was being shaken gently awake and always wishing she'd been left alone.

After she'd been at Aunt Margaret's for about a month, he wrote to say he'd reconsidered. He saw no reason why it couldn't work out. He would make it clear to his professors Edith's academic pursuit would in no way hamper his own advancement. He was willing to help with the housework. He could try his hand at slapping together a few meals. He just wanted her to come back. She wrote again to the dean and asked if her acceptance could be transferred to the following year. He replied it could not, she could reapply if she wished, but he made it a point to mention an increasing number of ex-servicemen were also applying and positions would be limited. Since the men would be given priority, she mustn't get her hopes up. After a good cry, she put the letter in her drawer. Then she went out and bought a new hat, a confection of satin and lace. She told Aunt Margaret they should dine out somewhere new and exciting. Aunt Margaret picked a French place where the waiters were clearly from Brooklyn, the lamb overcooked, and the wine sour, but Edith enjoyed it all with gusto. She'd made up her mind to stay in New York.

chapter three

Edith's mother didn't write nearly as often as Walter, which was a good thing, because of the cautionary tone she'd taken all summer.

I know Walter let you down, but you've been apart a long time now. If you're not careful, you'll end up divorced. With all the poor men who lost their lives, it might not be so easy to find another husband.

She went on to talk about Walter's parents, whom she'd seen working in their front garden when she drove by.

They waved politely, of course. They couldn't very well do otherwise, but they must have felt as awkward as I did. I can only imagine how they view the situation.

Edith was sure Walter's father assumed the separation was her fault because he was the kind of man who blamed women for everything. She couldn't guess what Walter's mother thought. She was reserved and seldom spoke her mind.

Her mother closed on a different note.

*I'm sorry if I sound harsh. I don't mean to bring you down.
I know you did what you felt you had to do. Please know I think
of you often.*

Edith put the letter away.

It was almost three in the afternoon. She'd gotten up early, served herself coffee, and climbed back into bed to read. She hadn't dressed. Bless Aunt Margaret for leaving her alone, except for slipping her mother's latest letter under her door. Those people were due soon, and she couldn't go on hiding out. Duty, she thought. Always duty.

Francine Green was like all of Aunt Margaret's friends—wealthy, impeccably dressed, and outraged by little things like the broken elevator, and the length of time it took to hail a taxi from her Park Avenue apartment. Her hair was dyed blonde, and Aunt Margaret had told Edith before she'd had her nose worked on. The Brooklyn accent she'd been born with had been studiously replaced with something sounding almost British. Like the good people in Boston, she didn't pronounce her "r"s, unless they came at the beginning of a word. She'd married a Jew against the wishes of both their families. The path of true love can be so very wretched, Aunt Margaret liked to say. Poor Saul! He'd been run down by a mad taxi driver years before.

Her son, Philip, was tall and pale. Below his probing blue eyes, faint shadows were etched in his white skin. His hands were clammy; there was a stain on his tie; his jacket was missing a button, and the crease had gone out of his slacks. Francine wore a raw silk suit in pale lavender and had a fox stole draped carelessly over one arm.

The weather had cooled overnight, and the open windows in the living room admitted a pleasant breeze. Aunt Margaret asked if anyone really wanted tea.

"Isn't that why we're here?" Philip asked.

"What about some refreshing cocktails, instead?" Aunt Margaret asked.

"What a lovely idea!" Francine boomed. Edith wondered if having money gave her the confidence to speak loudly. Aunt Margaret tended to project, too. Edith had been raised on the idea women should speak softly, gently, which she did. Usually, that is. She'd raised her voice several times to Walter. He'd cringed and looked stricken. In the home he grew up in his father yelled, not his mother. He'd said once he couldn't ever remember the woman raising her voice, which Edith found implausible. Even her own brow-beaten mother came out with a good squawk now and then—never at her father, heaven forbid—but at a cat who'd wandered into her kitchen and was found helping itself to a beautiful baked ham resting on the counter. Or the milkman who kept delivering salted butter when she always asked for unsalted. Edith's father suffered from high blood pressure.

"I'll make them. What does everyone want?" Philip asked.

Something about the eagerness in his voice made Edith regret choosing her dullest gray dress, embellished only by embroidered red roses around its pageboy collar. She wore her hair long and loose, though many women had the shorter style quickly catching on. She wanted to cut hers, too but didn't want to look too stylish at work.

"An old fashioned for me," Francine said.

"Ooh, that sounds wonderful! The same here," Aunt Margaret said.

"I'll help," Edith said. She and Philip went to the liquor cart at the other end of the living room and left Aunt Margaret and Francine to their discussion of the weather, the coming season, who would be returning from the Hamptons, and a couple named Dodge who was quietly splitting up. Edith looked at the glassware and bottles of liquor. She wasn't much for cocktails, herself.

"Ice," Philip said.

"This way."

They went down the hall into the kitchen. Philip opened the freezer and pulled out the ice tray. The lever was hard to release, and he strained. When it gave, several cubes of ice popped out and onto the floor. Edith bent down to collect them and tossed them into the sink. Philip asked for a bowl, and Edith handed him one.

"Awfully fancy, isn't it?" he asked. The bowl was hand-painted, part of an elegant set of dishes Aunt Margaret had had for years.

"It's all we have," Edith said.

"I don't know why everything has to be so posh."

Edith loved nice things. Everything she'd grown up with was cheap and ordinary.

"Oh, don't get me wrong," Philip said, when he saw her expression, "our place is full of pricey nonsense, too. Ma wouldn't have it any other way."

"Ma?"

"I tried 'Mumsy' for a while, then 'Mater,' which earned me more than a few scalding looks. 'Mother' is just too dull, so I settled on 'Ma.' She hates it!"

"You don't get along, do you?"

Philip dropped the ice cubes into the bowl one by one. "She's all right. She's just pinned all her hopes on me because she misses my father."

"How long has it been?"

"Fifteen years."

"I guess you never really get over losing someone."

"I guess not."

Philip asked where they kept the bitters. Edith said probably with the liquor. He stood looking at her, with the bowl in his hand.

"My mother says you're at the UN," he said.

"Yes."

"Must be fascinating."

"Not really. I type letters all day. And not very interesting ones at that."

He nodded. "You used to live in Boston."

"Yes."

Edith wondered if Aunt Margaret had withheld the fact she was married when she extended the invitation to tea. She'd removed her wedding ring her first week in New York.

"What were you doing there?" he asked.

"Going to graduate school."

"Where?"

"Harvard."

Philip whistled.

"In what?" he asked.

"American poetry."

"A real blue-stocking." He paused. "How old are you?"

"Don't you know it's rude to ask a lady her age?"

He grinned.

"Twenty-five," she said. "And you?"

"Twenty-three."

"Come on, let's go mix those cocktails."

He leaned in and kissed her. He put his free arm around her, and she put her arms around his neck. He was a good six inches taller than she was, though not as tall as Walter, who flashed maddeningly through her mind even as she kissed Philip harder. He stepped back and looked down at her.

"Do you always kiss women you've just met?" Edith asked. The heat rose in her face.

"Only when they're as pretty as you."

"I'm not pretty."

"Then I should see an oculist."

They returned to the liquor cart. Aunt Margaret and Francine were smoking and talking. They were still on the Dodges. The wife wasn't having it, according to Francine. Edith instantly thought of a baby, but then realized that wasn't the kind of thing you'd talk about so openly, even with a good friend, when there was a chance others might hear.

Edith set out four glasses. Philip asked if she had any sugar cubes, and she said they didn't. He asked her to bring him the sugar bowl. It was from the same set, decorated with butterflies and luscious rose blossoms.

Philip scooped some sugar into each glass, added the bitters, then a large amount of bourbon. When he came to the fourth glass, he looked at Edith. She shook her head.

"What for you, then?" he asked. He winked when he said this, and she blushed again.

"Scotch."

"A college girl who doesn't drink cocktails. Curiouser and curiouser."

Then he asked if she had any oranges they could slice for a garnish, although maraschino cherries would work just as well. They trooped back into the kitchen where a bowl of oranges sat brightly on the small table. Edith took one, then picked up a serrated knife, and went to work. Philip opened a cabinet and removed a plate on which to arrange the slices. He had a nice way of doing things, she decided.

Philip took out the plate of oranges. Edith stayed behind and poured herself a generous amount of scotch. Then she sat at the table and wondered what the hell had gotten into her, letting Philip kiss her like that. Even worse was how she'd kissed him back. Walter was romantic, but he was clumsy. And he was too fast. Her blush deepened as she thought this, but there it was. He made love like a desperate teenager. He never helped her get where she needed to be. She knew Philip would. His lips said it all.

Aunt Margaret appeared.

"What on earth are you doing sitting in here all by yourself?" she asked. The ice clinked pleasantly in her glass. She wanted to know if there were any salted nuts. Edith got them out of the cabinet and poured them into a silver bowl with scalloped edges.

"What's that you've got there?" Aunt Margaret asked, meaning the glass Edith had put down on the counter.

"Scotch."

"Well, bring it with you. I wish I'd thought to order some canapés. The idea of switching from tea to cocktails hadn't occurred to me until they came through the door!"

"I can call for some. That place on Lexington you use when your bridge club comes over."

"Dawson's. Clever girl! I have no idea where I put their number."

"I'll ask the operator."

"And in the meantime, I suppose these nuts will do. Have we any cheese and crackers?"

"I'll see what I can find."

"Thanks, dear. I best get back."

There was Brie in the refrigerator and some smoked salmon paste. Edith arranged everything nicely on a plate, hoping the crackers weren't stale. Then she called the caterer and asked if they could whip up an order on short notice. They could, but it would cost extra. Edith told them she wanted a dozen deviled eggs and a half dozen cucumber sandwiches. And please put it on their account. The woman on the line sounded put out but agreed.

Edith went into the living room, where something Philip was saying had his mother and Aunt Margaret in stitches. Everyone turned toward her.

"It's just not true!" Aunt Margaret shrieked after a moment.

"It is, it is," Francine insisted, sipping daintily from her drink.

Philip sat with one leg thrown over the arm of Aunt Margaret's favorite embroidered wing chair as if it were an old couch someone had brought down from the attic. His elevated leg jiggled nervously as he talked. His trousers had ridden up to reveal a shin thick with black hair. Edith sat on the loveseat next to the sofa.

"He loved that hamster more than life itself, at least that's what he told us. So, we held an elegant wake. What else could we do?" he asked.

Edith smiled politely until Philip caught her eye. He seemed not to recognize her for a moment, he was that lost in the story he was sharing. Then he focused.

"I refer to the beloved hamster of one of my fraternity brothers. Thaddeus. The hamster, not the brother. *His* name was Edward," he said.

"A hamster residing in a fraternity. How droll," Edith said.

"He wasn't supposed to have it, but no one had the heart to challenge him. It helped that he was clean and well-behaved."

"Thaddeus, I assume, and not Edward."

"Correct."

Philip sipped his drink and regarded Edith at length.

"Philip's a Yale man," Aunt Margaret said.

"Was," Francine said.

"I graduated," Philip said.

"I gathered that," Edith said.

No one spoke for a moment.

"What did you study?" Edith asked.

"Philip is a Medievalist," Francine said.

"Really? How unusual!" Edith said.

"I wrote my Honors thesis on Richard the Third," Philip said.

"The *last* Medieval King of England," Edith said.

"You didn't tell me your niece was so clever, Margaret," Francine said.

Philip put his glass on the table by his chair and removed a silver cigarette case from the pocket of his jacket. He opened it and extended his arm toward Edith. She took a cigarette. He took one for himself, put the case away, and brought out a silver lighter. She leaned forward until the tip of her cigarette met the flame. She leaned back and blew out the smoke she'd just pulled gratefully into her lungs.

"Clever is my middle name," Edith said. The scotch had hit bottom all of a sudden. She needed something on her stomach. She realized she'd left the plate of crackers, cheese, and salmon paste in the kitchen. She stood to get it. Philip took her hand and said, "You didn't hear the rest of my story." He dropped her hand quickly. Edith was sure Francine and Aunt Margaret had seen and hoped the bourbon in their system dulled the significance of his gesture.

Edith sat down. She stubbed out her cigarette. Philip drained his glass. His color was high. His eyes were full of sparkle.

He said the brothers got used to having old Thaddeus around. He became a kind of mascot. Someone's girlfriend was enlisted to knit him a sweater with the letters of the house—Alpha Delta Phi. It was harder than you might think, getting a sweater to fit a hamster, let alone holding him still long enough to slip it on. Did Edith know how to knit?

"Yes," she said.

"I didn't know that," Aunt Margaret said.

"Well, I can."

"Bet you do it well, too," Philip said. He looked around. Everyone's glass was empty. He offered a second round. Aunt Margaret asked Edith what was keeping the canapés. Edith said it hadn't been very long since she'd called. Philip asked if the place were nearby. If so, perhaps he could go over and save them the trip.

"They're in Midtown," Edith said.

"I could take a taxi."

"Darling, mix up some more of those old fashioneds. They're delicious!" Francine said.

Edith took the empty glasses to the kitchen, rinsed and dried them, and returned them to the liquor cart where Philip was busy crushing ice. She watched his hands work. He wore a gold band on the pinky of his left hand. The band held a small red stone which she guessed was a ruby. When she asked what it was, he said it was a garnet, and the ring had been his grandmother's. He said she'd come to America as a young woman, but a lot of her family stayed behind.

"Where?" Edith asked.

"Germany."

"And . . ."

"They were killed by the Nazis. Cousins I'd never met but had letters from, and two aunts."

"Horrible."

"People always say that."

"Because it's true."

"Many things are true that aren't said."

"Such as?"

"Never you mind."

He grinned, then added an orange slice to each glass. He'd obviously decided she'd have an old fashioned now, too.

He took Francine and Aunt Margaret their drinks. He asked Edith to show him around the apartment. With their glasses in hand, she led him into the formal dining room with the ornate cherry wood sideboard and table that could seat sixteen when the leaves were installed. She said she didn't want to turn on the light because the crystal chandelier was dusty. The cleaning lady didn't like getting up on the step stool to clean it.

"Let me," Philip said.

"That's very kind of you, but it's not necessary."

"I want to."

He asked where the step stool and duster were kept. She pointed to the pantry off the kitchen. He told her to hold his drink. He came back a moment later, set up the step stool, climbed on, and said to hand him the duster he'd dropped on the table. She put their glasses on the sideboard and gave him the duster. He ran it over each crystal pendant, making them swing cheerfully and occasionally clink against one another. Laughter was audible in the living room, and Francine said she was just going to go powder her nose. Aunt Margaret appeared in the doorway to the dining room and asked what in the world poor Philip was doing.

"Cleaning the chandelier, obviously," Edith said.

"A man who's good around the house. What a marvelous thing!"

Edith picked up her drink, sipped it, and told Philip the chandelier looked fabulous. He asked Aunt Margaret to please turn on the light. When she did, the room came to life.

Philip climbed down off the step stool and stood back to admire his handiwork.

"That is one nice piece of crystal you have there," he said.

"My husband objected to my buying it. He thought it was frivolous," Aunt Margaret said.

"Nonsense. It's quite a serious piece," Philip said. "Can you imagine if each of those small bulbs were a candle? Flickering light would be lovely in a chandelier, don't you think?"

"Sure," Edith said.

"Oh, Philip," Aunt Margaret said, and then laughed.

"Candlelight is quite inspiring. It's not just the poets who think so," Philip said.

"I like dining by candlelight," Edith said.

"And do you do so often?"

"No. I can't remember the last time."

"I'll take you out to dinner at the finest French restaurant in New York. There are sure to be candles on the tables there."

"Try Gerrard's," Aunt Margaret said.

"I've heard Emile's is the place to go," Philip said.

The doorbell rang. Edith went down the long hallway between the dining room and the door, aware she was tilting.

The delivery boy looked cross as he handed Edith a cardboard box. He said traffic had been murder, and not to blame him if the eggs didn't look right because Maribelle was the one who'd piped them, and she'd been rushed. He was sure they were delicious though, not to worry about that. Edith had trouble managing the box in one hand, so she put her drink on the table by the door. She thanked the delivery boy, told him to give Maribelle her compliments and the rest of the staff, too. After he left, she went along the hall to the kitchen where Philip was coming the other way. He took the box from her. She said she'd left her drink and was going to go back and get it. She asked him to put the box in the kitchen.

She joined him there a moment later. He'd opened the box and was looking inside. Edith looked into the box, too, and saw they'd forgotten the cucumber sandwiches. When she mentioned it, Philip said it wasn't a problem as far as he was concerned because he despised cucumbers.

"Really?" Edith asked.

"Absolutely."

"I adore cucumber."

"Must be the shape."

Edith blushed up to her hairline and was charmed a moment later to see Philip had, too.

"I must apologize," he said. "I'm not usually so, so . . ."

"Crass?"

"Something like that. I'm normally quite genteel."

They kissed again, longer and harder this time. Edith pressed herself against him. She loved how he felt.

"Don't," she said. She pulled away.

"Don't what?"

She arranged the eggs on a plate she took from the cabinet and put it next to the one with the cheese, crackers, and salmon paste. There was a bottle of champagne in the refrigerator, a special label Aunt Margaret had had for years, Veuve Clicquot, 1926. When Edith first arrived, Aunt Margaret had suggested they drink it to celebrate. Edith hadn't understood. Aunt Margaret said, "Your arrival, of course!" Aunt Margaret was lonely, despite her social whirl, and though Edith felt for her, she was under the cloud of leaving Walter and didn't care to celebrate. She did now, though.

"Can you pop a cork?" she asked.

"I beg your pardon."

She doubled over laughing, and he did, too. She held up her hand as a plea for calm.

"Did I hear the doorbell?" Aunt Margaret bellowed from the living room.

"Coming!" Edith called.

Edith asked Philip to carry in the food. She followed with the champagne. Philip set the plates down on the coffee table with a flourish. Francine and Aunt Margaret stared at them. Then Aunt Margaret looked at the bottle in Edith's hand.

"What's the occasion?" she asked.

"New friends," Edith said.

"Hear, hear," Philip said.

"Are there any napkins?" Francine asked. She'd tossed off her fox fur. One black velvet shoe lay on its side under the table. Her lipstick was smeared; strands of hair had come loose from her chignon. The hat she'd worn in, with a charming lace-patterned veil, was on the sofa next to her. Edith handed Philip the bottle, left, and returned with four napkins. They were white. Each bore an embroidered M. Aunt Margaret's towels, pillowcases, and shams were monogrammed, too.

Edith saw she'd forgotten the champagne flutes. She went to the china cabinet in the dining room. She had her choice of plain glass etched with roses around the rim or stunning cut crystal that threw the afternoon light. She chose the crystal. As she reached for the first glass, she heard the champagne cork release. She was filled with joy. She was still sober enough to realize the alcohol was lifting her mood, but Philip was, too.

Francine squealed, and so did Aunt Margaret. Edith thought the champagne must have flowed over onto the rug. When she arrived, Philip was on his hands and knees, patting away with a napkin. Aunt Margaret motioned Edith to bring the glasses to the coffee table. Edith lined them up. Philip got to his feet and poured champagne into each glass. Then he handed them around and took the last for himself.

"What shall we toast?" Francine asked.

"The future," Philip said and touched his glass to Edith's.

They drank. Aunt Margaret and Francine helped themselves to the salmon paste on crackers, then the deviled eggs. Philip flopped down in the chair he'd been in before. Edith sat, too. They finished the champagne and went back to cocktails.

Afternoon became evening. Francine and Aunt Margaret suggested dinner out but when they tried to stand up, realized they were too wobbly. Edith offered to make everyone scrambled eggs and toast. Philip thought that was a capital idea.

"I'm sure we have a side of bacon," Aunt Margaret said.

Edith cooked by herself. She set the table. Everyone ate quickly, and Edith cleared. Francine asked if she could lie down for a bit, and Aunt Margaret showed her the guest room. After another interval of time, the length of which was impossible to reckon, Aunt Margaret made her apologies and said she, too, needed a little time off her feet. Edith told Philip if he wanted to close his eyes, he should feel free to stretch out on the sofa.

Edith woke with a pounding headache, furious with herself for not closing the drapes. Her room faced east, and the August sun washed through the room. She was naked, and so was Philip. While how they got into bed was a blur, their lovemaking was recalled in detail. She even remembered the things they whispered. She blushed. She'd never blushed in bed before. But then, she'd never had sex like that before.

She needed aspirin badly. She got up and slipped into her silk kimono, loving its cool sleekness against her skin. She padded into the bathroom and discovered there was no water glass. She went silently into the hall. As she passed Aunt Margaret's bedroom, she listened. She heard nothing. Next door there was no sound from the guest room, either. In the kitchen, the clock on the stove said it was just past seven. She took her glass and returned to Philip, who was awake and lighting a cigarette. The grin he gave her made her weak in the knees. She forgot about her headache, put the glass in the bathroom, got out of her kimono, and back into bed. He raised his arm so she could lie right next to him.

"Good morning," he said.

"Good morning."

He offered her a drag on his cigarette. She took it. Walter wouldn't like her smoking. He thought it was unfeminine.

She chuckled. Philip asked what was funny.

"I was just thinking about my husband."

"Husband?"

She turned her head and met his eye. "Guess I forgot to mention him."

"Guess you did."

He turned away and smoked. He didn't offer her the cigarette a second time.

"Is it a problem?" she asked.

"That depends. Where is he?"

"Cambridge."

"That's part of Boston?"

"Yes."

"That's pretty far away."

She told him he should probably get going before his mother and Aunt Margaret started to stir. She'd say he stayed until around midnight when he felt sober enough to hail a cab.

He got up. She watched him dress. He had a beautiful body—muscled and lean.

"What do you do?" she asked.

"For a living?"

"Yes."

"Nothing at the moment. I'm thinking about graduate school, but it doesn't really appeal."

He went into the bathroom, ran the water, then took her comb from the counter, wet it, and dragged it through his hair. He held up her toothbrush as a request to borrow it. She nodded.

He picked up his tie from the floor and shoved it into the pocket of his jacket. He stood, looking down at her. She held out her hand. He took it and sat on the bed.

"Will I see you again?" she asked.

"If you want to."

He brought her hand to his lips and kissed it. Then he bent and put his lips to hers.

When he'd gone, she saw his lighter on the nightstand. Maybe he'd left it so she could think of him. Maybe he'd just forgotten. In any case, it was hers now, and she meant to keep it.

chapter four

Aunt Margaret didn't understand. She knew how hard it was to be parted from Walter, but wasn't her decision to return awfully sudden? Edith said she wouldn't be leaving for another three weeks, right around the middle of September. She'd just gotten off the phone with Walter, who was delighted.

They were having coffee in the dining room because the cleaning lady was busy scouring the kitchen and singing her fool head off. Aunt Margaret used a small silver spoon to distribute the cream she added to hers. Edith took her coffee black. It was Wednesday, and she'd called in sick. It felt strange not to be at work. She'd have to get used to it, she thought. In Cambridge, she'd have many hours to fill.

Aunt Margaret looked sad. Even the folds in her neck seemed heavier. She wore no bracelets, and her plump freckled arms looked undressed and vulnerable. She was due at the manicurist's later. There was a tiny chip in the red polish on her middle finger.

"Did something happen?" Aunt Margaret asked.

"Of course not. I just need to get back now."

"I rather assumed you weren't going back."

"Why?"

"Well, you've settled in so well."

Aunt Margaret meant what she'd done to her room. She'd added a charming vanity and arranged several bottles of perfume on it, as well as a new hairbrush and comb. Sometimes she put fresh flowers on the nightstand. There were also new pillow shams.

Edith didn't want Aunt Margaret to think she hadn't been happy there because she had. New York was a dream. Much more interesting than Boston or Washington, but Walter was up in Cambridge and well, the time had simply come.

Four days before, Aunt Margaret had emerged from her bedroom ruffled and seriously hung-over from mixing cocktails with champagne. She'd missed a button on her dressing gown, and it bunched over her round stomach. Francine didn't surface until around noon, wearing a borrowed nightgown and robe several sizes too big. Both accepted Edith's story about Philip making his way home around midnight; and when Francine arrived home that afternoon, after several cups of coffee and three aspirins, he confirmed it in an easy, off-hand way. He even invented a tired cab driver who waxed poetic about the charms of Manhattan at that hour. Philip called Edith that evening to say all was A-okay in the deception department. At the sound of the telephone, Edith jumped, knowing it was he. Aunt Margaret was taking a long bath, yet Edith feared being overheard. Philip asked her if she had any regrets.

"About what?" she asked.

"Cheating on your husband."

She wanted to say no, she didn't. She wanted to say so many things but instead begged him to leave her alone. The next day he phoned her at work. Personal calls weren't allowed, and she had to make up a story about a friend who hadn't understood the protocol. She told him he must stop.

"Where can I write to you?" he asked. She hesitated. The office hummed around her. She said nothing until Miss Grett looked at her over her bifocals with a gaze that could melt steel.

Edith gave him her address.

"Be careful," she said.

"I'll use my initials. Say I'm a girlfriend you ran into when you were buying shoes. Someone you went to school with."

"Clever."

"Not half as clever as you."

The following day she tendered her resignation to Miss Grett, who read the brief note she typed that morning with a disappointed sigh.

"Off to get married, I suppose," she said.

"Yes, as a matter of fact."

"I don't know how the world goes on turning when all an intelligent woman wants to do is marry and keep house."

Edith shrugged shyly. She felt like an idiot recalling it now.

Aunt Margaret sipped her coffee. Something clattered to the floor in the kitchen. Aunt Margaret winced.

"She's all thumbs," she said.

"Please know I'll always appreciate your generosity in taking me in."

"You make yourself sound like a refugee."

"More like a poor relation."

Aunt Margaret looked solemnly around the room. Edith could feel her dismay.

"You must come to see us in Cambridge," she said.

"Yes, of course. And we will make the most of your remaining time here!"

But they made little of it, in the end. Edith worked up until three days before her train was due to leave. She spent hours packing and repacking her few belongings. Walter wrote daily then, proclaiming his undying love and promising she would be happy.

On her second to last day in New York, the doorman buzzed to say a Mr. Philip Green was in the lobby and wondered if he could come up. The doorman was new. His predecessor never bothered to announce callers, and the sound of the buzzer was startling. Aunt Margaret was out with Francine, which is how Philip must have known the coast was clear. Still, it was brazen showing up like that. They'd had no contact since the day he called her at work. Edith buzzed the doorman back and said Mr. Green was coming to borrow some books, and she was happy to receive him. Then she rushed to her room, bent down to see herself in the mirror of her vanity, and was instantly disappointed. Her dark green blouse made her look pale. Her gray skirt was as dull as toast. Three months in New York had done nothing for her sense of style. She dug around in the right-hand drawer for a lipstick which she applied so quickly it smeared. She wiped where it had gone awry and dabbed a tissue between her lips. The shade was ridiculous, too pink and cheerful for what she had on, but it was too late to put another in its place because the doorbell rang, then rang again.

She walked slowly down the hall. As she got closer to the door, her pace slowed even more. She could ignore his knock and stay silent when he called her name. But then he'd go back to the lobby, alert the doorman something must be wrong, urge him to bring his keys up, and make sure Edith was all right. That would lead to more drama than she had strength for.

She opened the door. Philip stepped inside and took her in his arms. She resisted, he let her go, and she stepped back until there was a reasonable distance between them.

"Why did you come here?" she asked.

"Why do you think?"

He swept in for a kiss, and she pushed him back with the heel of her hand.

She turned away and went into the living room. He followed. She motioned to the sofa, and he sat down. She sat at the other end and turned toward him, her hands folded primly in her lap.

"Aunt Margaret will be home any minute," she said.

"She and Ma are tying one on. We've got lots of time."

"Philip."

The red tie from the other day had been exchanged for a blue one that matched his eyes.

"Look, I had to see you. Ma says you're leaving soon and—"

"Tomorrow. I'm leaving tomorrow."

"Golly."

She lifted her eyebrows. His disappointment seemed genuine.

Had it really happened, she wondered? Looking at him now as he leaned forward, elbows on knees, he seemed like a stranger. He *was* a stranger. She barely knew him. Since that night, she had asked herself again and again what had gotten into her. The answer was simple— she threw her good judgment out the window. And she'd taken no precautions. She had the diaphragm she'd used with Walter, but of course, hadn't thought to put it in. Her period started on time several days later, so she was relieved of that particular terror. She'd been stupid and vowed never to be stupid that way again.

"Did you decide to leave because of me?" he asked.

"I was leaving anyway."

"You seemed pretty settled here."

"I was, then I wasn't."

"What is it you're not telling me?"

"Look, Philip, I made a terrible mistake. There's no other way to put it. I admit I enjoyed myself. You're very attractive, and—"

"A demon in the sack."

"What?"

"That's what you said."

"I did?"

"You did."

"Oh, my god."

She brought her hands to her face for a moment, then returned them to her lap.

She begged him to understand. She'd been wrong to sleep with him and wrong to give him her address. They both had to forget what they'd done and go back to the lives they had before.

"That can't happen," he said.

"It can if you let it."

"Well, I'm not going to let it."

"Why are you trying to punish me?"

She stood up. Her temples throbbed. Her nerves were getting the better of her. She needed to collect herself and stay in control.

He stood up, too, and when he kissed her, she let him. Even as she yielded, she told herself in Boston, with all the miles between them, her heart would cool and logic would prevail. Half an hour later in bed, after lovemaking furious enough to send the covers to the floor, she lay naked beside him and thought she'd have to find a way to go on seeing him. This time she'd remembered the diaphragm. He offered to use the condom he brought with him, but she said she couldn't stand the damn things.

"You need to go," she said and got out of bed. Then she put on her robe. She sat at her vanity and combed her hair. It was wild, full of snarls. She could see him watching her in the glass.

"What's he like, this husband of yours?" Philip asked.

"Brilliant. Kind. Hardworking."

"Sounds like quite a catch."

She said nothing.

"Well, you're right, I should be on my way," he said. He dressed quickly, then took his time tying his tie.

"Don't write to me," she said.

"Whatever you say."

Before the sex, he'd been determined to keep this thing between them—whatever it was—alive. Now he didn't care.

She walked him out. At the door, he kissed her on the cheek.

She listened to his steps recede in the hall outside, then broke down crying. She pulled herself together, organized the rest of her things, and waited for Aunt Margaret. They were supposed to have dinner at Giovanni's, a cozy Italian place over on Eighty-third and Fifth. She'd make an excuse, say she was worn out from all her preparations, but that didn't seem fair.

Edith lay down on top of her newly made bed. She closed her eyes and forced herself to breathe deeply and slowly. The light had dropped in the room when she opened her eyes. Aunt Margaret was calling her name. Edith got up and went to the living room where Aunt Margaret sat on the sofa, in the same place Philip had occupied a few hours before and looked through the mail Edith had left on the table in the hall.

"There you are! What's the matter, don't you feel well?" Aunt Margaret asked. Edith noted she sounded sober.

"I'm fine, why?"

"Your color is high."

Edith sat down. She asked how the visit with Francine had gone and if she'd had a nice time. Aunt Margaret said they'd had lunch at a new place on Madison. The service was slow, the clientele nothing to write home about, but the soufflé was pleasing enough. After that, they'd gone into Tiffany's so Francine could have one of her rings sized. The poor thing had a swollen knuckle that never seemed to go down. Aunt Margaret couldn't understand it, either. How could you have just one bad joint? Didn't they all go bad at once? In any case, Aunt Margaret was grateful her own fingers had remained slim over the years, even if the rest of her hadn't.

Edith chuckled briefly. She'd miss Aunt Margaret's studied humility.

"It was a welcome distraction for her, I think," Aunt Margaret said.

"What do you mean?"

"She's awfully worried about that son of hers."

"Why?"

"It seems he's something of a womanizer. Frankly, I'm surprised. He never struck me that way before and certainly not when he was here the other day. He behaved properly with you, didn't he?"

"Absolutely."

Edith picked up Aunt Margaret's cigarette case from the coffee table and helped herself. Though she'd resumed the habit, she had yet to buy her own. Aunt Margaret opened a small pink envelope and removed a folded piece of paper, which she held at arm's length to read.

"Oh, drat. Laura is so tiresome. She's invited me to another one of those buffet luncheons she's so fond of. Well, I suppose I'll have to go and hear another tale of woe about her daughter and that Italian she eloped with."

"You said he was Chinese."

"Chinese, Italian, I'm sure it makes no difference, under the circumstances. I'm so glad you and Walter had a proper wedding, even if was just before the justice of the peace."

At the mention of Walter's name, Edith felt a weight settle in her stomach. When she arrived late tomorrow evening in Cambridge, he would be at the station with flowers. They'd be daisies because for some reason he thought those were her favorite, though she preferred roses or lilies.

They'd be cheerful, pleasant, and chatty. They'd go home and get into bed. They'd do what she and Philip had done that afternoon; he'd enjoy himself and she wouldn't, though she'd try. In the morning, she might sulk over coffee. He'd sense something and have no idea what it was. He'd probably think she was worried about coming back and settling into her old routine. As the days passed, he'd be nice to her, though gruff about the time she'd been away. If she asked him to forgive her for leaving, he'd feel bad, soothe, say he understood, even that it was *his* fault for making her go. But if she defended her decision, he'd find a new story to tell himself, centered around some selfless desire on her part, such as wanting him to be able to focus on his studies without her underfoot; or that Aunt Margaret had begged her to come and stay to ease her dull, sad life. Walter had only been to New York to visit Aunt Margaret once and that had been during the war. He had no idea how she lived, or what she really felt about anything.

It seemed as if everyone were just two-dimensional cardboard characters to him. Maybe it made things easier to see people as less complex than they were. But he had love in him, nonetheless. Sometimes great love. She had to hope she could shape it into something she could spend the next fifty years with.

"My dear, what on earth?" Aunt Margaret asked and passed Edith a handkerchief from her clutch.

"I don't know what came over me. I've just been so emotional. It's probably the thought of how happy I'll be to get home."

"Of course. You must write to me very often and let me know how you're getting on."

Edith went to change. She put on one of her better dresses, a pale pink, and wore open-toed shoes. For her last night in New York, her clothes mustn't reflect the darkness in her heart.

chapter five

Edith was reluctant, but Walter insisted. He wanted to invite some people to an informal get-together. He made his case by reminding her they hadn't hosted a single party since moving there. Then he referred to the glorious fall weather which put everyone in a great mood. She accepted his enthusiasm as pleasantly as she could. She'd been back in Cambridge for four weeks. Walter had kept the apartment reasonably tidy, but he never really cleaned. She'd done that, top to bottom. She missed Aunt Margaret's cleaning lady and her off-key renditions of popular Broadway show tunes.

She asked how many people there'd be. He said maybe eight or ten. She said that was a lot to cook for.

"You don't have to cook, darling. Just make one main dish, and everyone will bring something to share," he said. He drank coffee in his bathrobe and slippers. He'd taken up smoking a pipe, which for the moment lay in the ashtray by his elbow, unlit. Edith was grateful because the smell of it was awful. Walter had chestnut brown hair showing a bit of gray. He was twenty-seven. At first, he hated finding those hairs and plucked them out. Later, he said it was fine for a man to go gray early. It made him look distinguished.

"And where shall I put everything, dear?" Edith asked. Walter looked up from the textbook he was reading. He had a pencil in his hand and another tucked behind one ear. They sat at a small round table in their cramped kitchen. The apartment had no dining room, just a living room where they had a couch, a wingback chair, two lamps, a coffee table, and the radio. And the bedroom of course, next to the bathroom, where the medicine cabinet didn't close and the window wouldn't open.

"Well, I guess we can set up in here and press the coffee table into use, too," he said.

"And the liquor? Where shall I arrange that?"

"On the kitchen counter, I think. Won't that work?"

"Of course."

She asked when he wanted them all to come. He said on Saturday.

"That doesn't give me much time to prepare," she said.

"I'll put you in touch with Smith's wife. He says she's keen to give you a hand."

"Is she now? How *kind*."

Walter seemed to appreciate her sarcastic tone. He returned to the book in front of him. He underlined a sentence, then wrote something in the margin.

It was Tuesday, and his first class wasn't until one in the afternoon. He liked having the morning with her, he said, though all he ever did was work.

Edith didn't want to think about cooking for Saturday, or any day. She wanted to go to bed and read. She'd borrowed a stack of books the week she got back and had read through all of them. For the moment she was off new releases and had returned to her girlhood favorites—Jane Austen and the Brontës. The theme of unrequited love running through those pages made her think of Philip, but then she'd think of him, regardless. Her passing conversation with Aunt Margaret about his fondness for the female sex had left her struggling with a blend of rage and regret.

She washed the dishes. When Walter went off to campus, she took herself out for a walk. *Emma* had left her restless with all her matchmaking. She decided to visit the greengrocers first to see what inspired her, but one pass by the browning lettuce on display left her cold. She had half of a roasted chicken in the refrigerator. She would make sandwiches later. She might hard boil some eggs, too. Walter was fond of those, mashed with mayonnaise and mixed with salt, which she told him was essentially egg salad, but he ignored her.

She went further into Cambridge and the sidewalks were more crowded. A man she recognized from campus, a law professor she'd met last spring at a reception she went to with Walter, tipped his hat to her as he passed. She smiled back. When they were introduced, he asked what she did, an unusual question for a law student's wife. She said she was a graduate student. He expressed mild interest, then turned away.

Walter hadn't mentioned her abandoned doctoral degree since she came back. Sometimes she found him looking at her sharply as if trying to read her mind. He hid his concern well. It was part of his nature, something the war had further developed in him.

She went into a diner and asked for a cup of coffee. As she waited for it to cool, she watched a man and woman through the window. They stood close together on the sidewalk, their faces a study in tension and grief. The man put his hand on the woman's shoulder, and she shook herself free. Edith looked away. It was no good trying to understand the problems of other people when you couldn't do anything about them. Watching them a few moments longer brought Philip to mind, again. She was furious at the way she'd let herself be used. There, alone in the diner, all her failures crowded in.

She drank some of the coffee, left coins on the table, and went home. She would leave *Emma* be, change gears, and dive into *The Naked and the Dead*. Walter had recommended it to her. He wouldn't be home for hours, and she could indulge in a nice long read, then a luxurious soak in the deep clawfoot tub—the one thing she liked about their apartment.

The box contained two letters, one from Walter's sister, Kathleen, in Chicago and one with the initials PG and a Park Avenue address. She went upstairs and put Kathleen's letter on the breakfast table and took the other one into the bedroom to read.

The hand was elegant, full of loops and swirls.

Forgive my writing when you told me not to. Please be assured you are constantly on my mind.

He went on to say the fault lay entirely with him. He hadn't learned to temper his attraction to women and, naturally, alcohol didn't help. But she had to know she was different (here, Edith scoffed). He'd never met anyone like her. It wasn't just her intelligence he referred to, but her unabashed manner.

She folded the page away to finish later.

After they had their sandwiches, and Walter sat with his pipe and Kathleen's letter, Edith read the rest in the bath she'd put off. Philip talked about being promised a job in an advertising agency, something his mother had arranged, thinking a useful occupation would keep him out of trouble. He was certain that's not what he needed and begged for more time to consider his options. He wanted to come to Boston because he couldn't imagine what excuse Edith could make to come to him, after having so recently returned to her husband's loving arms.

Edith leaned back and willed the warm water to calm her. Did she detect jealousy in Philip's words or just sarcasm for the state of marriage? For any binding commitment, really. He might be the kind to always want freedom. To agree to see him now would be disastrous.

Feeling the tub water cool around her, Edith wondered what Kathleen would think of Philip. She'd probably admire his good looks, then size him up quickly as a wolf.

Edith rose from the tub, dried off, and put Philip's letter in the pocket of her bathrobe. She'd hide it in one of her books on the top shelf of their overcrowded bookcase. She didn't know yet if she'd answer him. She didn't want to think about it.

Walter looked up when she came into the living room.

"She says she wants to come out and see us," he said.

"Really? When?"

"You know her. She doesn't say. We probably won't know until she's bought the train tickets."

Kathleen worked at Marshall Field & Company in Chicago. She was engaged to be married and said she'd go on working until she jolly well wanted to quit. She did as she pleased and was often thoughtless.

"I wish we could put her up," Edith said.

"She's not much for sleeping on a couch."

Edith was sure Kathleen wanted to collect intelligence on their reunion and see how they were getting along. It was probably her own idea, though Walter's mother might have put her up to it. In any case, Edith was glad she'd come. She liked Kathleen and admired her free spirit.

But then Edith's spirit had proved to be freer than she'd ever suspected, hadn't it?

chapter six

The gorgeous weather gave way to rain about three hours before their guests were due. Edith had a headache; Walter was glum over something he wouldn't share. For a moment, she thought he'd discovered Philip's letter. She realized cheating on him would always mean this—fearing he'd find out.

While he bathed, she found the book, opened it, and saw the letter was still there. She removed it, took it into the kitchen, and dropped it in the sink. She used Philip's lighter, kept always in the pocket of her bathrobe, to set it on fire. The paper blackened and curled; the writing became lost; when there was a small handful of ashes, she ran the water.

Walter appeared in the doorway and asked if she needed help with anything.

"No, I've got it all in hand."

He stood, looking at her. His wet hair showed comb marks. Then he looked at the linoleum floor.

"What's the matter with you, anyway? You've been out of sorts all morning," she said.

"Just woke up on the wrong side of the bed, I guess."

"Did something happen?"

"Like what?"

"I don't know, something at school."

Walter ran his hand through his hair, ruining the comb's recent effort.

"I just feel a little overwhelmed, that's all," he said.

Edith told him it would be all right. He always rose to the occasion. What specifically had him worried?

"I think I did badly in the mock trial," he said.

"You said you were splendid."

"I thought so at the time."

"Did someone say something? A professor?"

"No."

"Well, then."

Walter nodded. He held out his hand. She went to him and took it.

"You're always so sensible," he said.

"Not always."

She held his gaze though she wanted to look away.

"I often thought it must have been hard for you, living with that silly soul," he said.

"Aunt Margaret?"

"You don't talk much about your time there."

"There's not much to talk about."

"I worried she might be a bad influence."

"Because she's silly?"

"Other reasons, too."

"She's just a middle-aged woman with too much time on her hands."

"But she has a lot of friends."

"She seems to."

Edith's letters to Walter had said little about her life away from work. She talked at length about the ambassador, though she'd had only glimpses, offering wry observations on the leaning way he walked, his bow ties, his passion for tea, and his pink silk handkerchief. She spoke often of Miss Grett's impatience with some of the typists. She embellished ordinary people in an ordinary place and made them sound exciting. When she tired of that, she wrote of the books she read and how much she loved lingering in the library on a Saturday afternoon. She took him with her on walks in Central Park, to the Cloisters Museum, to a performance of Beethoven's late quartets for which Aunt Margaret had kindly bought the ticket.

"You met her friends?" Walter asked.

"Only one."

Walter nodded. His gray eyes were solemn, but not sad.

"I'm sorry I ran away," Edith said.

"I know."

"Are you glad I'm back?"

"Don't be silly. Of course, I'm glad." He kissed her cheek.

Edith put on the pretty dress she wore for her last night in New York. Walter wanted her to impress his guests, a group of third-years he was close to. She was surprised to hear they'd gone out for bowling and beer once a week while she was away because Walter never mentioned much of a social life in his letters. She assumed he was always reading in the library, researching another case or at home, writing another paper. There was Smith from Alabama, Rawlins from

Indiana, and Blake from New Hampshire. These men were married and had had Walter to their homes to sample their wives' home-cooking. Walter said just the other day Clara Smith was a pretty good cook, though he hadn't cared for the black-eyed peas she'd served; Nora Rawlins was just awful—her potatoes were lumpy and her meat so pink he thought it would walk off his plate; and Luann Blake was just so-so, though he'd enjoyed her lemon cake quite a bit. At least one of these women was pregnant, Walter had said, and Edith hadn't made note of whom.

She'd made a big pot of chili because it was one of Walter's favorites. He was disappointed by her preference for red beans over black, but she assured him they were sweeter. To make up for her poor choice of beans, she added a bottle of beer. She'd read this made the meat more tender. Rather than using ground beef, she'd chosen chuck. It was less expensive. Walter had let several bills accumulate while he was on his own. She was in the process of settling them with the money she'd saved up working for the UN because their GI stipend was meager. The largest was from the dentist, for putting a crown on one of Walter's broken teeth. The next would be the grocery store where their account was two months behind. After that, the dry cleaners, who'd waited over a month. Walter attended Reserve Officers' Training Corp dinners on campus. He liked them because he could wear his uniform and brag about his brief tenure as an instructor at West Point. He wanted the uniform cleaned after each wearing, which Edith thought ridiculous unless it were soiled, which it never seemed to be.

She lined up the liquor on the kitchen counter—one bottle of scotch, one bourbon, one gin, and a smaller bottle of vermouth. She had a jar of green olives if anyone wanted a martini. She also had seltzer for the scotch and bourbon. The ice tray was full. Walter came into the kitchen and asked if there were any beer left from what she'd added to the chili.

"No. But I can make you a drink," she said.

"Swell!"

He asked for a scotch and soda. She mixed it and gave him the glass. He scooped up a bunch of salted peanuts she'd poured into a small blue bowl. She told him to leave some for their guests. He shoved the peanuts in his mouth and chewed, sending tiny bits everywhere. She told him to straighten up. He swallowed and laughed. He was looking forward to having people over, she could tell. She pretended she was looking forward to it, too.

She took out the trash and checked the mail. There was another letter from Philip. She folded it and slipped it into her sleeve, went upstairs, and put it in a different book. She wanted to wait for the right time to read it. She didn't yet know when that would be. She needed that little moment to anticipate and cherish before it slipped into the past and was forgotten.

The first to arrive were Clara and Joe Smith. Clara was hugely pregnant, and Edith realized passing on her offer to help set up for the party had been wise. When Clara warned Edith on the telephone she probably wouldn't be much good, Edith assumed she meant she wasn't very handy in the kitchen. It must have been hard for her to climb the three flights of stairs. Edith and Walter were on the top floor of a large house, which had been converted during the war.

Joe Smith's hair was so blond it was almost white. His jacket was made of lightweight wool, as were his slacks. His brown shoes gleamed. He shook Edith's hand, addressed her as "Ma'am," and said the pleasure was all his. She could tell at once he came from money. Walter admired people with money. It wouldn't have been evident in Washington, she thought. That was the brilliant thing about uniforms. But there in Cambridge, the cut and style of his clothes set him apart.

The diamond in Clara's engagement ring sparkled blue and red, sometimes yellow when she moved her hand. The wedding band was studded with smaller, equally fiery diamonds. Her nails were painted. Her palm was soft. She gushed over Edith and Walter's apartment and said it was just as cute as a Georgia peach.

"But you're from Alabama," Edith said, proud she'd remembered.

"Joe-Joe is. I'm from Atlanta."

Her lipstick was dark red; her teeth were perfectly even, and for a moment Edith wondered if she were wearing dentures. Edith drew her lips together. Her teeth weren't bad, but the bottom row was crowded like a fence whose pickets were out of line. Walter found it charming. He said stupid things like that, usually when he'd had a few.

Edith took the casserole in Clara's hands and put it on the stove. She lifted the lid. She couldn't tell what she was looking at.

"Black-eyed peas," Clara said from the doorway.

"Lovely."

Joe-Joe asked what the ladies would like to drink. Clara wanted a gin and tonic. Edith said they were out of tonic and offered to go down to the store on the corner. Walter told her to hurry. The others were due any minute.

Edith went into the bedroom to get her purse. She slipped Philip's letter inside it. Then she pulled on an old sweater that had a hole in the elbow. She called out she was leaving and got no answer. Everyone else was in the living room, laughing and talking. Clara said, "Seriously, Walter, you can NOT imagine!"

The rain was hard, and she'd forgotten her umbrella. She held her purse over her head and walked faster. Water splashed inside her open-toed shoes. They were new, bought on sale at a little store in Boston, whose prices were good to begin with. Black suede was all the rage. Since coming home she'd taken pains with her appearance, although Walter seldom said anything. When she came in with short hair, he lifted his eyes, stared hard, then went back to his work. Hair wasn't important. Neither were make-up and jewelry, though Edith wore little of either. A woman should look pleasant, but not enticing. Not if she were married. Clara Smith didn't hold to such thinking. She was attractive and knew it, flaunted it, even. And Walter seemed to enjoy it. His double-standard annoyed Edith. Confronting him with it would be pointless.

A couple passed her. The woman held a covered dish. The man said, "I'm not being silly. You know you have a bad habit of doing that."

The woman said, "It's not my fault! He starts it every time."

Edith stopped to see where they were going, and sure enough, they were just then climbing the porch stairs to her building. The man lit himself a cigarette then rang the bell. Edith almost called out the entry door was never locked but didn't want to give herself away. The woman turned the doorknob with her free hand, and they went in.

The store on the corner was closed, with a hand-written sign on the door stating a family emergency. The next store was two blocks away. Her feet were soaked. Why had she worn such stupid shoes?

Edith ducked into a doorway of a brick apartment building. She opened Philip's letter and was met by the same elegant script.

He began by talking about the weather, a party his mother had had, and some of the people that were there.

She stopped reading. Was he trying to tell her he'd met someone? A young woman who was unencumbered by a husband?

Do you think one can fall in love at first sight? I've been wondering this since you left. The moment I saw you, I just knew we were going to be tangled up for a long time.

Tangled up. That didn't sound promising, and it was hardly romantic. She and Walter were tangled up. Kathleen and the man she was engaged to were tangled up, though Kathleen's words on the subject had been they were "caught in a snare."

Philip said he'd taken the job at the advertising agency after all. He was working on a campaign for mouthwash. His first attempt, "for the freshest kiss you'll ever deliver," had been met with skepticism. His boss was a prude. And fat. Philip described a dull evening at the man's house and a butler with watery eyes.

He closed by saying he hoped to hear from her. He didn't urge them to meet.

Edith tore the letter into tiny pieces and dropped them in the gutter.

When she returned home, the apartment was full. Music played on the radio. Walter came into the kitchen and asked what had kept her. She explained about the first store being closed. He looked her over and asked if she wanted to change.

"Just my shoes and stockings," she said. "I'll be quick."

A few minutes later, she joined everyone in the living room. Walter introduced her to Steven and Luann Blake—the couple she'd passed on the street. Luann had a challenging, almost defiant air as if she resented being there. The husband had acne scars along his hairline and a heavy five-o'clock shadow. His eyes reminded her of Philip's, though they seemed less intelligent. Then, Edith supposed, Steven would have to be bright to be studying at Harvard.

Another couple was talking to Joe-Joe. The wife was pretty, the man looked dull. Walter didn't give their names. Edith made her way across the room to where Clara sat on the couch. She asked if she'd like that gin and tonic now. Clara had a glass in her hand which she said was scotch on the rocks and poor Edith shouldn't have bothered. Anyway, it was too late to switch. Didn't Edith think sticking to one liquor was always easier the next day?

"Never mix, never worry," Edith said.

People ate and drank. Polite comments were made about the apartment, which Edith thought a group of people made look even shabbier. Walter circulated, talked to everyone, encouraged someone struggling with a paper on constitutional law. Edith made the rounds, too. She refilled plates—Clara's black-eyed peas were wildly popular— she refilled glasses, hers especially.

She found herself alone in the kitchen with a fresh drink. She sat down, took a cigarette from the pack lying on the table, and lit it with a match from the book Walter kept there for his pipe. One of these days she'd liberate Philip's lighter from her bathrobe pocket and use it without explaining how she came by it. He seemed like a man who tried things on. First, he threw himself at her to see how she'd react, then he pulled back. He came at her again, then left in a cool frame of mind. His two letters were inconsistent. The first was full of keen interest, the second struck a blander tone.

Except for the question about love at first sight.

He had asked it to keep her on the hook and make her hope he was inching toward a genuine romance. He assumed that's what she wanted. He couldn't conceive she might be out for sex only. Being a woman, she would seek to involve her heart, too.

Rain beat against the glass. A flash of light was soon followed by distant thunder. The thunder approached, the lights flickered, then went dark. The radio was quiet. Drunken cries of glee came from the other room, and Walter said, "Hold on everyone. Edie's got some candles around here somewhere!" He came into the kitchen and said the lights were out. Edith said she knew.

"Why are you just sitting here?" he asked. The lights came on. There was also sudden, raucous music. He asked where the candles were and she said in the drawer under the toaster. Walter yanked it open.

"Is this all we have?" he asked. The candles were of different lengths. None were new.

"You won't need them now."

"What's wrong with you?"

"Nothing."

"Where are the matches?"

"Right there," she said.

She held out her hand to take the candles, and put them on the table. He asked what she was going to put them in. She stood up and pointed to an upper cabinet she was too short to reach. He opened it and said he couldn't see anything. She told him to go get the step stool from the closet so she could climb up and see for herself.

He came up behind her, grabbed her around the waist, and lifted her.

"What the hell are you doing?" she asked. He was laughing. Then she was, too.

"Just reach in."

"Lift me higher."

"Okay. Hey, you lost weight."

She leaned into the cabinet. There were three glass candlesticks. There used to be four, but she'd broken one. She grabbed two in one hand, one in the other. She told him to put her down.

"What if I don't?" he asked.

"I'll scream my head off."

"Won't matter. You're my wife. I can do what I want."

"Put me down."

He did.

Thunder continued to sound, and the lights and radio went out again. Edith handed a candlestick to Walter so she could pick up the matches from the table. They took everything into the living room. The Blakes stood at the window watching the sky light up and go dark. No one spoke. Edith arranged the candles and lit them. They didn't do much to brighten the room, but their glow was warm and pleasant.

"He died at Anzio," Clara said. She was still sitting on the couch.

"Who did?" Edith asked.

"Her brother," Joe-Joe said.

"I'm sorry."

Joe-Joe patted Clara's hand. "Don't think about that now," he said.

Clara said the storm was to blame. Every time there was lightning and thunder, she thought of her brother in battle. That's what a battle was like, wasn't it? Full of noise and flashes of light?

"It's a little different," the pretty wife's husband said.

Clara sobbed. Edith asked if there were anything she could do. Did she want to lie down for a little while? Sometimes it helped to put one's feet up.

Walter looked lovingly at her. He had a drink in his hand, and Edith wondered how he'd managed to pick it up again so quickly in the dark. She saw the glass was empty. Maybe he was refilling it for someone.

The pretty wife, sitting in their wingback chair, said she went to Texas once as a child and saw a tornado off in the distance. It came down from the sky like a black finger. When the storm was over, they got in the car and drove to where the tornado had been. A barn had been leveled.

"This conversation's getting awfully grim," Walter said. "How about another round?"

Edith said Illinois had tornados, too. Not so much where they lived, but out in the farmlands.

"You remember," Edith said to Walter.

"Not really."

"You're from Illinois?" the pretty wife asked. Edith and Walter said yes at the same time, and Edith realized from the way she looked pointedly at Walter the question had been for him alone.

"Really?" the husband said. "I thought you were from New England."

Edith laughed.

"Walter, a Yankee? Hardly," she said.

Walter's expression stiffened.

Clara sobbed again. "I'm sorry, I shouldn't be this upset, after all this time," she said.

"How much time do you need to get over losing someone?" Luann asked. "Some people never get over it. Maybe they shouldn't. Maybe people should remember a useless death. That way they won't forget how stupid and pointless war is."

The storm passed, and the room was so quiet Edith could hear the small clock on the bookshelf tick.

"My brother died for his country," Clara said.

"So did mine," Luann said.

"The war wasn't pointless," Steven said. "We liberated a lot of people."

Luann bowed her head as if to concede the point, yet her eyes were full of fire.

Edith brought Clara a glass of water, though she hadn't asked for it. Tears rolled down her face. Joe-Joe kept patting her hand. Then he said, "Honey, don't. Think of the baby."

"Seems only fair, don't you think? She'll be hearing *it* cry soon enough," Edith said. Everyone turned to look at her, even the people at the window.

Music blasted from the radio and the lights came on. A couple of people clapped. To Edith, everyone's face had a dull, sleepy look, as if they'd just woken up. She realized everyone had had a lot to drink. She had, too. Her candor was rising in a way that could end up badly.

She went from person to person asking if they needed anything. The pretty wife looked at Edith coldly and said, "You went away. To New York, Walter said. His aunt was ill."

Edith resented Walter had made up a story. But what else could he reasonably say?

"Yes. I got home several weeks ago," she said.

The woman lit a cigarette and blew smoke in Edith's direction.

Walter was at Edith's elbow, saying "You remember Babs, don't you, dear? She and her husband were over last winter." Edith didn't remember and said she did.

Babs' husband was now in a corner looking through the pages of a book. Edith approached him and said hello.

"Mrs. Sloan," the man said.

"I'm sorry I wasn't here when you arrived."

The man shrugged. Edith asked if he were enjoying himself. He said it was a swell get-together, but he wasn't much for parties, himself. His wife was the sociable one. It was hard for her, being cooped up at home all day while he was in class. He'd been trying to get her to get involved in something, a volunteer activity.

"How do *you* stay busy?" he asked. His eyebrows were reddish-brown, Edith noticed, looking at him more closely.

"Oh, I manage. Always lots to do, you know."

"I told Babs she should enroll in a class. She's a bright girl. She dropped out of college when we got married. Then when I went to the South Pacific, she lived with my parents. Hoo-boy, I think that wasn't too great for her, but she's a trooper, and kept everyone's spirits up."

Edith asked where Babs had been a student.

"Bryn Mawr."

"Is she from Philadelphia, then?"

"Yes."

No wonder Walter liked her. He probably thought she was some Mainline darling. So much more interesting than the midwestern cow he married.

She told herself she was being unfair. She wasn't a cow. Far from it. Philip had made her feel pretty. He'd made her feel *beautiful*.

"It's all about how people make you feel, isn't it?" Edith asked.

"I'm sorry, what is?"

"Literature. Poets, novelists, you know."

"I suppose that's true."

"Of course, it's more complicated than that."

"I'm sure you're right."

Edith asked him what made him want to study law. He said he hadn't always, but the disorder of the war made him see its value and necessity. The trouble was, he really loved literature, but there was no money in that. He'd always been a reader, which the book in his hands proved better than anything. It was a volume of Emily Dickinson, an author he had long admired, even loved. He said during the war he didn't have much time to read, and that was a shame. It left his mind looking for something to focus on and being on a destroyer wasn't a good place for an unoccupied mind. Books brought people together, but they weren't enough to keep them from ruining each other. That's what law was for. Didn't she agree?

"I think law is for punishing the people who break it."

He said nothing. Maybe he hadn't heard.

"Do you read Whitman?" Edith asked.

"No."

"My master's was on him, and Carl Sandburg. Comparing them, I mean."

"You have a master's?"

Edith nodded.

"That's amazing really." He paused and glanced back at his wife, who sat smoking, talking now to someone else.

"I'm Andy, by the way," he said.

"I remember."

"We've never met."

"No, I didn't think so."

Edith excused herself and went into the kitchen. She lifted the window enough to let some fresh air rush in. Blood pounded in her ears. She was aware of being hungry, yet the idea of eating made her queasy. Andy followed her in and asked if she were feeling all right.

Edith said she'd make some coffee. She filled the glass pot with water and put it on the stove. She didn't turn on the gas because she remembered the matches were in the other room. She went out to get them. Walter was dancing with Babs. Steven and Luann Blake danced, too. Edith got the matches and returned to the stove. She lit the flame, then sat down at the table.

"I'm sorry, what were you saying?" Edith asked Andy.

"Nothing important. May I?"

"Please."

He sat down, too. Edith asked if he had a job lined up when he graduated.

"I've been interviewing, of course, but nothing's certain."

Walter was going through the same thing, Edith said. He'd been to a number of the bigger Boston firms. One, Hopkins, Drake, and Lowe, seemed interested.

Andy said it took a certain type of person to do well in a law firm. A consistent, unquestioning type. He wasn't running himself down by that, or Walter either, of course. From what he could tell, Walter was a very dedicated person who would really cater to a firm's partners and clients.

"And their wives," Edith said. Then, "I'm sorry, I don't why I said that."

"It's all right. Babs can be overly friendly sometimes."

"So can Walter."

"But only with members of the opposite sex."

"Bingo."

Andy said he knew he was a pretty dull person, and Babs didn't like dull people as a rule.

"She married you, didn't she?" Edith asked. Her left temple throbbed. Her headache had never gone away.

Andy looked at his hands. Edith did, too. Like the rest of him, they were clean, ordinary, and suggested a capable person.

He said he probably shouldn't be telling her this, but the truth was Babs got pregnant, and he married her. That's all there was to it. Then she lost the baby. He didn't feel trapped, exactly. Disappointed, certainly. He didn't know how Babs felt about it. He assumed she was relieved. He made it clear he'd give her a divorce if she wanted it, but she said no. She's been a good wife, but sometimes he wondered if she wouldn't be happier on her own, playing the field with no strings attached.

"Some women find shelter in marriage, even when their eye wanders," Edith said.

"Because nothing can get serious," Andy said.

Edith nodded.

Walter came into the kitchen and asked what she was doing.

"Making coffee," she said.

"Good idea." He was flushed. Beads of sweat stood out on his forehead. He asked her if she wanted to dance.

"Sure."

The music had softened into something slow and romantic. Walter held her close as they swayed. Edith was glad for his embrace. She put her head on his shoulder. Everyone was dancing except Clara and Andy. Joe-Joe danced with Luann. Steven was with Babs. The music picked up speed, and Walter sped up, too. Edith watched Joe-

Joe change his beat. He was courtly, prescribed, but not familiar. She wondered if people thought Walter were a fool for the way he'd shown how much he liked having Babs in his arms. But everyone was lost in the music, themselves, in what they hoped would come, and in what was gone. She looked over at Clara, who seemed calm at last.

Edith hoped her baby would be a boy, and she'd name it after her dead brother.

chapter seven

On the Monday before Thanksgiving, a foot of snow fell over most of New England. Classes were scheduled to end on Wednesday and were canceled the day before. Walter didn't mind. He was in high spirits. He had a research paper due before Christmas, which he felt he had a good handle on. He wanted to go sledding. Edith said that sounded fine—if they had a sled. Did she remember sledding on the golf course back home? She did. And almost landing in a freezing creek.

The telephone rang. Walter left the kitchen to answer it. His buoyant tone turned polite, almost deferential. The caller did most of the talking.

"Well, sure, we'd be glad to," Walter said.

Edith sighed. Walter didn't believe in consulting her first about anything.

She lit a cigarette. She'd been smoking more, something Walter commented on. He told her to take it easy. She didn't. She enjoyed liquor a little more these days, too. Walter had also commented on that. Clara had had her baby, a little girl they named Noreen, which Edith thought was a hideous name. Joe-Joe brought cigars into class, and Walter enjoyed his that same evening at home. Edith had had to open all the windows afterward.

Walter returned to the kitchen looking merry.

"We've been invited to Thanksgiving dinner," he said.

"By whom?"

"Henry McCormick."

Walter explained he met him at the college bookstore, wandering idly through the new releases. At first, Edith thought Walter might have been looking for something to get her, but he typically didn't buy her gifts. She asked what had taken him there, and he said he had some time to kill, the weather was bad, the library had gotten old. He and McCormick—Henry—were looking at the same book, *Cry, the Beloved Country.* Henry said he had an uncle in South Africa, which is why he read the dust jacket. Walter noticed at once Henry was English and asked what he was doing at Harvard.

"You didn't," Edith said.

"By way of a polite inquiry. I didn't interrogate him."

"And what *is* he doing at Harvard?"

"Studying Shakespeare."

Edith didn't see why an Englishman would come all the way to Boston to study one of his own. There must be a backstory. There was always a backstory.

Naturally, Henry and his wife, Mary, didn't know anything about Thanksgiving and wanted to give it a try.

"He's very excited about it," Walter said.

Edith said fine. It would be nice to have someone else cook. Then Walter said Henry had asked if they could bring a nice bowl of mashed potatoes.

"Oh, honestly!"

"And maybe a tray of stuffing?"

"Do they want me to bring the turkey, too?"

"No, they seem to have that in hand."

"Or gizzard."

"Oh, you."

Walter could sense Edith was put out and called Henry back to say perhaps stuffing was all they could manage. He said their stove was iffy. Henry said they would be happy to handle the potatoes themselves, which made Edith wonder why they'd been asked to contribute them in the first place.

Edith looked forward to meeting some new people. The gang that came over the other night wasn't too interesting. And before that, the people they sometimes visited or went out with were all concerned with school, money, and getting ahead. Not that she had anything against that, of course. It's just there was so much more to life! If only she could find it. She was bored. She spent her time in the library or bookstores. A little place in Cambridge, The Turned Page, had become her favorite. As you entered, there was a large round table covered with a Persian rug. Usually, a vase of flowers stood in the center, and more often than not, they were wilted. The owner had arranged a comfortable seating area where customers could sit and browse the books they considered buying. Edith seldom bought anything. The owner, an elderly gentleman whose white hair was always ruffled as if he often ran his hand through it, didn't mind. He was friendly and impressed with her knowledge. He said he was looking for a part-time clerk and asked if she were interested. Edith shocked herself when she said she'd have to speak with her husband about it. The owner, Mr. Samson, was curious about Walter, so Edith described his military service, and what he was studying at Harvard. Mr. Samson had lost two grandsons in the war. He said it was hard to understand why the young had to die when they were the future, after all.

Once, Mr. Samson offered her a cup of tea. He ushered her into a back room he used as an office. It was a charming place with books stacked everywhere, an elegant desk with carved legs, and a small fireplace surrounded by blue and green tiles. The chair he suggested Edith sit in was upholstered in velvet and extremely comfortable. He boiled water on a hot plate. A side table held the pot, cups, and tins of tea. He apologized for having no cream. There was no way to keep it fresh. He did have lemon if she liked. She said lemon was lovely.

It was a slow day. The bell on the door tinkled only once. Mr. Samson went out and told the woman who'd come in if she needed anything, he was just in the back. Edith asked if he were worried she might help herself to something while he wasn't able to observe her. He said in his experience people who loved books didn't tend to steal them. Then again, if she did steal one it would be because she couldn't afford it, and, in that case, he'd feel as if he'd done a good deed.

She never told Walter about the tea or the offer of a job. She wanted to take it, though. Very much. Maybe she'd just announce she had. Giving up her academic career made her deserve to have what she wanted. Thinking that brought Philip instantly to mind. He hadn't written again; she never wrote once. Aunt Margaret had and mentioned him. Edith understood Aunt Margaret was savvy to what had taken place that night. Maybe she didn't know all the details, but she knew enough to know something significant happened, which she hoped her words, *he seems to have settled down now, much to Francine's great relief,* would gently underscore. Edith felt like a child who'd been offered a slice of cake and turned it down, thinking she could have it later when she really wanted it. She supposed if she wrote and asked to see him, he'd try to arrange it. But think of the complications! It would be very difficult to tumble into bed without involving other people, a hotel desk clerk, if no one else.

Edith made the stuffing. Walter read his textbooks. While the stuffing cooked, she read, too, a novel by Ernest Hemingway, *A Farewell to Arms.* The tragedy of unmarried lovers gnawed, as did the descriptions of the First World War, which everyone then thought of only as The Great War. She'd read Ford Maddox Ford's *Parade's End* and was so moved by its elegant yet dismal slant. Everyone could relate to war. That is, war seemed to provide a reliable subject for art of all kinds. What were people her age going to make of what they'd all gone through together? Was their generation lost, too? She looked at Walter, bent over the table, taking notes. His concentration was fierce, and he didn't look like himself. Or rather, he looked like a version of himself—the person he would have been deciphering a code, perhaps.

They were invited for three o'clock on Thanksgiving Day. Just after two, Walter began fussing about which suit to wear. He only had four, so it seemed to Edith the choice should be simple enough. He hadn't shined his shoes, and she offered to do it for him. When he asked what she was wearing, she said her green velvet. This was a jacket and matching skirt. It's what she'd worn on her wedding day. For her birthday, the week before, she'd received a silk scarf from her mother she thought she would add. By then Walter had lost interest and was going through his shirts one by one, checking the cuffs and collars for wear. Edith said she kept an eye on everything when she did the washing and ironing. Didn't he trust her?

"Of course, I do. I'm just nervous, I guess," he said. He'd moved on to his socks, making sure the pair he chose had no holes.

"Why?"

"They're classy people."

"I thought you only knew the husband."

"I do. I figure the wife has to be upper crust, given what he's like."

"And what's he like?"

"You'll see."

In the cab over, Walter begged her to make a good impression. She was miffed. Didn't she always make a good impression? Well, of course, she did. He was sorry for suggesting otherwise. Edith was annoyed with him and with the tray of stuffing balanced on her knees. She hoped it wouldn't leave a stain. She'd wanted to bring a dish towel to put under it, but Walter said that was tacky. She should have asked him to manage the tray. His lap was empty. She hoped their host had good liquor and wine. An Englishman should know about wine, she thought.

The McCormicks lived in an apartment near the Charles. There was a wide brick walk leading to the door and manicured hedges on either side. It was the kind of place where a businessman might live, not a student.

A crystal chandelier hung in the lobby. The floor was marble, and Edith thought it would be difficult in snowy weather. But then some handy person was probably employed to keep everything clean and dry.

They took the elevator to the top floor. The apartment was at the end. There was no noise coming from behind any of the doors they passed, and Edith wondered if everyone had gone away for the holiday or been invited out. The carpet was so thick Edith's heels left little round marks. The soft lighting came from brass and crystal sconces along the wall.

Walter knocked, then straightened his tie. Edith handed him the tray and adjusted her scarf and smoothed down her hair. Right before leaving home, she'd sprayed herself with perfume and she worried it was too strong. Walter had said nothing, but then his nose was usually full, from some allergy or other.

The door was opened by a man in a white shirt and black jacket, black tie, and black trousers. It took a moment for Edith to realize he was a butler. Walter gave him their name, and the butler ushered them in. They stood in a foyer with inlaid tile in the shape of a circle. A charming cherry-tone table with three drawers was nearby, also two side chairs and a hall leading to what must be the kitchen. Edith's thought was confirmed when the butler took the tray of stuffing from Walter and headed down the hallway. Walter and Edith didn't know what to do when he didn't come back right away. Neither wanted to walk further into the apartment, so they waited. Then they removed their coats and draped them on one of the empty chairs. When the butler was still gone after a few more minutes, they crossed into a large room with heavy pleated drapes on either side of a floor-to-ceiling window. Through the window was a direct view of the river. Edith was instantly reminded of Aunt Margaret's place.

A fire danced in the fireplace. The mantlepiece had a series of small abstract sculptures. The furniture was upholstered in light gray and pale blue; the wood floor was broken up with large area rugs. Edith felt at home. She could tell this was an easy, comfortable place. With a pang, she reflected on the small rooms she and Walter lived in. One look at him then, as he, too, took in his surroundings, said he also was very impressed.

"Walter!"

They turned and were greeted by a tall man in an exquisite double-breasted blazer and cuffed slacks. The crease in his pants looked sharp enough to cut. His cufflinks were gold and navy-blue enamel. He wore no other jewelry. He shook Walter's hand, then turned to Edith.

"Mrs. Sloan, what a pleasure," he said. Edith adored his accent. She'd developed a good ear at the UN, and knew at once this was a cultured, educated person from the British upper class.

"The pleasure's all mine," Edith said.

"Mary's having some trouble in the kitchen, I'm afraid. Alistair's in there with her. Our butler. You didn't know that was his name, of course."

Edith was surprised he was nervous when it was she and Walter who should be worried about not measuring up. Yet she didn't feel that way. Something about him put her at ease.

"Darling, this is Henry McCormick," Walter said.

"So I gathered," Edith said.

"Or do you prefer Sir Henry?" Walter asked.

"Lord Henry, but just Henry's fine."

"Henry's an Earl," Walter told Edith.

"I see," she said.

"You Americans couldn't care less about such nonsense. It's so very refreshing, I must say!"

Henry was pleasant looking enough but plain, Edith thought. His eyes struck her as too small for his long face. His chin receded.

Henry offered drinks. Walter wanted a scotch and soda. Edith did, too. Henry said he had some very fine single malt scotch he'd been saving for a special occasion, and he couldn't think of anything more special than celebrating his first Thanksgiving.

"Oughtn't we wait for your wife?" Edith asked.

Henry looked as if he'd forgotten about her.

Something clattered to the floor in the kitchen.

"Let me see if I can help," Edith said. Henry pointed to the hall they'd identified a few moments before.

The kitchen was behind a pair of hinged doors that made Edith think of a saloon. She pushed her way in. The room was large and done all in white, except for the floor which consisted of black-and-white tiles in a checkerboard pattern. Alistair wore an apron and was staring at a turkey in a pan sitting on the stove. Next to him stood Mary. She was tall, almost as tall as Walter, with raven black hair. She turned at the sound of Edith's heels and looked down at her with an angry gaze. In an instant, she regained her composure and held out her hand for Edith to shake.

"Mrs. Sloan! You find me in quite a predicament," she said.

Mary's wrists were decorated with multiple gold bangles. On her ring finger was a large square-cut diamond. Her palm was soft, her nails unpolished. She gave off a sweet, floral smell, which Edith could tell at once was perfume much more expensive than her own.

Edith asked what she could do.

"Well . . ." Mary glanced helplessly at the turkey and explained she was a fair cook but had no experience with these things. Edith asked how long it had been in the oven.

"About two hours."

"Well, I think you've got a little bit more to go. Do you have a meat thermometer?"

"Have we?" Mary asked Alistair.

"Yes, Milady."

Alistair was British, too, but there was a hint of Cockney on his tongue.

"And what is the oven set at?" Edith asked.

Mary looked blank.

"The temperature."

"Oh, I have no idea."

"Three hundred degrees," Alistair said.

"Turn it up to three-fifty, wait a few minutes then put the turkey back in. In about forty-five minutes, poke it with the meat thermometer. If it reads a hundred and eighty degrees, it's cooked."

Alistair looked critically at Edith.

Mary said she wasn't sure how to prepare the potatoes. She usually baked them, but that didn't seem right for the occasion. Edith asked where they were. Mary pointed to a bowl full of fat russets. Edith told Alistair to wash and peel them, then to cut them into quarters, and drop them into cold salted water and bring the whole thing to a boil. Then when he could pass the tines of a fork through one, they were ready.

"I assume I'm to strain them," Alistair said.

"You assume correctly. Do you have a masher?"

Alistair dug through a drawer and pulled one out.

"Butter? Milk?" she asked.

"Yes."

"You're all set."

Mary pushed open one of the swinging doors, allowing Edith to pass through it. She followed. They walked in silence to the living room where Henry and Walter sat, one in each wing chair, by the fire. They stood up.

Henry introduced Walter to Mary. They shook hands. Facing each other Edith realized Mary was slightly taller than Walter. After they dropped hands, Walter folded his arms across his chest, demonstrating this fact made him uncomfortable. Edith was much shorter than the other three. She felt like a child in a room of adults, but only for a moment because Walter burst out with, "Golly, this is a swell place you have here!"

Edith and Mary took a seat on opposite ends of the sofa. Henry gestured to the drink on the coffee table he'd prepared for Edith when she left the room. There was no glass for Mary.

"Have we no champagne?" Mary asked.

"I'm certain we must," Henry said, and lifted a small silver bell from the side table next to his chair and swung it. The ring it made was surprisingly loud. A moment later Alistair appeared, without the apron, looking flustered. Henry asked about the champagne, and Alistair said he believed they had a 1940 Dom Pérignon, and also perhaps a 1943.

"Which is better?" Henry asked Alistair.

Alistair stood perfectly straight. He wasn't a young man and the folds of his neck rolled over the top of his starched collar.

"I believe that would be the 1943, Milord," he said.

"Right you are. Lady Mary cares for some."

"Right away, Milord."

After he'd gone, Walter whistled. He said he'd never seen a genuine English butler before.

"Nor perhaps a genuine lord and lady," Edith said. Walter flushed.

"You mustn't test him like that," Mary said.

"How else will he learn?" Henry asked.

They were talking about the butler, Edith realized. She asked if he'd come with them from England. Henry said he had and was grateful for the chance to see America.

Edith then asked how Mary and Henry liked it here.

"Like a breath of fresh air," Mary said, but something in her tone suggested she didn't care for it much.

Henry explained he'd had a choice of where to earn his graduate degree—Oxford or Harvard and he, too, was keen for a chance to see how the Yanks did things.

"And how do we? Do things, that is," Edith asked.

"Splendidly!" Henry said. Mary smiled thinly.

She asked Walter if he were also a graduate student.

"I'm in law school," Walter said.

"Ah," Mary said.

"A man with a practical calling. I very much admire that," Henry said.

"You're practical too, darling, in so many ways," Mary said. Henry sipped his drink. He looked around the room in a detached way, as if the items in it meant little to him. His gaze rested on Edith.

"You're a poet, I believe," he said.

"No, no. I wrote my master's thesis on Whitman and Sandburg. Sometimes I *felt* like a poet or wished I could be one."

"I apologize. I was certain Walter said something about you and poetry, so naturally I assumed . . ."

"Henry tends to assume," Mary said.

Everyone paused. Edith wondered where the butler was.

"Are you still in school, or perhaps teaching?" Henry asked.

"School. That is, I was. I had to quit."

"But why?"

"My aunt got sick. In New York. Edith was gone all summer," Walter said.

Edith thought they would need to come up with another story because she was tired of that one.

"I'd always heard American women were very devoted to kith and kin," Mary said. "And here you are, living proof!"

Edith asked her how she spent her time.

Oh, doing this and that, Mary said. Decorating mostly. She'd found some wonderful little shops around. She'd be happy to show Edith some afternoon if she liked. She could come by for tea first.

"That sounds lovely," Edith said.

Alistair returned with the champagne and four glasses. He asked if he might open it. Henry said he'd prefer to, and Alistair handed him the bottle and withdrew. Henry certainly knew what he was doing. He had the cork out in no time without spilling a drop. He poured four glasses. Edith mentioned she wasn't sure it was a good idea to combine scotch and champagne.

"Well, leave off the scotch, enjoy the bubbly, and we'll have wine with dinner. All right?" Henry asked.

Mary said they must drink a toast to their new American friends. They raised their glasses. Everyone drank except Edith. She told Walter you weren't supposed to drink when you were the one being toasted.

"Oh, well, too late. My word, this is awfully good stuff," he said. His glass was empty. Edith inwardly cringed. Henry refilled Walter's glass.

Mary asked what Edith did while Walter was studying.

"I work part-time in a bookstore. Well, I'm starting this week."

Walter stared at her.

"Since when?" he asked.

"I told you that ages ago."

"No, you didn't."

"Darling, you have so much on your mind, you just forgot."

Henry said he had a collection of first editions Edith might like to take a look at some time, including a volume of Walt Whitman's.

"Really? That's amazing!" she said.

"You're boring our guests," Mary said.

"Not at all. I love first editions."

"Me, too," Walter said. He had never expressed any interest in first editions.

Mary said old books didn't particularly interest her. Horses, that was another story. She'd always been mad about horses. She was thinking about buying one or two if she could find a suitable stable for them. She wanted to drive out in the country and take a look.

"Do you have a car?" Walter asked.

"Not yet. I think we'd like to get a Cadillac," Henry said. "Have you a car?"

"No. It's too difficult, living in Cambridge," Edith said.

They talked about driving in England, and how odd it would feel to switch sides of the road. Then came a brief survey of words that differed—*elevator* here was *lift* there; a car's *trunk* here was a *boot* there; an *apartment* was a *flat*; and the oddest of all, at least to Mary who suffered from them on occasion, was no one in England would ever say a *bloody nose*. The correct term was *a nosebleed*.

The conversation turned to the war and how it had changed things. Edith said she appreciated the greater opportunities women now had. Privately she thought things had swung again in men's favor, at the expense of women, as always. Mary said as far as she could tell, women were still stuck in the same old rut they had always been in. Your highest duty wasn't to king and country, but to find a husband and have children. Henry reminded her she wasn't interested in having children and that was okay with him.

Edith thought it strange they would share this information with people they'd just met, but maybe the English were more candid about that sort of thing than Americans were. A man at the UN, some undersecretary, told her during a reception she'd been required to attend, that despite all their alleged openness, Americans were very private and prudish. Edith couldn't remember where he was from, some Scandinavian country, she thought. She'd considered that remark from time to time as it related to her own experience. Walter wasn't a prude, but he couldn't talk about sex. She tried to tell him he was too fast, and he always turned away or changed the subject. She supposed it wasn't the easiest thing to talk about. What made everything worse was this idiotic notion that a woman should enter the marriage bed a virgin. She'd wondered many times if she would have married Walter if she'd slept with him, first. She knew she wasn't supposed to be caught up in her own pleasures, but where sex was concerned, what else was the point? Children, of course. But why couldn't there be both pleasure and progeny? And why was she supposed to feel ashamed of what she wanted?

Like Walter, Henry had done intelligence work during the war, which meant he couldn't go into detail. Edith asked what it had been like in London, with bombs falling all around.

Henry considered her question.

"Terrifying," he said.

"Were you there, too?" Edith asked Mary.

"I stayed in Shropshire with Henry's parents."

Edith asked Henry if he planned to look for a teaching position, once he'd earned his degree.

"No, I shouldn't think so," he said.

"What will you do?"

"Engage in a life of quiet scholarship, I think."

"Sounds lovely."

Mary looked out the window and sighed. The champagne had brought color to her face, but she wasn't relaxed, Edith could tell. She was thinking about the future, Edith thought, wanting one thing while Henry wanted another.

"How long have you been married?" Edith asked.

Mary, Walter, and Henry looked at her.

"Eight years," Henry said.

"Nine," Mary said.

Henry asked if anyone wanted a refill. Walter did. The ladies did, too.

"And you?" Henry asked Walter.

"Me, what?"

"How long have you been married?"

"Three years."

"Three and a half," Edith said.

Henry chuckled.

"Women are always exacting about these things," he said.

They finished the champagne and opened a second bottle. Henry rang the bell, and when Alistair appeared, Henry asked for the hors d'oeuvres to be served. Edith was glad. The alcohol was hitting her pretty hard, and Walter, too, from the way he was listing in his chair like a dinghy taking on water.

Mary was saying something to her about a professor who'd invited them to dinner recently, an older man who was acquainted with England. Apparently, he'd lived there for a time after the First World War. His knowledge of the countryside where Mary grew up made her homesick. She supposed it wasn't just missing what she was used to but being separated from her brother.

At the mention of this brother, Henry, who'd been talking to Walter about a local place that did marvelous tailoring, fell silent. Edith thought it was quite a talent, being able to talk to one person and monitor another conversation at the same time.

"You were saying?" Edith asked.

Mary said her brother, George, had been with the RAF and was shot down during the Battle of Britain. He'd been badly burned over his hands and arms and spent a long time in a convalescent home in Kent. Mary got down there every chance she got. Her parents were both frail and couldn't make the trip. Gradually George healed, but not really in his mind. Mary knew it was awkward to speak of such things. She hoped Edith understood what she meant. Maybe she'd known someone, too, who'd left a part of himself behind once the fighting was all over and things had more or less returned to normal.

"Things will never be normal again. Not the way they were," Henry said. He lit a cigarette and extended a carved box that had been on the table to Walter. Walter helped himself.

"Not with the Russians making trouble," Walter said.

"They're not happy with the Marshall Plan. Or with Kennan's idea of containment."

"No choice *but* to contain them."

Alistair returned with a silver tray bearing a bowl of caviar on ice, small pancakes Edith assumed were blinis, linen napkins, small plates with gold around the rim, and a mother-of-pearl spoon. He asked if he could prepare a plate for Edith. She said yes. She took the napkin and spread it on her lap before taking the plate Alistair handed her. She'd never had caviar before. Walter said he did once, at a fancy dinner in Washington.

She nibbled a corner of the blini topped with caviar. All she could taste was fish and salt. Maybe her palette was too coarse to appreciate the delicate flavor. Walter ate his in one go. Edith could tell he didn't like it much.

"We should have had salmon sandwiches. But I don't know how they'd go as a prelude to a turkey dinner," Mary said. Her speech was slightly slurred. Edith thought about her brother, gone off his rocker. She imagined a good-looking man, padding around a large country house in a smoking jacket and slippers, with an absent, preoccupied air.

Mary asked about Edith's family, and where she was from. Edith wondered how to describe Illinois to a foreigner. She said she was from the Midwest, the heartland of America.

"I've heard it called 'the breadbasket,'" Henry said, helping himself to more caviar.

"Yes."

"Because of all the wheat it produces."

"And corn," Walter said.

"Is it farm country, where you're from?" Henry asked Edith.

"Not in the town itself, obviously."

"I should think not."

Walter said it was a lovely place. He'd never said that to Edith. When they'd lived there, he hated it and couldn't wait to leave. Maybe with time Urbana had taken on some charm. Yet he never suggested going back to visit. He wasn't close to his parents. His father was demanding and critical. His mother was needy. Edith had suffered through many family dinners with his mother trying so hard to please, and his father withholding the smallest nod of approval.

"Darling, Mary asked you a question," Walter said.

"I'm sorry."

"I asked if we should take a look at dinner," Mary said.

"Yes, if you like."

Alistair had removed the turkey and mashed the potatoes. Edith's dish of stuffing was warming in the oven. From somewhere a bowl of creamed spinach had appeared. Edith nodded her appreciation to Alistair, who stood at attention, waiting on her word. She said everything looked wonderful, and when he went to tell the others dinner was served, she took a quick taste of the potatoes. They were lumpy.

The dining room table was at least ten feet long. In the center was a silver candelabra, which Alistair was in the process of lighting when they took their seats. Henry had decanted a good French wine and filled their glasses. Walter offered to carve the turkey. Edith hoped he was sober enough to manage it and not make a mess. He did well.

When they were all served, Henry asked if they usually said a prayer.

"No," Edith said.

"Not raised on it?" Henry asked.

"My father is an atheist."

"You never told me that," Walter said.

"Was religion a part of your childhood?" Mary asked Walter.

"His mother is a Quaker," Edith said.

"Was. She doesn't go to meetings anymore," Walter said.

Henry said he was raised in the Church of England, but then everyone was. In England, anyway.

"Yes, dear," Mary said.

They ate.

Henry asked if it always snowed so early in the year. Walter said it did, sometimes. Mary poked suspiciously at her turkey but enjoyed Edith's stuffing.

The men talked about school and their respective programs. Henry's thesis advisor was pushing him in a direction he didn't want to go, which was to analyze the use of comedy and comedic themes in Shakespeare's plays when he'd much rather focus on the sonnets and their treatment of romantic versus spiritual love. Walter said his Evidence professor gave him a low mark on his last paper for noting the judge in the case in question had improperly instructed the jury. It wasn't a recent case, something dating from the 1920s, but it took place in Boston, so naturally, Walter assumed his professor might know that particular judge, or be related to him somehow, or just didn't like the idea of some upstart student questioning anything a judge did.

"But isn't that the basis of American law? To question everything?" Henry asked.

"You give us too much credit. We're just as concerned with upholding tradition as you Brits are."

Henry flushed just a little. Edith wondered if the remark irritated him.

As the two men continued to talk about school, Edith sensed a subtle rivalry developing. Henry would make a mild complaint about a professor, or a classmate, or the library not having a copy of a book he very much needed to have, and Walter would cite a student in his study group who never pulled his weight or another who tapped his pencil most annoyingly during a recent exam. It was as if each wanted to convince the other that his plight was worse, his circumstance more harrowing, and thus more deserving of the other's—what, exactly? Sympathy? Respect?

Later, after the store-bought pumpkin pie no one liked and barely touched, they sat again in the living room. Snow began to fall, and Walter and Henry went to the window to admire the view. Mary leaned toward Edith and said, "Henry can be very competitive. Try not to mind too much."

Edith didn't share that with Walter. She was pretty sure he'd figured it out for himself.

chapter eight

Edith didn't admire other women or feel jealousy toward them, except for one—Kathleen Sloan. How could she not? Where Edith was a pipsqueak at five foot three, Kathleen commanded whatever room she was in at five foot ten. In high heels, she was over six feet tall. When she wore them, she and Walter were less than an inch apart, but then he always wore a hat, which gave him an advantage.

Kathleen phoned from the train station to say she was taking a cab to her hotel. Did they want to join her there for a drink?

"I'm on my way," Edith said.

"What about the darling boy?" Kathleen asked. Her nickname for Walter derived from a long-ago visit from their grandmother, who called him that every time she addressed him.

"He's on campus. I'll leave him a note."

"Swell. See you soon."

Edith wondered if she should change into a pair of wool slacks. The weather was brutal. But slacks in the lobby of the Copley Plaza would draw the evil eye from the doorman and probably everyone else, so she stayed in her light flannel dress and heavy stockings. How did Kathleen afford such a fancy hotel, anyway? Edith didn't know much about her fiancé, Dennis, except he was what her mother called a "maker of deals." Well, clearly the deals were paying off. Edith reflected when she first got to know Kathleen, she wasn't interested in money. She was a free spirit who wanted to act, or paint, or write brilliant novels. And she spoke her mind, which made her father take his belt to her more than once. She discovered she had a good head for figures and worked her way up at Marshall Field & Company. She was now in the accounting department. There was a chance she would go even further up the ladder into middle management. She was one of the lucky ones, Edith thought. The door opened to her by the war hadn't closed afterward. But then, Kathleen was the kind to keep it open with her foot, if she had to. A well-shod foot, to be sure.

The train took a little over half an hour. Edith had been cooking a pot roast and turning off the fire meant the beef would get cold and tough. Walter would be disappointed. She thought Kathleen might invite them both to dinner, which would solve the problem. It was already close to three in the afternoon and flowing into dinner would make sense. If they didn't drink themselves silly, first.

Edith had only been in a grand hotel a couple of times. Their honeymoon had been spent at the Willard in Washington. The room must have set Walter back quite a bit, even though it was small and had no view. In New York, Aunt Margaret sometimes took her to tea at The Plaza, but she'd never been upstairs. Had she remained there, and not returned to Cambridge, she might have had long luscious afternoons in beautiful hotel rooms with Philip. The only news she had of him had come in a recent letter from Aunt Margaret in which she mentioned Francine's summary of the new girl he was seeing—*a horse-faced dud with a nice figure.*

She went to the reception desk and endured the critical gaze of the man behind the counter. She asked for Miss Sloan's room. He lifted the receiver of a white telephone rimmed with gold around the mouthpiece and rang.

"Your name?" he asked Edith without looking at her.

"Edith Sloan."

"Relation?"

"Obviously."

Edith could hear Kathleen's voice on the other end of the line. "Well, send her up, for the love of Pete, and quit making her cool her heels!"

The man put down the phone and pressed the bell on the counter. The bellboy appeared. His cap's elastic was tight under his chin, and he tugged at it with his forefinger. The man ordered the bellboy to escort Edith to the fifth floor.

"Oh, I can manage," Edith said.

The bellboy marched off toward the elevator bank without a word, and Edith went after him. He pressed the button on the wall. The sand in the columnar ashtrays on either side of the door had been raked into elegant curving lines. Edith took out the pack of cigarettes she kept in her purse. She took a cigarette for herself, then offered one to the bellboy. He looked hungrily at the pack before shaking his head. Edith lit her cigarette with Philip's lighter. She put the pack away as the elevator door slid open. They entered and the bellboy told the operator the lady needed Floor Five.

When they reached Kathleen's floor, the elevator operator opened the door and Edith got out. The bellboy stayed behind. Edith asked him for the room number. He looked at the palm of his hand, where he'd written it down.

"516," he said, then made a formal nod.

Edith wondered how many numbers accumulated on that palm over the course of a day.

Kathleen's room was at the end of the hall, a suite with a large sitting room. Kathleen was in a spectacular silk suit the color of jade, which brought out the red in her hair perfectly. At the sight of Edith, she squealed and hugged her hard. Pressed against her, a plume of floral perfume went right up Edith's nose, causing her eyes to suddenly tear.

"Look at you! You're marvelous," Kathleen said. "Great hair, by the way!"

"Look at me? Look at *you*. You're a fashion plate."

"In-store discount."

On a wheeled cart were bottles of liquor, seltzer, glasses, and a crystal bowl of ice with a pair of silver tongs. There was a fire going in the fireplace. Edith asked how she could afford such a nice room.

"Oh, Dilbert put it together," she said vaguely, looking around as if she'd misplaced something.

"Do you call him that to his face?" Edith asked.

"That, and other things."

Edith asked what Dennis was like. Kathleen said rich, at least for the moment. No, she wasn't a gold digger. She was truly in love. She was walking on air. Everyone in the whole world should be just as happy as she was right then.

"Oh, Kathleen."

"Too thick?"

"A bit."

Edith took off her coat and tossed it on the sofa. Standing there in her plain dress she felt as she always did in Kathleen's presence—like a daisy next to a bouquet of long-stemmed roses. She went to the window. The lights were coming on; the street below was full of cars; the sidewalks were crowded with people. She looked in the direction of Cambridge. As the crow flew it was probably only two miles between where she was then and her apartment, a surprisingly short distance between two entirely different worlds.

Kathleen offered her a drink.

"Isn't it awfully early?" Edith asked.

"It's five o'clock somewhere, right?"

"Right."

Kathleen mixed herself a gin and tonic. Edith noted the large quantity of gin that went into the glass. Her scotch and soda was more moderate. They sat.

"Should I ring down for some nuts?" Kathleen asked.

"I'm fine."

They sat on either end of the sofa with Edith's coat now on a side chair.

Kathleen got right to the point. She wanted to know how things were going with Walter. Edith said everything had been smooth sailing.

"Not to hear him tell it," Kathleen said.

"What do you mean?"

Kathleen got up and went into the bedroom. She returned with an envelope she'd taken from her suitcase. She handed it to Edith.

"I don't think I should," Edith said.

"Oh, go on. All's fair in love and war."

Edith took the envelope and removed Walter's letter.

November 2, 1948
Cambridge
Dear Kat,

How funny your last letter was, full of zany remarks about the people you work with! Miss Dillington sounds like a real character the way she covers for Mr. Parks all the time. Sort of reminds me of my professor's secretary. We were to meet the other day and he stood me up. Mrs. Smithson said he'd been called away on urgent business, which is a fib as big as the Ritz since I saw him walking across the quad as I left the building.

You ask how we are. Well, we're fine. I'm so glad to have Edie home, I can't tell you! Yet it's been an adjustment, of course, much like after we were first married. First, I got used to having her around, then I was used to not having her around. I remembered how to be a pretty good bachelor after all! Thank God for my friends and their wives. They all seemed so keen to take me under their wings.

But there is something else, and I know I can tell you because you're a woman of the world, despite Pop's efforts to the contrary (and I agree, he was awfully hard on you too much of the time.) Something happened when Edie was in New York. Happened to her, I mean. Maybe it was just the time away or having such an important job at the UN, or the nutty influence of dear Aunt Margaret (I know you think I'm too hard on her.) She's just not the same girl she was before. I can't ask her about it, but maybe you can when you come to visit.

Edith stopped reading.

"You don't have to tell me anything, you know," Kathleen said.

"I know."

"But whatever you do tell me will stay between us. As fond as I am of my brother, we girls have to stick together."

Kathleen knew how to keep a secret. She'd taken the blame for her mother's broken bottle of perfume back in high school when Edith was the one who dropped it. Edith was a junior then, Kathleen a senior. Edith and Walter had just started dating, and she and Kathleen became friends. Kathleen thought Edith was great and just what Walter needed. The family wanted him settled. Being brilliant alone wouldn't make for a good life. He needed a companion, someone sensible to guide him. He had blue moods. Even then, Edith had shown herself capable of navigating them and waiting for them to pass.

Another time a boy asked Edith on a date. She liked him a lot. She knew she should refuse, but she went with him because Walter was safe at home, sick in bed. As they walked back from the movie theater Kathleen drove by. Edith hoped they hadn't been noticed. Kathleen knocked on Edith's kitchen door a little later. Edith's parents had gone up for the night. Edith let her in and decided to be truthful. Kathleen didn't want an explanation. Rather, she said Walter had asked after her and said he hoped she'd visit him the next day, if only for a few minutes because he really depended on her. The incident was never mentioned again.

Kathleen was in Chicago during the years Edith and Walter were in college. She didn't know about the affair with Reynolds. Edith had wanted to confide in her and almost confessed more than once. She trusted Kathleen's affection for her yet didn't want to test it. That still held true.

"There's nothing to tell. I just felt. . . free, that's all," Edith said.

"From Walter?"

"From everything."

Edith said Aunt Margaret's standard of living was very comfortable. Aside from slapping together a few meals a week, she didn't have any boring chores to tie her up. Her job, while not fascinating, nonetheless made her feel a part of something important, just as she had during the war, making maps. In her free time, she could read as much as she liked. Walter didn't approve of how much she read. Didn't Kathleen think that was ironic, given what he was doing with his life? Lawyers read a lot, didn't they? Though what they pored over were casebooks and wills and contracts, not novels and short stories. Kathleen shrugged and finished her drink.

"You're sure that's all?" she asked.

"Did you come all the way out here to interrogate me?"

"Of course not. I came to see you. And Walter. But his letter left me wondering, naturally."

Edith said she understood. She admitted their situation wasn't exactly usual. Wives didn't just up and leave. Husbands did the leaving. At any rate, it was more acceptable when the man moved out for a while.

"You were brave, to go against the grain like that," Kathleen said.

"I didn't see it that way. I was just so mad at him."

"For?"

"Going back on saying I could stay in school."

"But didn't he change his mind?"

"Yes."

"So, in the end, the decision to quit was yours."

"Well, it's a little complicated. They said they wouldn't hold my place, I'd have to reapply, and that spots would go to ex-servicemen first."

"*Did* you reapply?"

"No."

"Do you regret that?"

Edith said only now and then, and less as time went by. She just felt, well, life wasn't all that amusing, or interesting, or whatever she always assumed it could be.

"You don't like being a lawyer's wife," Kathleen said.

"Law student's wife, you mean."

"He'll be a lawyer soon enough."

Edith nodded.

Kathleen said the world was full of things to keep her busy. Edith told her about the job, which had been pushed back until after the first of the year because Mr. Samson was ill and not available to show her around the place, though she knew the layout pretty well by now. His niece had taken over, and he'd hinted in his note she wasn't exactly a patient person and shouldn't be approached until he was there to intercede on Edith's behalf.

"She sounds like a nuisance," Kathleen said.

"Just territorial, I expect."

"Let's go in together. Tell her you've been given the job and are ready to get started."

"Oh, I couldn't do that."

"Listen, you'll never get what you want in this world if you wait for it to come to you. You have to go after it."

She didn't go after Philip, he went after her. She'd been lucky. She didn't admit it to herself right away, but the truth was she'd wanted a romance with another man for a while. Maybe if Walter were spectacular in bed, she'd never have strayed. *Strayed.* She didn't like that word. It made her sound like a cow who'd found a break in the fence and wandered through it.

"Mr. Samson will be back soon," Edith said. She finished her drink. She went on holding the empty glass instead of putting it on the table next to Kathleen's. Kathleen offered her a cigarette. She'd heard from Walter she was smoking again. Edith put down the glass to take it. Then Kathleen said she didn't know what had happened to her lighter. She took the book of matches from the clean ashtray provided by the hotel, but by then Edith had removed Philip's lighter from her purse and lit her cigarette. She extended the flame toward the end of Kathleen's cigarette, and Kathleen leaned forward.

"Fancy. Not from Walter, I imagine. The darling boy has no taste," Kathleen said.

"I found it on the bus."

"The owner must have been mad as a hornet when he realized he'd lost it."

"Or she."

"It's clearly a man's lighter. Can't you tell?"

Edith said she supposed the thick carved lines along the side were more masculine than feminine.

"Very Deco, actually. It's probably worth something," Kathleen said.

Edith put the lighter away. She returned to Walter's letter and skimmed the closing paragraph in which he talked about his classes and the end-of-term jitters everyone was starting to feel. He hoped Dennis was well and asked if they'd set the date yet.

"Have you?" Edith asked.

"Have I what?"

Edith showed her the passage in question.

"Not yet," Kathleen said.

"Why not?"

"He wants to see how his latest investment pans out before getting saddled with my expensive habits."

Edith knew this was nonsense since Dennis covered a lot of Kathleen's bills already. She was pretty sure it was Kathleen who was delaying things, another bold move, since she was pushing thirty. Edith's mother had already called her an old maid more than once, then hastened to qualify that remark by saying she was a real beauty and could take her pick. She assumed she and Dennis weren't interested in having children, given their ages. Dennis was in his early thirties. Edith, who'd just turned twenty-six, was getting less than subtle hints from several quarters, among them Clara Smith, whom she'd seen at the market with her brand-new pram.

"I'm all for waiting for the good things in life, but some joys just aren't to be put off," Clara had said. The baby was red-faced and looked like a human squash, though, of course, Edith cooed and fawned over it.

Then their landlady said just the other day the tenants on the second floor would be leaving after the first of the year, and would Edith and Walter possibly be interested in having a second bedroom?

"It's got a lot of natural light—just perfect for a nursery," she said and adjusted the red scarf she wore over her hair whenever she vacuumed the entry hall carpet.

As to Edith's mother, she hadn't broached the topic for a while, probably because she'd pressed her enough on the matter of their separation.

Edith gave Kathleen back the letter. Kathleen dropped it on the table and had more of her drink.

Kathleen asked how her parents were. She hadn't stopped by the last time she was down from Chicago. Edith said they were fine. Kathleen said she'd always liked Edith's mother. Her father was harder to read.

"I think he disapproves of me," Kathleen said.

"He disapproves of anyone who doesn't worship him."

"My dad's the same way. Walter better not end up like that. I'll tell him what for."

Edith saw her ash was about to fall, and quickly moved her hand toward the ashtray.

Someone knocked on the door, and Kathleen got up to answer it. It was the maid asking if Kathleen wanted her to unpack her things for her. Kathleen said sure, why not? Kathleen and the maid went into the bedroom and Edith stayed behind. She was uneasy all of a sudden, being there. She had wanted so much to see Kathleen, and now she just wanted to go home and be alone. She got up and put on her coat, then realized she couldn't leave without saying goodbye. She stood in the doorway to the bedroom and watched the maid laying each of Kathleen's dresses on the bed so she could decide its relative importance among the others and where it would hang in the wardrobe. The dresses were exquisite, particularly a black strapless evening gown with a tulle skirt. Where would she wear it in Boston? Did she have glamorous, exciting plans? The opera? A reception? Watching Kathleen direct the maid, a stout middle-aged woman with arthritic hands, Edith realized she was outside whatever world Kathleen had conquered and probably always would be. She wished knowing where you *didn't* belong meant knowing where you *did*.

She closed the door as quietly as she could and went quickly to the elevator, which happened to be waiting. She sped through the lobby and out into the street, thinking she should get around the corner as fast as possible so Kathleen wouldn't look out the window and see her down below. But that wasn't likely, was it?

She began walking, hoping the rhythm of her footfalls would calm her. She didn't know why she was agitated. She supposed she'd hoped for a warm reunion, a pleasant visit, and then a light-hearted evening with Walter joining in. In the past, she'd been able to talk to

Kathleen easily, but the talk was always about their respective next steps. For Edith, that was school, the war, marriage, more school. For Kathleen, it was to get the hell out of her hometown, enjoy life in a big city, meet someone fun with a fat wallet who would let her do what she wanted to do, not what he wanted her to do. Kathleen had succeeded. Edith had failed. Once, she had been proud of herself. Now, she was ashamed.

Was it her affair with Philip that pulled her down? The drudgery of being Walter's live-in servant? Or that her commitment to poetry hadn't been enough to make her pursue her doctoral degree, no matter what?

She'd walked past the train stop and was in a neighborhood she didn't recognize. It was cold, and she wanted to go home. She didn't have enough money for a cab, and she didn't want to go back to Kathleen's hotel. She went into a drug store where the sudden brightness hurt her eyes. She asked the woman behind the counter where the nearest station was that would get her into Cambridge and was told she only had another two blocks to go.

She went into the phone booth by the door, dug out a nickel, and dialed her number. Walter answered after the first ring.

"Edie? Where the hell are you?"

"I'm on my way."

"Kathleen said you left the hotel without saying goodbye."

"She was busy with the maid."

"What maid?"

Edith explained. She said she was worried about her pot roast and thought she should get back to it.

"Well don't bother. Kathleen was kind enough to invite us out to dinner, despite your abrupt departure," he said.

Walter said the plan was Kathleen would come into Cambridge, and they'd eat at that little French place off Harvard Square. Then she'd take a cab back. They were to meet at six, so there was time for Edith to get home and freshen up.

"I don't have anything nice to wear," Edith said.

"Sure, you do."

"No, I don't. Everything I have is old and plain and boring."

"Are you all right?"

"Don't I sound all right?"

"How many cocktails did you have with Kathleen?"

"Just one."

"Okay, then. Shake a leg."

They hung up.

Edith went out of the booth. Her eye fell on a small table where scarves for sale were neatly folded. One was blue with a pattern of white dots. She found it very cheerful, though impractical for the winter season they were locked in. She brought it to her face, held it for a moment against her cheek, then put it back. She left the store and walked to the train stop. The platform was crowded, but there was a spot on one of the benches. She sat down.

Her mind wandered. She thought about Mary, who'd recently invited her to tea. Edith didn't particularly care to go. Walter wanted her to. He wanted to deepen his friendship with Henry because Henry was wealthy and had class, the kind of class Walter wanted to have someday, though of course, he would never say so. Instead, when she expressed her reluctance, he made it a failure on her part, something she needed to fix. He said she lived like a hermit. It was good to get out and see people. She had to get used to accepting invitations and returning the favor. That's how things between people flowed. It's what held everything together.

She knew his tension stemmed from fear of the future. He'd gone on several interviews with firms who might hire him after school, and none had expressed specific interest. Classmates were already being given offers. She felt again his gnawing doubts had been fueled by her leaving him. But she was back and playing the good wife twenty-four hours a day, wasn't she? Except for bailing out on her pot roast this afternoon, everything she did was picture perfect.

She was especially dutiful in the bedroom. He seemed to want sex all the time—even on the weekend, in the middle of the day. Too bad all that practice wasn't improving his technique. Every time they made love she thought of Philip.

The train came. She boarded, grateful for a seat by the window. Everyone seemed to be carrying something—groceries, books, or Christmas parcels. She hadn't thought about Christmas at all. Last year they bought a tiny tree and put it in the corner where the tall window it stood next to made it seem like a silly afterthought.

A man and a little girl got on the train, holding hands. The aisle was crowded, and the man picked the child up and bounced her a little. Her small face was tight with worry, but as she was held aloft and snuggled closely, she relaxed and even giggled. Walter would be a good father, despite having had a poor role model. Walter Senior was hard, just like Edith's father. How could two men, who professed such a deep love of teaching and learning, be so mean? Walter Senior taught the great philosophers. His freshman class was called Discourse of the Mind. Edith had taken it. He was articulate, patient, and with a winning manner that put students at ease. His verbal probity in the classroom fell away over the dinner table, where he routinely berated his family, even with Edith present. He called his son a nincompoop;

his daughter a floozie; and his wife a scatterbrain. He never insulted Edith. She didn't know what she'd have done if he had.

The train rolled on through the gathering darkness. Though the walk to her apartment building from her stop was short, her feet were freezing by the time she looked for her key in her purse. The door was unlocked. Walter told her to always keep it locked, even when she was home, and there he was, going back on his own silly rule. He was in the living room with Henry. Both men got to their feet.

"Darling, there you are!" Walter said. He'd been drinking. "I brought Henry home with me. He was so disappointed to find you'd stepped out."

"I'm here now," Edith said. She hung her coat in the hall.

"I've invited Henry to join us for dinner with Kathleen."

"Oh. Where's Mary?"

"I'm afraid she's under the weather," Henry said. He'd been drinking, too, even more than Walter, judging from the slight sway in his stance. Edith asked them both to please sit.

"I'm not feeling top-notch, either. There must be something going around," Edith said.

"Oh, you're not going to cancel, are you?" Walter said. Something in his tone was forced, Edith thought, spoken for Henry's benefit. Before, on the phone, he'd sounded like himself. Maybe Henry had been in the bathroom, or the kitchen, somewhere Walter thought he might not be able to hear his side of the conversation.

"I'm afraid I may have to," Edith said.

"That's why you ran out on Kathleen."

"Yes."

"You do look a bit flushed if you don't mind my saying so," Henry said.

"I thought I might."

At that point, Edith thought she really could be ill. She asked if they'd excuse her. She went into the bedroom, took off her dress, put on her bathrobe, and crawled into bed.

She heard Walter and Henry talking in the other room. Henry said something about having them both over at their place for Christmas Eve. Edith liked the idea and was annoyed when Walter said he'd have to check their schedule. They didn't have a schedule.

She reached for her book on the nightstand. Her current read was *As I Lay Dying*. It had taken her a while to warm to Faulkner's prose, and now found his sentences had the loveliest lilt. She quickly became immersed in the dark image of Addie Bundren watching her coffin being built. Yet as dire as that sounded, she read on, carried along by that hungry, desperate family trying to do the right thing and not being able to overcome their misfortune.

When the clock by the bed said five forty-five, Walter leaned into the bedroom to say they were leaving. Edith asked him to make her apologies to Kathleen, both for not being at dinner and for leaving the hotel without letting her know.

"Make sure you ask her how long she'll be in town," Edith said.

"Oh, I think it's just for tonight."

"What? Why would she come all this way for just one night? Besides, she brought stacks of clothes."

"I'm sure she did. She said Dennis phoned to say his plans had changed. He was supposed to be in Philadelphia, but some developer in New York just had to see him about something, so he'll be there the day after tomorrow. She's going down to meet up with him." He paused. "I can't help wondering what he's like."

"Dennis? Well-off, I think."

"I'm not talking about his bank account."

"No, of course not. Well, he must be nice, or else Kathleen wouldn't like him."

Walter's expression said being nice wasn't necessarily high on Kathleen's list.

"I still don't understand what he does," Walter said.

"Something to do with real estate, obviously, if he's meeting with a developer."

Edith hoped Kathleen wasn't leaving because of her, but that seemed unlikely. She'd come to see how Edith was, and she had. She'd assess Walter over dinner, form whatever opinion she was there to form and be on her way. Boston wasn't Kathleen's kind of town, in any case.

"Do you think they'll stay in the same room?" Edith asked. She didn't know why that occurred to her. Obviously, Dennis would reserve two rooms.

"They'll have to be discreet about it if they do. Those hotel dicks don't mess around with things like that."

"Oh, if one knocks on the door, I'm sure Dennis will slip him something to keep him quiet."

Walter blew her a kiss on his way out.

She read for hours. She got up once to make herself a piece of toast and pour a large glass of scotch, then got back into bed. She closed the book, turned out the light, and reveled in being alone. She tried not to love it too much, but she did. There was no denying it.

chapter nine

The silver garland draped in the display window of The Turned Page looked dingy and sad. So did the paper snowflakes taped to the glass. Whoever had made them was clumsy or rushed—or possibly in his cups, Mary suggested quietly in Edith's ear as they entered to the tinkle of the bell fastened to the door.

The store wasn't tidy the way it usually was. On the large table in the center of the room, the vase of flowers had been replaced by books. Bigger books had been stacked atop smaller ones, making an uneasy balance that could topple. The books were dusty. The floor needed to be swept. On the counter, by the cash register, a coffee cup with a lipstick imprint spoke further to lack of interest.

The store was empty. Edith and Mary walked around, picking up a title here and there, and putting it back. There was a light on in the back room and Edith headed that way, hoping to find Mr. Samson's niece. The niece must have heard Edith's approach because she appeared before Edith reached the door.

"May I help you?" she asked. She was about Edith's height, older, with pouches under her eyes. Glasses hung from a chain around her neck.

Edith introduced herself and stated why she was there.

"He didn't tell me he'd hired anyone. I don't see how he could have, anyway, given the state of his finances."

"I see."

The niece explained Mr. Samson was confined to bed. His heart was bad. He was to avoid all stress. That's why she'd taken over the store, only now what she needed was a buyer. You'd think there'd be interest in a nice place like that—all stock and furnishings included—in a college neighborhood. But, so far, no one had expressed any.

"You're selling the store?" Edith asked.

"I just said so."

"Oh, dear."

"What's the matter?" Mary asked. She'd overheard them talking and was now at Edith's elbow. Edith introduced her as Lady Mary McCormick. The niece gave her name, Patricia Wilkins.

Edith explained.

Mary opened her handbag and removed a tortoiseshell cigarette holder. She put a cigarette in it from her gold case and lit it. She wore a stylish red wool coat with black and white buttons. Her beret was also made of red wool. Just as at Thanksgiving, Edith felt like a frump standing beside her.

Mary turned around and stared into the room they'd just come through. She gazed from one wall to the next. One of the bookcases leaned, suggesting the floor wasn't level. Mary looked down and studied the wooden planks.

"I think it would be jolly fun," Mary said, exhaling her smoke toward the ceiling.

"What would?" Edith asked.

"Having this, of course."

"Yes, but—"

"Henry's been after me to find a useful occupation."

"But, Mary, how can it even be possible? I mean, financially, you know."

Mary looked down at Edith. Her false eyelashes were thick yet seemed quite natural. If Edith hadn't seen her without them, she wouldn't have known she was wearing them. Mary's expression was patient, one of stoic forbearance with Edith's gaffe as if she'd just asked the color of her underwear.

Mary said she didn't know anything about running a store, but was a quick study. Was Edith any good with figures? She had to think that would be important. Edith said she could pick up what had to be done. In college, at the urging of her mother who feared the impractical nature of majoring in Classics, she took a class in bookkeeping, one of the few vocational courses offered to women at the main campus. She kept those details to herself.

"I'd think part of the deal would be to have you stay on long enough to show us the ropes. Ordering inventory, for instance. I wouldn't know how to begin," Mary told Patricia. A small column of ash fell from her cigarette to the floor. "Oh, I beg your pardon," Mary said and wore the ash away with the heel of her boot.

Patricia said she would be happy to provide details if their interest were genuine.

"Yes, quite," Mary said.

"Fine. But just let me say, a bookstore is a business and requires a business-like attitude," Patricia said.

"Which you suspect I lack?" Mary asked.

Patricia said nothing.

Mary opened her purse again. "Here is my card," she said.

Patricia stared at what Mary had handed her, then looked at Edith. Edith shrugged.

A customer came in, and Patricia turned away.

Edith and Mary walked slowly around the space, looking at everything in detail—the rubber tree in the corner, the drapes in the front window, the titles on the tables and shelves, even the counter by the cash register, where the finger of Mary's glove left a line in the dust. Customers could walk from the main room into another small one separated by an archway. That, too, was lined with bookshelves. The light fell from chandeliers whose white opaque glass reminded Edith of her childhood schoolrooms. The paint was chipped in places. There was a water stain down one wall. Edith told Mary the office was just beyond, and they could go in there if they wanted. Patricia probably wouldn't mind. Mary said she'd rather take a look at what was behind the door at the other end of the room. They opened it and discovered a set of wooden stairs leading to the basement. The light switch turned on a dim bulb hanging overhead. Mary said the door should be kept locked against wayward customers. They went down, holding tightly to the metal rail. This was where the extra books were kept, all still in boxes. Edith said if the basement ever flooded, they'd all be ruined. Mary said shelves could be built so the books could be elevated.

"That's going to cost money," Edith said, and again received the same patient expression from Mary.

The basement smelled musty. A cockroach scuttled along the floor. Edith didn't like old buildings. Boston was full of them.

They returned upstairs, looked for Patricia so they could say goodbye, and found her speaking to a middle-aged woman with a tired, expressive face.

Mary was quiet as they walked back to Edith's apartment. Edith could see her thinking. She hoped she wasn't having second thoughts. The idea of buying the store was growing on her—rapidly.

Walter was out. Edith asked Mary if she wanted to call Henry and tell him the news. Mary removed her coat and hat and sat on Edith's lumpy couch with a new cigarette, again in the elegant holder.

"I'll have to give some thought as to just how I should put it," Mary said.

"You said he wanted you to find something to do."

"The trouble is, it's all Henry's money."

"Oh."

Mary asked if there were anything to drink in the house. Edith said, of course, she'd be right back. She returned with two glasses of scotch, neat.

Mary told her to sit. Edith did. As they leaned back and enjoyed the warmth of the liquor, Edith thought upper-class breeding must make you feel entitled to order other people around, even in their own homes.

The truth, Mary said, was her own family was more or less penniless. The estate she'd grown up on had gone for taxes before the war. Her parents lived well enough in a smaller country home, but not as they had back in the day. It was hard with her brother on their hands, too. They were down to just a handful of servants, where before the house had staffed as many as twenty at one time.

Henry's family held on to their money, even when their estate didn't produce as much as it used to. They'd sold some of it to their tenant farmers; another plot went to a developer who put up some ghastly row houses common people seemed to be mad for; and his father had taken some of his own money and invested in a string of high-end car dealerships that catered to the wealthy foreigners, many from the Middle East, it seemed.

Henry had inherited a lump sum from his maternal grandmother on his twenty-fifth birthday. It was substantial and put in trust. That trust came under his control the summer before when he turned thirty. He didn't know what he wanted to do with it yet. He thought he should finish school, first.

"What do you suppose she wants for the store?" Edith asked.

"We should have asked."

Edith stood up and went to the telephone. She removed the directory from the lower shelf of the phone table, opened it, found a listing for The Turned Page, and dialed the number. There was no answer. Edith tried again. Patricia answered on the fourth ring. Edith stated her name and referred to their recent meeting. She asked how much Patricia was hoping to sell the store for.

"Well, my uncle said three thousand, but I'd be willing to let you have it for twenty-five hundred."

"For the whole building?"

"Of course not. The building's not for sale, just the business."

"So, the building is owned by someone else?"

"Yes."

"And he charges rent?"

"Of course."

"And how much is that?"

Patricia paused. "One hundred and ten dollars a month."

"And the purchase price includes exactly what?"

"The name, inventory, and furnishings."

"Thank you very much. I'll be in touch."

Edith told Mary the hoped-for sum. Mary said she didn't know how many pounds that translated into, but if her recollection were correct, the current exchange rate was something around one dollar to three-quarters of a pound sterling.

"So, roughly seventy-five percent," Edith said. She took the pad of paper and pencil by the phone and calculated.

"Which equals about one thousand eight hundred and seventy-five. Pounds, that is."

Mary nodded.

"Can Henry afford that?" Edith asked.

"Most certainly."

By the week following New Year's Day, the talk had grown serious. Henry thought owning a bookstore might be amusing but could prove to be frustrating and perhaps more trouble than it was worth. Mary cited it as a marvelous opportunity to become part of the academic community. Their customers would be mostly made up of professors and students, alike, wouldn't they? Walter liked the idea of being able to announce his connection to the store, possibly hosting a reception there. Edith asked him for whom, and for what, and he ignored her. He was talking to Mary, nodding, as she wondered if stocking paperbacks were a good idea, or if they would seem too plebeian. Edith looked around their silly little apartment and wondered what made her think she could bring grace to a rundown bookstore. But she wanted to try. Very much. She found Henry watching her and she asked him how he would feel if she and Walter were to have a small ownership stake, say five or ten percent? They wouldn't be able to contribute to the purchase price, not yet, at any rate, but over time they would.

"Now, wait just a minute. I'm not sure I want to put any money into the place," Walter said.

"But darling, Henry and Mary are doing so much! They're making it possible. The least we could do is contribute what we can."

Walter thought about it for a moment. Edith could see him calculating the amount.

"I think we would need at least a year to come up with it," Walter told Henry. "That is if you don't mind waiting."

"Not a bit. Glad to have you on board!"

"For the time being, we'll put only Edie's name on the title."

"Why?" Edith asked.

"It's your project. Let's see how you do with it. If all goes well, I can add my name later."

Edith said nothing. Everyone looked at her.

"Is there something else?" Henry asked.

"Well, yes, actually. I'd sort of hoped I could manage the place," Edith said.

"What about Mary?" Walter asked.

"Oh, I don't need to manage anything. I'll just be on hand to help," Mary said.

"Are you sure?" Edith asked.

"Quite."

The next day, with Walter on campus and Mary at the beauty parlor, Henry took Edith out for a drink at the Copley Plaza bar. On the phone, he said they could talk more about the store, but when they'd been seated in a quiet corner, she could see something else was on his mind. She understood men well enough to know when their eye wandered, it was toward something wholly different from what they had at home. During her interrogation of Reynolds, at the end of their affair, she got out of him that his wife never opened a book, was nervous, and loved all manner of domestic pursuits, like knitting, collecting pictures, often cut from magazines, of something she found pretty like a piece of furniture or a view of someone's garden, to put in a scrapbook, and cooking. Her beef stew was superb.

"You must know how attracted I am to you," Henry said.

"To be honest, I had no idea."

"Have I offended you with my candor?"

"I don't know. I don't think so."

She didn't know what she felt. Flattered, obviously. But worried, too. Had he suspected she was a philanderer?

The waiter appeared. Henry asked if Edith might enjoy a champagne cocktail. She said she would. Henry told the waiter to bring two. When he'd gone, Henry asked if he could take her hand. She let him.

Henry hinted Mary was aloof. Since Edith hadn't found her to be so at all—if anything she put herself a bit forward, especially when she was nervous or unsure of herself—she assumed he meant in the bedroom. Then Henry said Mary subscribed to the Victorian edict of closing one's eyes and thinking of England. He said he very much hoped his remarks weren't disturbing her. She shook her head.

"Why me?" she asked and reclaimed her hand. Her face was warm.

"He doesn't tell you how lovely you are, does he?"

"Of course, he does."

Henry's mouth went up slightly on one side. She could see lying to him would be hard.

"The world is full of lovely women," she said.

"Yes, and I have had some of them."

"Does Mary know?"

"She may suspect but says nothing."

"How very modern of her."

"Not really."

"Is this how things are done among the British upper classes?"

"I couldn't say."

Her concept of him fell away. She'd thought of him as surrounded by cronies, people of the same background and experience, like-minded young men whose money put them at ease; but the way his gaze hardened and became cold as he sought to penetrate the particular whiteness of the tablecloth spoke of deep isolation.

"You think I'm a common cheater?" Edith asked.

"I think you want what you don't have. Maybe I can give it to you."

"What makes you think I lack for anything?"

"I've observed you and Walter together. There is affection, but no passion."

Edith's cheeks grew hotter.

"Ah, now I have overstepped. I do apologize," Henry said.

The waiter brought their drinks. He asked if they cared to see a menu. Henry looked at Edith. She said she wasn't hungry at the moment. Henry told the waiter they were fine.

When he left, she sipped her drink. She'd never had a champagne cocktail before. She found it bitter, and not what she had hoped for.

"Would you like to order something else?" Henry asked.

"No, this is lovely, thank you."

Edith asked how it would all work, assuming she agreed.

"I've joined a club, right here in Back Bay. Lovely place. Discreet. Mary doesn't know about it," he said.

"How do I manage it?"

"That's up to you."

She asked if he intended to forgo the purchase of the bookstore if she said no. He said it was already in the works. He'd found a good solicitor in town who was going over the papers.

"Lawyer, you mean," she said.

"Yes."

Edith wondered why Walter hadn't been involved in that part of it. Maybe Henry didn't want him involved, or maybe Walter didn't care to bother since he'd already said his name wouldn't go on the documents.

She asked Henry how much money he was willing to spend on renovations and redecorating.

"I hadn't given it any thought, but I gather from the gleam in your eye that you have."

She had indeed. And done some checking. She thought an extra thousand would do it. He said he would keep that in mind.

She wanted to know how the money would flow.

"I'm not sure what you mean," he said.

"Will I be authorized to sign checks?"

"Yes, if you like."

Edith looked around the room. On either side of the door stood a tall rubber tree plant; on each table, an opaque vase held a single pink carnation. The waiters were silent, the drinkers genial. The afternoon light through the tall arched windows faded and softened into a charming blend of purple and gray. She felt at ease with Henry, and with herself—a woman who didn't have to pretend or hide anything.

And yet.

"I can't do it. It's not right," she said.

He shrugged and smiled as if to say he couldn't be blamed for trying.

She expected him to pressure her, and not give up so easily. She didn't like realizing she wanted him to.

They took a cab back to Cambridge. Walter was still on campus. Henry said Mary was probably home by then. They'd meet at the lawyer's office when the papers had been drawn up. They parted cordially, with no reference to the conversation in the bar.

Edith had a growing sense she'd made a mistake by turning him down. As she went up the stairs to her building, she told herself it didn't matter. She'd throw herself into the store and make it a great success.

A letter from Aunt Margaret sat in the box. Edith read it after removing her coat. It was chatty and warm and made Edith miss her. She asked how things were in Cambridge and if the weather were getting to be too much. She'd seen Kathleen and her fiancé in New York when they came through. Kathleen looked marvelous, but then she always did, and as to Dennis, she wasn't sure he was the right one for her. Aunt Margaret then described him in detail, focusing on his pencil-thin mustache which had gone out of style some years before. Clearly, he just wasn't with the times. She closed by giving her very best wishes to both her and Walter for the new year and saying she'd just heard from Francine Philip was engaged to be married. Edith considered this information and then went to make Walter's dinner.

chapter ten

The doctor said he'd never seen such swollen glands. He didn't think it was the mumps, nor anything particularly serious, just a bad infection penicillin would cure. Walter had been sick for days with a high fever and a raging sore throat. Edith was at her wit's end tending to him. He came home from campus out of sorts with a glassy look in his eye. Edith took his temperature, told him to get undressed and into bed. Then she made him chicken soup. He didn't like it because it came from a can. She went to the store and got everything she needed to make chicken soup from scratch. In the meantime, to keep up his strength, she fed him scrambled eggs and toast. He said he wasn't hungry, then wanted another serving.

Doctor Mosher said it was going around, and Edith should take care lest she, too, fall ill. He cleaned his glasses with the end of his tie. He recalled the Spanish Influenza of 1918.

"Whole families wiped out. Nothing we could do but provide good nursing, and wait," he said. There was no grief in his tone, just an objective reporting of fact.

He took a glass vial of penicillin from his bag, broke off the top, then inserted a syringe into the fluid. He pulled up on the plunger, and the syringe filled. He removed the syringe and depressed the plunger until a small amount of fluid spurted out the end of the needle.

He asked Walter to roll over on his side. He told Edith to hold the syringe while he sterilized the injection site, and to be careful to keep the needle from touching anything. When he took it back from her, he inserted it and pressed the plunger. He asked Edith if she thought she could repeat the procedure. She said she'd never done it before but thought she could manage.

He put his instruments away, wrote her a prescription, and told her to have it filled at once. Walter should be given aspirin every four hours. Edith should call in the morning and report his condition. Edith went with him into the hall and handed him his hat, which he'd dropped on the small table. His coat was on the rack by the door, and she helped him into it. He was an elderly man, who smelled of lavender.

Edith got Walter settled and then went to the drug store around the corner. The snow fell; the sidewalk was icy. Just the other day Henry had slipped on campus and turned his ankle. They'd spoken on the telephone the day before about signing the papers for the bookstore. Edith said Walter was down with the flu, and she might not be able to get away for a few more days. Henry said they could bring the papers to her. The idea of something so important taking place in their small, dingy apartment gave her pause. She said she'd let him know.

The line at the druggist was long. A woman held a weeping child in her arms. The man behind her coughed constantly. It was no surprise Walter got sick, given how everyone else seemed to be faring. But he got sick more often than most people, even in the summer. He'd been delicate as a child and given to such bad anxiety his mother put him to bed and darkened the room. His father took a dim view of his frailty and declared a weak body was the result of a weak character. Walter loved and feared his father, which Edith supposed was fairly normal, for a man, at any rate. As to her own father, she'd be happy if a hole in the earth opened up and swallowed him.

The line inched forward. She thought about her parents. Their relationship had always been a puzzle. Her mother deferred yet didn't yield as much as her father assumed she did. She was stubborn about things, usually, things he didn't care about, like the color of a new pair of curtains, or how much to tip the milkman. He always voiced his opinion and by doing so made it clear he expected her to honor it. She seldom did. Edith hadn't seen that for a long time. Now that she understood this dynamic better, she couldn't decide if her mother were clever, or foolish for not pushing harder for the things she wanted.

They'd married late. They met in Huron, South Dakota, where her mother grew up and her father taught at the college. He was from Minnesota, and though he went to school in the East, he never liked it much. Her mother was thirty when he proposed and had resigned herself to being an old maid. Maybe it was her gratitude to Edith's father for saving her from this fate that prompted her to be subservient, but Walter's parents had married in their twenties, and his mother was as meek as a wren. The problem was what the world expected women to be, Edith thought, which was always less than a man. It enraged her. But what did that rage get her? Wasn't she just as trapped as her mother and the other Mrs. Sloan?

Her turn at the window came, and she passed over the prescription. The man said it would be a few more minutes, and her name would be called. Until then, she was welcome to visit the soda fountain at the other end of the store or catch up on some shopping.

Soda fountain. Shopping. Would he have suggested these to a man?

She wandered past the cosmetic counters. Many things appealed, all too expensive. Rich hand creams from England; cologne from France; further on a compact with tiny seed pearls from Ireland.

Imported goods had been impossible to get during the war. Now they were everywhere—but still beyond reach.

"It'll be a while before I make any real money," Walter had said the day he proposed. She said she didn't care, as long as their life together was interesting. His life was interesting, at least it was when he calmed down enough to let it be. Hers wasn't. It could be, once she got her hands on The Turned Page.

The first thing she wanted to do was line up an events calendar. Book clubs could use the small room for weekly discussions. Local authors could read from their new works. A whole section could be devoted to children's books, which the current store lacked, and a monthly story time could be held. The idea of kids running around the place didn't appeal, but Edith reckoned with them temporarily under someone else's control, their mothers would be free to browse books for sale. Another idea she had was to form a buyers' club where purchases would be recorded, and after someone had bought nine books, the tenth would be free or discounted at something like fifty percent off the regular price.

Finally, her name was called, and she was given a syringe in a metal case, vials of penicillin, and instructions. The man told her where the vials were concerned it was easy to snap off the top but to be careful not to cut herself on the glass edge. He also gave her a bottle of rubbing alcohol and a bag of cotton balls. Edith took everything and went home. Walter was asleep. She put the medicine in the refrigerator, filled a pot with water, and put it on the stove because the needle of the syringe would have to be boiled after each use.

What a nuisance, she thought. Worse than having a baby around!

Her days were filled with tending to Walter. He got better, but his recovery was slow. He complained his backside hurt from the injections. He complained about the food she made. He complained about being bored, about needing his pajamas washed and the sheets changed, and fretted about being away from class. Another law student, Charles Blackman, promised to take lecture notes, type them up, and bring them by when Walter was able to receive him.

When Edith passed along this information, he opened his feverish eyes and glared.

A few days later, he was on his feet and back on campus. Edith opened the bedroom window as wide as it would go and enjoyed the blast of freezing air.

Edith went to the lawyer's office to sign the papers. The reception area was furnished with deep leather armchairs. The receptionist invited her to sit in one while she waited. Edith sank deeply into it. Her feet barely touched the carpeted floor. Henry came through the door wearing a double-breasted wool coat and a fedora with a deep green band. He was dashing, there was no doubt.

He explained Mary had already signed, just about half an hour before, in fact. Edith was certain she'd gotten the appointment time correct, then realized Henry hadn't wanted her there when Mary was. Edith smiled politely and said she was sorry she'd missed her.

"Oh, you'll see her later, I imagine. She's over at the store now, consulting with the decorator."

Edith said nothing but was exasperated. She wanted to be in on all choices made concerning the store. Watching her, Henry said Mary was just acting in a most preliminary way and wouldn't commit to anything. Final decisions would be made with Edith. Edith couldn't tell if she were particularly transparent, or if Henry were especially perceptive, but his understanding her concern calmed her.

Finally, they were shown in. Bradley Sturgis was a short, unassuming man, with a fiercely whimsical look in his eye. He gestured to a pair of chairs on the other side of his wide, heavy desk. Edith and Henry sat.

"Well, you were just here, so there's no need to explain the fine details," Mr. Sturgis said to Henry.

He put what Edith was to sign in front of her. Below the signature line were the words *Mrs. Walter Sloan*.

"Excuse me, but shouldn't I sign with my real name?" she asked.

"Isn't that your real name?"

"Yes, I mean my first name."

Mr. Sturgis stared at her.

"Wouldn't that be just as legally binding?" Edith asked.

"Yes, of course. But to have the secretary retype the page will require some time—my partner's got her busy with last-minute probate instructions, and I understood you wanted the matter concluded this afternoon." Mr. Sturgis consulted the watch he pulled from the pocket of his vest.

Edith signed.

Mr. Sturgis said he'd file the papers at the first opportunity. Then he congratulated Henry on his purchase and wished him every success.

On their way out, Henry offered to buy her a drink.

"Don't you have class?" she asked.

"Not this afternoon."

"Ah."

She said she wanted to get over to the store right away and see how things stood. Patricia Wilkins was to show her the books and walk her through the inventory lists.

"What about the decorating?" Henry asked.

"Oh, that can wait!"

Edith had thought Mary would be there, but Patricia said she hadn't been in. Edith thought Henry had misunderstood. Maybe she'd gone riding. She'd recently found a large indoor ring attached to a stable that rented horses by the hour. She'd formed an attachment to one of the mares, a Miss Lizzy B, whom Edith explained was no doubt named for Lizzy Borden, and might therefore have a fiery temperament. But Mary said the horse was calm and sweet, and a joy to ride.

Edith hung up her coat on the rack in the office. Patricia had pulled up a second chair to the desk so they could sit together and go over the books. The accounting system was simple and clear. Edith had no trouble following it. Patricia asked if they were considering hiring any salesgirls.

"I hadn't thought of that," Edith said.

"I only ask because I know you're both married. With husbands to take care of, your available time here will be limited. I suggested to my uncle we hire one or two, but he wouldn't hear of it."

"I think that's a good idea."

"They should be attractive, but not too attractive. They should love reading. I say English majors are your best bet. Stay away from art students. They tend to be loose."

Edith didn't know whether to laugh at this or not, but Patricia was clearly being serious.

"Why not you?" Edith asked.

"Why not me, what?"

"I'll hire you."

Patricia leaned back in her chair. She said nothing. Had Edith insulted her? Hurt her feelings? After a few more moments had passed, Edith asked if she were all right.

"I just hadn't really taken it in, until now," Patricia said.

"Taken what in?"

"That the store's not ours anymore."

Edith asked her what a fair salary would be. Patricia said something around sixteen hundred dollars a year. Edith glanced down at the ledger on the desk. Cash-on-Hand showed a balance of one hundred and twenty-two dollars. The business account at the bank had about half that sum. Edith saw then she'd have to talk to Henry about cash flow. He'd agreed to the improvements she'd raised, but there needed to be more operating funds. She asked Patricia if she would excuse her for a minute because she needed to make a telephone call. Patricia said of course, and went out into the store. Edith didn't know Henry's number and asked the operator to look it up.

"It's Edith," she said when he picked up.

"Have you changed your mind about that drink?"

"I'm calling about business."

"I see."

She got right to the point. She wanted him to put five hundred dollars into the store's account. He said nothing. Then he said he'd take care of it the following day.

"How's it going with the decorator?" he asked.

"They're not here."

"Oh? Perhaps they finished early."

"Perhaps."

They said goodbye. Edith left the office. Patricia was watering a trailing ivy plant she'd recently bought and put next to the cash register. A young man came through the door wearing an overcoat that was too big for him, and mismatched rubber boots, one was black and the other dark blue. His hair was thick and wild; his eyes, too, had a feral, desperate look. Patricia stopped watering when she saw him, clearly uneasy. Edith thought in that neighborhood there were plenty of unkempt young men, usually with a notebook in hand, jotting down an idea for a book they were going to write one day when they got around to it; students or former students, or just general hangers-on, people who liked the academic atmosphere; who lived on who-knows-what, probably the charity of their tired families or more energetic friends. Patricia would have seen a lot like him before today.

He moved over to one of the wall shelves and took down a volume of Tennyson poems. He turned the pages slowly with fingers that had a slight tremble. Edith wondered if he were a drug addict and decided if so, he probably wouldn't bother visiting a bookstore.

She smoothed down her hair and approached him.

"Are you looking for something in particular?" she asked.

He continued to turn the pages of the book. She repeated her question, then put her hand lightly on his arm. He closed the book.

"I'm sorry," he said. "I was lost in the words."

He didn't sound like a local. His tones were flat and twangy, like hers, she supposed. Boston seemed to attract Midwesterners. Up close, she saw he was older than she first assumed, maybe just on the other side of thirty. His forehead had a deep crease as if he were constantly raising his eyebrows in astonishment.

She asked again if she could help.

"Say, where's the old guy that's always here?" he asked.

"Mr. Samson retired. He sold the store. I'm the new owner."

"You?"

The man looked her over. His eyebrows went up. His expression was wry.

"Don't I look like the owner of a bookstore?" she asked. She smiled to soften the edge in her voice.

"Frankly, no."

"What do I look like, then?"

"A secretary, maybe."

"Really?" The man picked up her left hand, stared at it, then dropped it. "I'll change that to a housewife.

"Just because of the ring?"

"No." He stood back and regarded her at greater length. "You look sensible and hard-working, as if you could bake a darned good cake with one hand and iron a shirt with the other."

Edith was infuriated. She said nothing. She refused to lower her gaze.

"I'm sorry. That was rude," he said.

"Yes, it was."

He put the book back on the shelf. He said he was looking for something by W. H. Auden. Had Edith heard of him?

"Of course."

She realized she didn't know how to find a particular title in the store. She'd been so focused on the financial arrangements that a simple thing like locating a single book among hundreds hadn't occurred to her. She looked around for Patricia, who had vanished.

Edith excused herself. She went into the office where Patricia was making a cup of tea. She asked how the books were organized. Was it alphabetical, by author and title? Or by subject and genre?

Patricia asked which book she wanted. Edith told her. Patricia stood up and turned off the electric ring under the tea kettle.

She went into the main room, turned right, and went to the three bookcases at the far wall. She brought over a step stool that had been resting in the corner. She climbed up and took a book from the top shelf of the middle bookcase. She put it back, then ran her finger across the spines of the other books and pulled out another one. She came down off the step stool and handed the book to Edith.

"He just won the Pulitzer. Uncle doesn't approve of literary prizes, so he put it a bit out of reach," Patricia said.

"Thanks for finding this. We're going to have to come up with a better system," Edith said.

When she returned to the main room, the man was gone. Edith left the book on the central table. She went back into the office and asked Patricia about inventory. Was there a master list? Patricia said yes, there was a ledger that listed titles and the number of copies ordered and received. Then, when a book sold, that number, usually just one, was entered in a different column and subtracted to show the number currently on hand. She cautioned her uncle seldom checked whether his ledger matched what was on the shelves. For all Patricia knew, people could have helped themselves from time to time and he'd never know.

Edith asked to see the ledger, and Patricia said it was right there, in the desk drawer. Edith removed it and flipped through the pages. The handwriting, all in pencil, was hard to read, but she gradually got a sense of it. She wanted to know how books were purchased. Was there a file of publishers, addresses and telephone numbers? Was there a standard form one submitted, or did a letter have to be written?

Patricia poured herself a cup of tea and sat in a chair opposite the desk. She said as far as she knew, when a new title came out, her uncle wrote a letter asking for an order of so many copies.

"How does he know how many copies to ask for?" Edith asked.

Patricia didn't know. Common sense said you'd request more copies of a title likely to sell well, and fewer of those by a lesser-known author.

Edith sat in the chair behind the desk and rubbed her forehead. She found Patricia looking at her with a blend of humor and sympathy.

"I guess I really didn't know what I was getting into," Edith said.

"You'll get the hang of it. Your friend will help you, won't she?"

Where was Mary, anyway?

The jingle of the front door and the firm stride of high heels across the wood floor said she'd arrived at last. She swept into the office with a wave of perfume. She wore a charming velvet hat with a veil that fell just below her nose. She removed her fur coat and tossed it on the empty chair next to Patricia. Then she removed her leather gloves and tossed them, too. She realized there was nowhere for her to sit, so she collected her coat and gloves and held them in her lap. Patricia stared at the coat.

"Where's the decorator?" Edith asked.

"Who? Oh, we met at her office."

"I thought she needed to take measurements."

"She'll do that another day."

Mary said she'd had a chance to review some fabric samples for the curtains in the front window. Did Edith think a pale green chintz would do well?

Edith said she'd have to give that some thought. In the meantime, they had several more pressing issues.

"Like what?" Mary asked. She lit a cigarette and blew the smoke toward the ceiling. Edith saw she was flushed. She must have realized she was running late and hurried herself along.

"Inventory, record-keeping, hiring a couple of salesgirls, to start," Edith said.

Mary waved her hand. She crossed her legs, causing her hose to make a faint rasping sound.

She asked how Walter was. Edith said he was fine, with no relapses. Then she said she wanted to work on a new way to organize the books, which would first entail establishing exactly what was in the store, and *that* would mean going around and writing down each title in turn.

"Sounds tiresome," Mary said, then agreed to help. Patricia said she'd be glad to help, too. She sipped her tea and asked if Mary wanted any.

"That would be lovely!"

Patricia offered to hang Mary's coat on the coat rack.

"Thank you so much," Mary said.

Patricia took the coat. Then she turned on the hot plate.

Edith pulled out the cash box from the desk and saw while it had a hasp to accommodate a lock, there was none. Another thing to fix. She scratched some figures on a pad of paper and removed thirty dollars from the box. She told Patricia this was her first week's salary, and soon she hoped to be able to pay her monthly. Patricia asked what she planned to do about withholding.

"I'm sorry?" Edith asked.

"Social Security, state and federal tax, that sort of thing. Although I suppose you could just pay me, what's that phrase?"

"Under the table," Mary said.

"We'll have to, for now," Edith said. Why hadn't that stupid lawyer raised these issues as he handed her his engraved pen for her to sign her name? Why hadn't Henry? Why did they assume she had the business knowledge to carry this thing off?

Edith suggested they close the store for two or three days, to give them a chance to record on-hand inventory and then rearrange it. They would also clean the place from top to bottom. Since the books would be taken off the shelves, now was a convenient time. As she laid out her plan, she realized Walter was going to object because she might not be home to make dinner. She'd leave him a sandwich and a slice of cake for dessert, or she could invite him to come down and help them, and they could grab a bite before or after. He wouldn't want to do that, though, would he? Even in high school, Walter avoided boring chores. Kathleen, because she was female, got stuck with spring cleaning and tidying up the attic. She hated it but was energetic. She could whip this place into shape before you knew it.

Obviously, Edith couldn't beg her to come all that way, but she could ask her those accounting questions.

She made sure the wobbly typewriter on the desk had a decent ribbon, slipped a piece of paper in, and rattled away with the skill she'd practiced last summer at the UN. Mary and Patricia stared at her while she worked. Her letter was brief, and cited the payroll issues Patricia had raised. She promised to write more later when she had time. She removed the page and read it through. Not a single mistake. She found an envelope in the desk drawer and typed Kathleen's address on it. She took a stamp from the drawer, wondering if she should leave three pennies to cover the cost. Then she realized she would only be reimbursing herself. It washed over her again, all that she'd committed to. The most important thing now was to replace fear with action.

chapter eleven

Edith wrote to her mother about the bookstore. Her mother wrote back with congratulations and said it was a bold, daring move. She worried it might prove to be a far greater demand on her time than she anticipated, then praised Edith's courage in taking it on.

I suspect Walter's not happy with the idea, and if that's the case, then he should look at things from your point of view.

That will be the day, Edith thought.

Edith assumed cleaning the store would take three days, and it consumed an entire week. Patricia apologized over and over for the dirt and grime on the shelves, the counters, the windowsills, the window glass itself, behind the file cabinets in the office—everywhere—then she stopped. It was as if some accumulated grief had been let out, and once freed, she became sunnier and easier to be around. She wore brighter colors, too. The gray sweater had been replaced with a soft plum she said she'd made herself, and which she protected with a cloth smock, the kind an art student would wear.

Mary restacked books and noted titles in a brand-new ledger; hummed while she ran a clean cloth up and down table legs and tabletops; steered the broom around the floor. But by the end of the week, her mood suffered. Edith didn't know why, and she didn't ask. All she hoped was she wouldn't be left dealing with everything on her own.

Which is just what happened. Mary announced she needed a few days off. Edith looked at her closely and saw no sign of illness. Fatigue, certainly. And a dark glimmer of sadness in her eyes, which made Edith wonder if things were all right with Henry. Given the distant nature of their relationship, she didn't think a loss of marital bliss was the cause.

Patricia was called away to take care of Mr. Samson, who'd taken a turn for the worst. Edith hired two salesgirls from Boston College, Eloise, and Isabelle, both of whom had clean, shiny skin and beautifully manicured nails. Each was twenty, a fact that made them giggle when they discovered it. Of the two, Eloise had a better grasp of the cash register and writing receipts, while Isabelle had a deep knowledge of literature, female novelists in particular. They took over each day at three o'clock so Edith could shop, go home and clean, then make dinner. They closed up at six. Sometimes, when Edith opened up in the morning, always promptly at eleven, she found things out of place in the office—the chairs moved around, or a teacup on the desk. She didn't like the idea of the girls messing about in there. She was glad she'd gotten a lock for the cashbox.

When the store reopened not many people came, but gradually those who'd been temporarily turned away wandered in and looked around. Many were regulars, people who lived in the neighborhood and who knew Mr. Samson. Some, men in particular, looked at Edith suspiciously when she said she was the new owner. The women, especially the older ones, were more sympathetic.

Kathleen answered Edith's letter and told her to hire someone to handle the payroll taxes for her. It was a time-consuming process and had to be done correctly. She said to look for a smaller firm because it would be less expensive. The weather in Chicago was horrible; she didn't think she could stand another winter there; Dennis was talking about an investment opportunity in Florida that sounded simply heavenly. The only thing was, she didn't want to give up her job.

Was there friction between them over Kathleen's career? Edith couldn't read between the lines but assumed Dennis would expect her to quit and be at his beck and call once they married, despite Kathleen suggesting otherwise. That's how it worked. Married women were servants. Single women were disdained. Only wealthy widows like Aunt Margaret had any freedom. Patricia seemed to have her share of fun, though, despite being a spinster and not exactly flush. She talked about an informal choir she belonged to that met at the home of a friend. They'd tired of the classics and wanted to try a couple of show tunes. The idea of Patricia belting out Cole Porter or Irving Berlin struck Edith as highly improbable, but who knew?

On Kathleen's advice, Edith engaged Black and Associates for the tax work. When she went to their office, which was just two blocks away, she expected the same wry expression she always got when she introduced herself as the store's new owner. Black turned out to be Mathilda Black, who'd inherited the firm from her father. Her associate was a much younger man, just out of school, who was clearly terrified of her. As Kathleen predicted, their rates were reasonable.

Nothing had come of redecorating, and Edith was glad. She didn't want to spend money on new curtains and rugs when the old ones were fine. In fact, she sensed there was only so much the place could be spruced up and still hold the interests of its loyal clientele. When she mentioned this to Walter one evening, he said she wasn't forward-thinking enough. The store should attract new people. That was the goal of business, wasn't it? To grow?

Edith sipped the wine he'd brought home. He had been offered a job the week before and felt more liberal with money. And he was trying to develop a taste for good French Beaujolais, no doubt to impress Henry at some future dinner party. She enjoyed the wine and found it a nice change from scotch.

"Well, I think people come in for the charm of the place, to enjoy that old-style atmosphere," Edith said. She gave Walter another serving of boiled potatoes.

"Can't it have new charm?"

"I suppose."

She wondered if he regretted not being a registered owner. He'd mentioned a couple of times he was ready to become one. Edith said he could consult Sturgis, who might waive whatever fee would normally be charged, sort of as a professional courtesy. At the time, Walter asked her where she'd gotten that idea. She said she just thought of it—wasn't that what lawyers did? She couldn't remember if he'd answered. She'd been busy with something else.

Walter asked if Edith could pour him some more wine. She did.

"You know, I was talking to Hawkins about you the other day, and told him about your little store," Walter said. Hawkins was his Evidence professor. He referred to all his professors by their last names, though she was sure in person he still addressed them as Professor So-and-So.

"Did you?"

"Yes. He knows it. Said it used to be a meeting place for Communists, back in the day."

"Really?"

"I'm surprised the old fellow's niece didn't mention it."

"She might not have known."

"Hawkins said he might drop in sometime, maybe with his daughter. She's studying art history at Wellesley. Do you have any texts she might like to look at?"

Edith was able to cite four titles she'd seen during the rearrangement. Walter marveled at her memory, then said she'd always had amazing recall. Edith asked what kind of art the girl was studying. Had she a particular focus?

Walter didn't know. He was looking at the evening paper then. Edith thought he might have been testing her about the book titles to reassure himself if Hawkins and his daughter did indeed visit, she wouldn't prove to be an embarrassment.

Walter put the paper away and lit his pipe. Edith cleared the table. When she returned she sat down. She didn't want to do the dishes yet. She was tired, and her feet hurt. Walter took her hand. He noted her skin was dry. Was she still using her hand cream?

"Yes."

He asked if she were looking forward to moving out of Cambridge when he started working. She said she hadn't thought about it at all.

"You'll want to start looking for a new place by mid-summer. Our lease is up in August," Walter said.

"Well, where do you think I should look? I don't want to be too far from the store."

"I was thinking Newton maybe, or Lexington."

"They're miles away!"

"You can cut back your hours."

"I can't do that."

"Why not?"

"Because I'm the manager. And part owner!"

"Well, what about Mary?"

Edith reminded Walter she was at home, taking some time off.

"She'll be back," he said.

It wasn't that. Mary wasn't committed the way Edith was. She didn't need it the same way.

Three days later, Mary still hadn't returned to work. Henry called the store and asked if Edith might come by and say hello.

"What seems to be the trouble?" she asked.

"Just run down, I think."

Mary hadn't worked hard enough to be run down. If anyone should be exhausted, it was Edith. She agreed to come that afternoon.

The winter sunlight was thin and low. The glimpse it gave of the warmer season ahead was a cruel tease. It made one long for what was still so far away. Edith had read a short story once, a piece of science fiction, where the orbit of the Earth was thrown off by a passing meteor whose gravitational pull caused it to slip. The Earth went around the sun in a wider and wider ellipse, slowly and steadily freezing, while the hapless souls on its icy surface struggled to stay warm and alive. In the end, they failed.

Edith took a cab because Henry said he'd reimburse her for it. He didn't like to think of her messing about with the train. Edith was used to the train and was sure Henry knew that. The bell was answered by Henry, not Alistair, who was out fetching something to cheer Mary up, Henry said, as he took Edith's coat. She looked into his face for signs of worry, but his expression was smooth, almost bland. Yet it was a studied calm, she thought. Something in his eyes said his heart was sore.

"Can I offer you something? Some tea, or perhaps you'd like a drink?" Henry asked.

"I'm fine."

At the end of the living room, an open door showed a wall of tall bookcases. Edith asked Henry if this were his study. He said it was. She wanted to go in and browse the shelves but hadn't come there for that. She asked if she could look in on Mary.

Henry led her down the hall past two closed doors to the end where another door stood ajar. He leaned his head in and said Edith had come for a visit. Mary must have gestured her assent because Henry told Edith to go on through.

Mary was lying propped up in a four-poster bed. Her bed jacket was quilted red satin embroidered with flowers. On the table by the bed were a crystal pitcher and a glass. A paperback book lay face down on the bedspread at her side. Mary told Edith to bring the armchair that sat in front of the fireplace over and to put it by the bed.

The chair had a lovely petit-point seat that brought Edith longingly back to Aunt Margaret's living room. Mary looked at her keenly. She was pale, with smudges under her eyes.

"How do you feel?" Edith asked, cheerfully.

Mary told Edith to go and close the door. When Edith had returned and sat down, Mary said, "What I'm going to tell you stays between us. Is that clear?"

"Of course."

Mary brought her hand to her forehead and closed her eyes for a moment. She dropped her hand slackly on the bed.

She'd been to see a doctor. She was late, and that could only mean one thing. The doctor confirmed what she suspected. She thought it wasn't possible. They'd tried for a long while back in England.

"You're pregnant?" Edith asked.

"Not anymore."

"Oh."

Naturally, the doctor she first consulted wanted nothing to do with it. She said she'd been attacked one night—raped—and the baby she carried was that of her assailant. He didn't believe her at first, so she had to spice up her story. She hadn't gone to the police because she didn't want her husband to know what had happened. She wasn't supposed to be out that time of night. A dear friend, someone the husband didn't like much, was having a hard time, and Mary had gone to spend time with her. Really, she told the doctor, handholding and giving comfort came quite naturally to her. Her husband would be angry to learn she'd walked certain streets alone. She could have called for a cab, but she'd been so distracted by her dear friend's troubles she just didn't think of it until later.

She could never tell her husband the child she carried wasn't his. Did the doctor really want her to have it, and pass it off as the result of a loving union?

The doctor had her write down a name on a pad of paper. He cautioned there could be complications. Then he sent her on her way.

"And?" Edith asked.

"And I went to this other man, who took care of it."

"So, why are you in bed?"

"Because it was awful. Not to mention embarrassing."

"You'll be all right, though."

"Soon."

"What does Henry think is wrong with you?"

"Nerves. Overwhelmed by the stress of the store."

Edith wished Mary had used a better excuse. She could have said she'd fallen off a horse, or something, but then Henry would probably have wanted her looked at, and that would have meant another doctor asking questions about what ailed her.

"I'm sorry," Edith said. She didn't know what else to say.

"Thank you."

"And the day you were supposed to be meeting with the decorator, you saw this first doctor?"

"You're very clever."

"But that was what, three or four weeks ago? Why did you wait so long?"

"I kept hoping it would just take care of itself."

Edith wondered what it was like to hope your body would do something against its own nature and design. Then she wondered if Mary had any regret over the life she ended. Despite the deeply personal nature of the news she'd just heard, she didn't think she could ask.

"So, what happens now?" Edith asked.

"I'll be on my feet soon."

"No, I mean what happens between you and Henry, you know, about babies."

"How do I avoid another pregnancy?"

"Yes."

"Separate bedrooms."

Edith watched Mary closely to see if she were joking. She didn't seem to be.

Was this the aloofness Henry alluded to before? Being willing to give up sex because it was inconvenient? Edith reflected on the difference between her and Mary. Edith would never want to do without sex altogether. Even bad sex was better than no sex.

Mary asked how things were at the store. Edith said they were fine, the new girls were working out well.

"Don't you find them silly?" Mary asked.

"They do giggle a lot, I admit."

"I'd hoped for more serious types."

"They were the only ones who applied."

"A few years ago, all young women wanted to have a little job on the side. Remember?"

Edith was sure her life during the war was quite different from Mary's. But Mary had opened the door, so Edith asked politely how she'd spent her time then. Mary had worked in a tea shop. Her mother was shocked, of course. Women of her class just didn't do that sort of thing. Mary had to remind her mother Princess Elizabeth drove an ambulance. And besides, with Henry in London, and her stuck out in the country, she needed something to do. It hadn't been easy, living with Henry's parents. Oh, the house was quite large and very comfortable, but one had to sit with them over dinner. They were also a bit skeptical of her working, but much less so. They understood she needed to keep going, and, in a way, she was doing her bit.

Her face had taken on a softness as she remembered. Edith thought those had been happy days for her, even with Henry gone. Or perhaps because he was gone, though she hesitated to believe that.

Mary closed her eyes. Edith took this as a signal she should go. She stood up and said she looked forward to having her back, which was true. Her excellent taste in clothes and her British accent gave the place a degree of class Edith couldn't. A couple of customers had asked for that "nice English lady" and were disappointed when Edith said she was away.

Henry emerged from his study when he heard Edith come up the hall. He asked how it had gone.

"Oh, fine. She'll be right as rain in no time," she said.

As he helped her on with her coat, he rested his hand on her shoulder. She looked up into his face.

"This has been hard on you, hasn't it?" she asked.

"Yes."

"You mustn't worry. It's nothing serious."

"I wish I could believe that."

"You'll see."

Henry leaned down and kissed her on the cheek.

"What's that for?" she asked.

"You."

She said she had to be going and would be in touch.

He asked if five dollars would cover the cab fare. She said yes.

All the way home she wondered if she'd made a mistake, turning down his offer of an affair.

chapter twelve

Edith spent the morning removing the red paper hearts from the store's windows—ones she'd cut and decorated herself with glue and glitter. Two days before, when Walter came to take her to dinner for Valentine's Day, he said they looked childish. Edith didn't normally work on Saturdays, but one of the salesgirls had a big date and needed hours to get ready. She thought her boyfriend had bought a ring and was going to pop the question. Walter's remark about the decorations sat in Edith's stomach during the French meal he kept saying was magnificent. She praised everything on her plate, and barely touched it. He asked if she were well. Had she contracted what Mary had? She was tempted to laugh or be cynical, and in the end said no, she was just a little tired and looked forward to an early night.

It was the Monday after, and a lot of the merchants around Harvard Square still had hearts and cupids everywhere, but Edith wanted to move on and think about the next big holiday, which was St. Patrick's Day. She and Mary planned to promote Irish authors and display their titles in the front window, even if they'd been released years before. She imagined an arrangement of green carnations, and the staff all dressed in green. When she mentioned this to Mary, Mary said she had a lovely emerald pendant she'd gotten as a wedding present from Henry's mother. Would that do?

Edith threw away the decorations and went into the office where Mary was drinking a cup of tea. Unopened bills were piled on the desk. Edith thought Mary would have opened them, but no, she just sat, sipping and gazing coldly into space. These icy silences had become more frequent since the baby, or since the end of the baby, to be specific.

Edith sat at the desk and picked up the issue of *Publishers Weekly* that had arrived that morning. As she flipped through it, one item caught her eye.

"We should stock this," Edith said.

"Stock what?"

"Shirley Jackson's story collection."

"Who's that?"

Edith looked at Mary.

"Really? You didn't read 'The Lottery?' in *The New Yorker* last year?" she asked.

"I don't read *The New Yorker.*"

"Then you must start."

Mary's face tightened. Edith smiled. "You need to know who's saying what about what."

"You sound like Henry."

"Well, he's onto something."

Mary asked about the story's plot, and Edith told her.

"Golly? That's positively macabre," Mary said. "Though I could see some of our esteemed English villagers partaking—even enjoying a good stoning now and then." She looked amused, then chuckled quietly.

She told Edith about a Miss Norris, a former schoolteacher, proper old spinster and all that, Ludlow's finest example of dignified celibacy, who observed a group of boys throwing mud on her freshly washed sheets hanging in her yard, and confided to the vicar over tea they should all be castrated.

"She used that word?" Edith asked.

"She did. And from what I understand, the vicar went red up to his thinning hairline."

"Oh, she sounds like quite the character."

"Ripping sort, what."

Edith looked through the correspondence at her elbow. One envelope contained a letter from a local author who wanted to come and read her poetry. The name meant nothing to Edith, and she realized she'd have to get to know her immediate pool of writers. There had to be a lot of them around. The author, Clara Levy, had recently published a volume called *Holocaust*. It sounded dreary and tragic, but maybe it wasn't. Then again, how could it be anything but?

The bell on the door jingled and Mary went out to see if whoever had come in wanted something. Edith was glad she'd gone, rather than waiting for her to get up and go. She slipped a piece of paper into the typewriter and tapped out a quick note to Miss Levy saying she was welcome to bring her book by anytime, and she would read it with pleasure. She couldn't guarantee an author event at this time and asked for her patience. She had plans to put a calendar together soon. With luck, Miss Levy might be their first reader.

Mary returned and said it was just the gas man, wanting to read the meter. He was new, apparently, and didn't know the meter was accessible by the alley behind the building. Edith told her about Clara Levy. Mary sat down.

"Do you think that's wise?" Mary asked.

"Certainly. Why not?"

"Well, you know."

"Because she's Jewish?"

"Well, yes, frankly."

"Oh, Mary."

"I've got nothing against them, but I'm not sure they'll promote the right kind of atmosphere."

"And what kind is that?"

"You're having me on. You know perfectly well what I mean."

"Communists used to meet here in the thirties. Did you know that?"

"Really? How colorful."

"It's our duty to not only serve but to reflect all parts of our community, wouldn't you agree?"

"Edith, darling, I just said I've got nothing against them!"

Edith typed Miss Levy's address on an envelope. She signed the letter, put it in the envelope and put a stamp in the corner. She'd leave it on the counter by the register for the mailman to collect.

Mary wouldn't let the matter go. She said during the war Henry's parents hosted a pair of girls, refugees, from Poland, much to the dismay of their neighbors. Of course, that was before everyone really knew what the Nazis had been up to with their camps and all. Henry's father hadn't understood what he was getting at the time. He hadn't understood the girls were Jewish.

"And?" Edith asked. Her face was hot. The bell on the door rang again. She didn't budge. Neither did Mary.

Mary explained Henry's father was in business with a man who had been a Nazi supporter before the war. Naturally, the man was never candid about it, but Henry's father remembered him saying Hitler was getting a raw deal. Anyway, they were partners in a housing development, and this man had put up a larger share of the money than Henry's father had, and Henry's father thought he might be tempted to pull out if he got wind he was harboring two little Jewish girls under his roof. Of course, it all came to light when the local vicar said in his Sunday sermon Henry's father was doing the Lord's work by taking them in. The business partner threatened to dissolve the partnership, and Henry's father told him to go ahead. He wasn't going to be bullied. He also told him his pro-Nazi sympathies would be made known to everyone—Henry's father would see to that, and no one would want to do business with him in the future. So, the girls stayed, the houses got built, the war ended, Henry's father bought out the business partner for very favorable terms, and the girls eventually became British citizens.

"A happy ending, don't you see?" Mary asked.

"Yes, with a lot of unnecessary stress and strain."

"It's inevitable."

"What do you mean?"

Mary paused. She stared at the floor for a moment. "They create problems. Just by being Jewish. It's not their fault. It's the fault of others. But there you go. It's a fact of life," she said.

"So's tolerance, acceptance, and making a difference."

"I'd say those are conscious choices."

"Made possible by a sense of moral obligation."

Mary leaned back and regarded Edith at length. As she did, the fingers of her right hand played with the pearl choker she often wore.

"I can see why Henry admires you," she said.

"Who says he does?"

"It's obvious."

"Not to me."

"You sell yourself short."

"No, I don't."

"Well, let me just say you're quite a clever girl, and I'm glad to be in business with you."

Mary seemed genuine. Yet Edith remained disgruntled and kept conversation to a minimum for the rest of the day.

She had to pick up Walter's dry cleaning on the way home. She'd forgotten it the day before, and he complained because he was waiting for his new suit to come back. He hadn't even worn it. She didn't understand why it had to be cleaned and didn't want to waste her time listening to a long explanation. She carried the suit home, hung it in the closet, and went right out again. She still had groceries to buy for dinner. Walter had said he wanted some of her wonderful spaghetti and meatballs, and she'd make them for him when she had more time. For the moment, he'd have to be happy with stuffed pork chops, creamed spinach, and baked potatoes.

The man at the butcher counter recognized her and gave her a charming smile. His name was Greenberg. She was curious about what life was like for him—how often he'd had to deal with prejudice, being blamed for things he didn't do, kept out of places other people didn't think twice about going into. She thought of Philip and his family members the Nazis murdered. The declaration of Israel as an independent state last year had caused ripples everywhere. Walter said it was a strategic move. Edith was all for it, too. She wondered about the displaced Palestinians, though, being told to leave where they'd always been. The gloom that settled on her then was deep, and she told Mr. Greenberg she didn't care which chops he took from the case, anything would be fine.

Walter returned in a bubbly mood. They'd been invited to a reception at the firm where he'd accepted a job. Well, it wasn't going to be at the firm itself, but in the home of one of the senior partners.

"When?" she asked.

"This Saturday."

"I don't have anything to wear."

"You always say that."

"Because it's true."

"Well, can't you borrow something from Mary?"

Edith slid a pork chop onto his plate, followed by a baked potato.

"If you haven't noticed, we're not exactly the same size," she said.

Walter asked why she was in such a bad mood. Had something happened at the store? She told him about Clara Levy, and the awkward conversation she'd had with Mary. He ate slowly, which meant he was thinking about what she'd said.

"She's right," he said.

"What? How can you say that?"

He held up his hand, asking for a moment to explain.

There was a growing anti-Semitic sentiment afoot in the country now, he said. It was wrong, absolutely wrong, but it needed time to work itself out. People needed to get over blaming the Jews for the war. The only thing to do was wait, bide one's time. Eventually, people would move on to some other, more pressing concern, and this would all be forgotten.

"And in the meantime? Am I supposed to tell Clara Levy she's not welcome to read in my bookstore?"

"You'll do what you think best."

"I already did. I asked her to send me her book."

"Well, she'll be very pleased, I'm sure."

"Not as pleased as she'll be when I schedule her author event."

Walter looked at her. He could see she wasn't going to budge.

"Might be bad for business," he said and heaped butter onto his potato.

"I'm not out to make money."

"How does Henry feel about that?"

"I have no idea."

"Hm."

Edith didn't pursue it. Her mood darkened. She told Walter to leave the dishes, she'd get them in the morning. She went to bed with *The Sun Also Rises*. She'd read it before and was giving it another look. Great novels could be read many times, she'd found.

Two days before the reception, Edith took herself out shopping. She was determined to have a brand-new outfit to wear, and she didn't care how much it cost. Walter had been going on and on about what his first year's salary would be, close to six thousand dollars, and there was enough in their checking account for something reasonably nice. Mary was at the store, along with Patricia, who reported Mr. Samson had returned to his usual self but didn't have the strength to do much besides sit and read. Edith envied him this pastime, not the condition that made it necessary. The day was mild for a Boston February, and she decided to walk over the bridge from Cambridge. Her spirits lifted. Soon the first buds would be on the bare trees; crocuses would pierce the ground; the birds would wake them in the morning.

As she passed a bakery, and the smell of fresh bread filled her inexplicably with hope, she recalled the last February of the war and the mood of cautious optimism in Washington. Four years ago.

Sometimes it felt as if not that much time has gone by; then there were moments when she felt as if a decade had passed since then.

She'd recently had a letter from her former roommate, Mary Jane, who now lived in Dallas with her husband and three children. She wrote, *I've been busy, as you can see!* She said she'd had a devil of a time finding her address, then remembered Edith saying she'd grown up in Urbana, Illinois, so with some persistent checking and a friendly telephone operator, she got the address of Edith's parents. She wrote to ask where to reach Edith, and Edith's mother wrote her back right away.

She sounds like such a nice lady! How lucky you are. As you know, my own dear mother passed away when I was quite young, and now all I've got is Tom's mother, and let me tell you, what the Nazis could have done with her! She'd have been running the show in no time flat!

Edith hadn't seen much of Tom when he was living with Walter, but he always struck her as a nice, quiet fellow. He worked in a bank. Mary Jane was energetic and wholesome. She'd probably end up with five more children, before demanding separate beds. Edith wondered why her mother hadn't mentioned Mary Jane wanting her address, but then her mother's letters had become increasingly distracted. She jumped from topic to topic as if trying to find enough news to fill the page. Her latest worry was Edith's father, whose doctor had warned him to cut back on salt because of his blood pressure. Edith wrote back and suggested her mother put sugar in the saltshaker as a joke. She could see her quiet smile as she read that.

The wind picked up. She took a taxi into Back Bay and the store she wanted to visit. Chatsworth's tried to be glamorous with its velvet sofas, glass chandeliers, and fresh-cut flowers on the counter, but the floor was worn and the paint was dingy. Edith went to a rack of dresses on sale and found a blue silk with a silver waistband. She didn't think blue was her color, though Walter liked her in it. She wanted something bolder—and that meant red. She chose a charmeuse with a deep neck and rhinestone buttons. She felt like a movie star in it. The fifty-four-dollar price tag made her pause. Walter would want her to look good and make him proud, but, in the end, she chose a simple black satin dress with fake-pearl buttons for thirty-seven fifty. The sales clerk who rang up her purchase told her it was a lovely choice. Then she asked if there were a special occasion coming up. Just as Edith was about to explain about the reception, she paused, cash in hand, and realized their anniversary was that very day.

How could she have forgotten? Had Walter remembered? Last year they went out to a little Italian place and toasted each other with a glass of Chianti. The year before, they stayed home because of the weather. She didn't remember the year before that. She had to pause for a moment to calculate they'd been married for four years. Edith didn't answer the clerk and gave her two twenty-dollar bills. She took her change and her package and left.

She had to make something special for dinner. Otherwise, Walter would be unhappy and blame the bookstore for distracting her. She'd forgotten to launder his handkerchiefs the other day, and he told her he couldn't very well use them in the condition they were in. Then he said she needed to make sure the house was running smoothly first and tend to the store second.

"What about Mary? Do you think Henry says the same thing to her?" Edith asked.

"They have a butler. Mary can do as she likes."

"Well, when you start your job, and we're in a different apartment, maybe I'll hire a maid."

Walter said nothing.

Edith looked at her watch and decided she had just enough time to buy a standing rib roast and get it in the oven. She'd make potatoes au gratin, and creamed spinach again. Walter was wild about creamed spinach. And maybe a good bottle of champagne?

By the time she got home, her feet were killing her. She got the roast in, the champagne cooling, and arranged the little bouquet of carnations she'd chosen at the last minute. She waited until a few minutes before Walter was due home and changed into the new dress, thinking she'd have to be careful not to stain it so she could wear it again for the reception.

The telephone rang. It was Walter.

"Listen, Edie, I'm having a beer with some of the gang, and I won't be home for dinner. You don't mind, do you?"

"Walter, do you know what day it is?"

"Thursday."

"Besides that."

"No."

She sighed. She asked what the occasion was. He said Charles Blackman had just been offered a job at the same firm that took on Walter. Wasn't that a scream? Forest and Parks didn't know what they were getting into, letting the likes of them through their doors.

She told him not to be too late.

"Oh, I won't. I've got an early class, remember?"

She hung up.

She changed out of the dress and into her robe. Then she picked at the delicious dinner she'd made. She opened the champagne and drank a couple of glasses. She put the food away but left the dishes in the sink.

She read for a long time and fell asleep.

Walter nudged her awake.

"You made roast beef! Why didn't you tell me?" he asked. He was gnawing a piece he'd carved off and slapped onto a napkin.

"It's our anniversary."

"Oh, Edie, you're right! Why didn't you say something?"

"Because you should have remembered."

Her head hurt from the champagne. She got up to get herself a glass of water. Walter went into the living room and flopped down on the couch. He asked if she'd mind heating a plate for him. He hadn't had anything to eat except a bowl of beer nuts.

"I'm tired," she said. "I ate dinner alone, and I'm tired."

Walter stared at her. "You're wearing lipstick."

"I bought a new dress, too. I was looking very fancy there, for a while."

"Come here."

She went to him and perched in his lap.

"I'm sorry. I really did forget," he said.

"I know."

"Say you're not mad."

"I'm not mad."

"Now, mean it."

She stood up and went into the kitchen. She called out it would be a few minutes before his food was ready unless he didn't mind eating it cold. He said he didn't.

She brought him his plate, then went back for the champagne. She hoped it hadn't gone flat. She poured them each a glass. She tasted it. It was still cool because she'd set it on the sill by the drafty kitchen window. She gave him his glass, and he put it on the coffee table so he could go on eating. He told her it was delicious, and he wished he'd been home sooner. She joined him on the couch.

"Charles is over the moon, I expect," she said.

"About the offer? He is. And guess what."

"What?"

"They're paying me more."

"How do you know?"

"He told me what they're starting him at."

"Why are they paying him less?"

"Because he wasn't in Naval Intelligence, like yours truly."

Edith couldn't see how a war career translated into monetary value for a law firm, then thought Walter's credentials might give him an edge when courting a prospective client. He'd be described as particularly analytic and insightful, or so she assumed.

She said she hadn't gotten anything for dessert. Walter said that was fine, her dinner had been first-rate. He apologized again for forgetting their anniversary. She said they should probably turn in.

She lay awake a long time. Walter had insisted on having sex, and she could hardly refuse him. He dropped off immediately afterward. She thought about turning on the light and trying to read, but that would probably wake him. Gradually, she felt fatigue take over, and she fell into a hard sleep with uneasy, sometimes frantic dreams.

He nudged her awake.

"Another nightmare," he said.

"Did I cry out?"

"You always do."

He got up for his early class and made a lot of noise about it. He wanted to know if the coffee were ready. He was dying for a cup. She gave it to him and offered to make breakfast, but he said he'd grab something on campus. He had his coffee standing up and went into the bedroom to dress. She looked at the mess on the table from the night before and sighed. Then she got everything into the sink full of warm, soapy water.

There was a knock on the door. She had a telegram. It was from her mother.

Father seriously ill. Cable if you can come.

The man at the door asked if there were any reply.

"Yes."

He wrote down, *Will let you know which train.*

She found her purse and paid him for the message.

Walter was in the living room.

"Who was that?" he asked.

She handed him the telegram. When he'd read it, he said, "Oh, Edie. I'm so sorry! It doesn't say what's wrong with him. He might be right as rain in no time."

"My mother wouldn't have sent a telegram for something minor."

"No, I suppose not."

She told Walter she'd have to make arrangements. He asked if she wanted him to stay home and help her. She said she'd rather be alone if he didn't mind. He looked hurt but said nothing. After he left, she called the train station. She could go first thing in the morning.

chapter thirteen

This nightmare, unlike so many others, stayed with her after she woke up.

She stood in the front hall of an empty house. It wasn't her house or one she'd been in before, but she knew the layout. The living room was to the left, the dining room to the right, and the kitchen was at the back. As she went from room to room, she saw the walls were cracked and crumbling in places, while in others they were smooth and solid. She assumed the home was being rebuilt and the owners had gotten called away in the middle of their efforts. The kitchen was brand new, sunny, with cut flowers on the table. The bouquet was made up of carnations, lilies, roses, snapdragons, and iris, all in shades of white. Their scent was almost too strong, but after she stood there a moment, she found it delicious. The flowers shriveled, their petals dropped off, the water in the vase turned brown. The floor trembled, and one wall fell away. She feared for her life, thought to run, and couldn't. The sky, now revealed, knotted and swirled. The wind was fierce, yet she was able to stand. The wind died and the clouds became wisps tinged with shades of orange and yellow. They reminded her of decay, yet were beautiful, too, so gorgeous she was moved to weep.

In the morning she boarded the train. She had a sleeper car in which she barely slept. It was strange to think of her father being ill. She couldn't remember a single time when he had to stay in bed for anything. She was worried about her mother and what the stress of seeing him suffer might do to her.

The drive from the station didn't instill the same painful nostalgia as it had the last time. The town had grown. New stores stood along Main Street, many of them selling clothing and appliances. The taxi driver commented on the mild winter they'd had and said his wife was hoping for the crocuses to sprout soon.

The hedge in front of her house was taller. A bird feeder had been installed on a low hanging branch of the oak tree that stood on the west side. There'd been a tree on the east side, too, but Edith's father had declared it blocked the morning light and had it cut down years before.

Her knock on the door went unanswered, so she went in. Her mother came up the hall from the kitchen. Her navy-blue dress and black shoes seemed appropriate for the crisis at hand. She looked so much older, Edith thought. She kissed her on the cheek, then gave her a hearty hug. She felt solid in Edith's arms, which was reassuring. Edith put down her bag.

"How is he?" she asked.

"Sleeping now."

"What's wrong with him?"

"Stroke."

"Oh, my god."

"Come," her mother said and took her into the living room.

Her mother said it happened on campus. He collapsed in the lecture hall. That the stroke hadn't been fatal was a miracle, really. They did everything they could do for him in the hospital, then sent him home. He would probably recover, but it would take time. His speech had been affected. He was difficult to understand. They didn't know yet if he would walk.

"Was it because of his blood pressure?" Edith asked.

"Most likely. He was given something for it, but I don't know if he took it. He might very well have decided he didn't need to."

Edith had strep throat once and was prescribed sulfa. Her father objected and said her body should be strong enough to fight off the illness on its own. Her mother ignored him and gave her the medicine. She couldn't recall her father ever taking an aspirin, even when he complained of a bad headache.

"How are you holding up?" Edith asked.

"Tired. In poor spirits, of course. Betty has been a great help."

"Betty Blake?"

"Yes."

That was an old friend, a spinster. She and Edith's mother had been in school together in South Dakota. Betty came to Illinois just a year after Edith's mother did, having no family of her own. She'd been a constant presence in Edith's life when Edith was young. Then her father decided he didn't like her and told her mother to keep her out of the house. Edith didn't know they'd remained friends and was glad they had.

Edith offered to make coffee if her mother would like some.

"I'd rather have a drink, to tell you the truth," her mother said.

Edith went into the kitchen where a bottle of scotch stood on the counter. There was no seltzer bottle. She didn't mind drinking it straight, though she'd never known her mother to take it that way.

She returned with two glasses, gave one to her mother, and sat on the other end of the couch. The stuffing in the cushions had flattened years before. All the furniture in the house was old. Her mother had wanted to replace it for years, and her father always refused.

Her mother's face relaxed as she gazed softly at her.

"I'm so glad to see you. It's been too long," she said.

"I know. I'm sorry."

"You've been busy with your bookstore."

"Yes."

"Is it going well?"

"Reasonably well, yes. I think I'm a born businesswoman."

Her mother smiled. "So perhaps an academic life wasn't for you, after all."

"Perhaps."

Her mother turned her head, listening. There was nothing to hear.

"I should have come sooner. Before he got sick," Edith said. "What happened that Christmas . . . I just couldn't take it anymore, I guess."

"You'd taken enough."

As a girl, Edith adored her father. Then her love for him gave rise to self-hatred. She had to be bad because he punished her so often. When she was nine or ten, had angered him yet again, and had received her slap and insults, she fled to her room and screamed. The release of her physical and psychic anguish was wonderful. Her voice echoed off the bedroom walls. It was as if she had let loose a spirit waiting too long to rise from her stomach and slip furiously from her mouth. Her mother came into the room and took her by the shoulders. Edith went on screaming, and her mother did nothing to stop her. Eventually, she ran out of energy and threw herself down on her bed, empty and spent.

"Why is he so cruel? I've never understood it," Edith said.

Her mother shrugged. She said cruelty was a habit some people fell into because they didn't know any better. Maybe it served him well once, in his youth. Maybe he had to defend himself against something or someone and never learned to drop the aggressive stance.

"Does he love you? Did he ever love me?" Edith asked.

"I think so. I also think love means different things to different people."

Edith asked her to explain.

Her mother said for some people it meant passion or nurturing, or some combination of those. For others, it meant control and ownership.

"One thing I've learned is kind people love kindly; careless people love carelessly; cruel people love cruelly," her mother said.

And how do I love?

She'd never thought about it. If she had to say anything, it would be she loved passionately. But passion couldn't sustain by itself. Love needed gentleness. Fairness and consideration, too. Altruism, perhaps. A lack of selfishness.

Henry would agree. She could sense it.

"So, what's the plan?" Edith asked.

"Plan?"

"For taking care of Papa."

Her mother said there was a rotating staff of nurses who came in every day. One stayed overnight on a cot in the downstairs hall; another came in the morning to handle breakfast and lunch, whatever he could manage of those two meals; and the third came in the afternoon to bathe him.

"Isn't that expensive?" Edith asked.

"Yes, but there was no choice. He didn't want me to touch him."

"You said he had trouble talking."

"He made it clear."

"But how can you afford it?"

"We have savings. And Betty gave me a fair amount."

"That was very generous of her."

Edith tried to remember what Betty did for a living. She couldn't, so she asked her mother.

"She's a writer."

"Really?"

"Mystery novels."

"I had no idea! We must get her books in the store."

"You probably already have them."

"I don't think so. I'm sure I'd have recognized her name."

"She writes under the name of Marion Holt."

"You're joking! *Betty?* Of course, we have her. I've read a lot of her books!"

Edith remembered Betty's hands being stained with ink from her fountain pen; and a conversation about the problem of finding replacement typewriter ribbons. She had a kind face, a soft voice, and loved the color green. When Edith was very young, Betty always brought her a book when she came to visit. After Edith's father barred her from the house, her mother sometimes went to see her. Once, Edith went, too. She couldn't have been more than eight or nine. Betty's house was even smaller than Edith's, but it was a sunny, cozy place, with an orange cat and a row of African violets on the windowsill.

"Why did you never tell me who she was?" Edith asked.

"I'm sure I just didn't think of it."

Edith doubted that were true. Not that her mother was lying, she just didn't want to think about it too much at the moment.

Someone knocked softly on the back door. Her mother went on sitting. So did Edith. The door opened, and a moment later a youthful-looking woman in a nurse's uniform appeared in the doorway to the living room. She wore a blue cape. Edith's eyes were drawn at once to her sturdy white shoes.

"Hello, Doreen. Please allow me to introduce my daughter, Edith Sloan. She's come all the way from Boston to see her poor father," her mother said.

"How do you do?" Doreen asked.

"How do you do?" Edith answered.

Doreen asked if there had been any change, and Edith's mother said Connie reported a relatively peaceful night. Nancy said she hadn't been able to get him to eat much, though he had a couple of bites of oatmeal.

"And how do you find him, dear?" Doreen asked Edith.

"Me? Oh, I haven't seen him yet."

"She just arrived," her mother said.

For a brief moment, a look of mild disapproval paced over Doreen's pink face. Then she turned her head in the direction of the den, which must have been converted into the sick room. Edith listened closely and heard nothing. Doreen went on her way. Her mother looked at her watch, and then Edith looked at hers. It was almost three-thirty. Her mother explained her father tended to wake up a bit in the late afternoon. That's when all of his necessary tasks were seen too, like a sponge bath and a shave. For a moment, Edith considered the rough, brutal man her father had always been, now in a weak, submissive state. She wasn't glad, but neither was she sorry. Had she stopped hating him?

Her mother asked how things were with Walter. Edith shrugged.

"I'm sorry you're not happy," her mother said.

"I'm happy enough."

Edith said Walter had forgotten their anniversary.

"Men do that," her mother said.

Doreen returned to say Edith could go visit now if she liked. He was expecting her. Doreen bustled off, her heavy tread growing fainter as she went into the powder room and ran water in the sink.

"Do you want me to come with you?" her mother asked.

"No, it's all right."

"He's . . . quite changed."

"I should think so."

"Don't be alarmed."

"I won't be."

But as Edith approached the den, she felt cold. She raised her hand to tap gently, then slowly pushed the door open until she could see into the room. The bed was parallel to the window, which meant her father lay in profile. He was propped up on several pillows, his hair grayer than before, and neatly combed. His right arm lay on the bedspread, palm up. His eyes were closed, and his chest rose and fell in a regular steady rhythm. She entered. He opened his eyes but didn't turn his head. She advanced as quietly as she could, though it was pointless since he was clearly awake. She felt like a child again, coming into that room just to be near him while he graded papers, and soak up the serious, elevated atmosphere he fueled with his concentration and hasty pencil marks.

"Papa," she said. He didn't move. She went to the foot of the bed and looked down at him. He seemed so small! He wasn't a tall man, but he was broad-shouldered, at least he used to be. He lifted his eyes and met hers.

How easy it would be to kill him, she thought. She could hold a pillow over his face or press her hands to his throat. The idea didn't shock her. She'd wanted to many times before. His eyes took on a keener light, and one side of his mouth moved, but no sound came from it. He lifted his left hand. She assumed he meant she should sit in the chair by the bed. She did. Up close, his skin was yellow around the eyes. His face was slack, where once his jaw had been firm and square.

"I came to see you," she said.

Her father swallowed. There was a glass of water with a straw in it on the table by his bed.

"Are you thirsty?" she asked.

He stared at her.

She lifted the glass and brought it to where the straw could touch his lips. He drew his lips together against it. In that moment, he looked like himself, but then his mouth fell open. She put the glass back on the table.

She heard Doreen walk up the hall. Her head appeared in the doorway. She smiled. Edith didn't smile back. Doreen left.

Rain beat against the window. Edith didn't remember if it had been raining before when she came in from the station. The rain would probably turn to snow as night fell. The idea of them together in the house under snow aroused nothing in her—neither dread nor a sense of comfort. She wasn't used to feeling empty. Shock, she supposed, or just not knowing where to put the image of this weak, shrunken man.

She looked around, remembering the room as it had been. Where was his desk? A solid piece with shelves on the side. He used to put things there he no longer wanted—an ashtray she made him in kindergarten and an almost empty inkwell. She'd sat on the floor once and picked it up. She removed the stopper to look inside. He coughed, which startled her, and she dropped the bottle. Ink spilled. There followed the usual shouts and slaps and an order to her mother to come at once and clean the mess. Edith's mother used seltzer water and a towel. A lot of the ink came up, but a small stain remained. The carpet hadn't been changed. Where was the stain? It must be under the bed.

"Do you remember when I spilled the ink?" Edith asked.

He didn't move.

"It was an accident. I didn't do it on purpose."

He looked at her.

"All the things you punished me for were accidents."

Doreen came in and fluffed up her father's pillows. Her father made a sort of growling sound, followed by an open vowel.

"Walter," Doreen said. "He wants to know about Walter."

"That's my husband."

"Ah."

"He's a law student at Harvard."

"Is he now? Well, isn't that something! You must be very proud."

Doreen took the water glass and left the room.

Her father's head was turned to the side as if he wanted to look out the window. Edith didn't understand why the bed didn't face that way. Wouldn't you want to let someone see the sky if they were confined to a single room? Or maybe the thinking was it would be too hard, too disappointing.

"Walter's fine," she said. "He has a job lined up."

Her father blinked.

"I'm happy for him, of course. He deserved it. He works very hard."

Her father stared into space.

"I don't love him. I don't think I ever did."

The staring continued.

"I'm fond of him, don't get me wrong. I always will be. But there's no passion there. There never was."

Doreen came in again. She said she wanted to change the sheets, and she wouldn't be a minute. Edith stood up and left the room.

In her absence, her mother had poured herself another drink and turned on the radio. A Mozart symphony played cheerfully.

Edith flopped down on the couch, sending up a plume of dust. She put her face in her hands. Her mother asked if she were all right. Edith lifted her head and said yes, she just needed a minute to pull herself together.

"It's not easy, seeing him like that," her mother said. Edith detected genuine grief in her voice.

"He's not the same person."

"That's just it, isn't it?"

Doreen could be heard moving around the sick room, making cheerful remarks as she told Edith's father she was going to roll him first this way, then that, to get the old sheets off and the new ones on.

"This all must be so hard on you," Edith said.

"It's much easier than it was a week ago."

"But I only got your telegram the day before yesterday."

"I didn't send it until he came home from the hospital."

"Really? What day was the stroke?"

Her mother paused to think. "On the eighteenth."

"That was ten days ago! Why didn't you let me know sooner?"

"I wanted to wait and see."

"Wait and see what?"

Her mother's face stilled.

"If he'd die, you mean," Edith said.

"Yes. I hope that doesn't shock you."

"It doesn't."

"Good. I hope what I'm going to tell you won't, either."

Her mother put her empty glass on the table and said she was leaving Edith's father. She knew how it would look—she abandoned him in his time of need. She didn't care. She'd worried too long about the opinions of other people when the only person she needed to be concerned about now was herself. And Betty.

"Betty?" Edith said.

"It was never what your father thought."

"And what did he think?"

"That we were lovers."

They might have been, she supposed, if either of them had that particular grain. They just didn't. In fact, if she were ten or fifteen years younger, and the right man came along, well, that would be different. They'd discussed it, she and Betty. Betty had had her share of suitors and physical relationships, and was still open to life with a man, but was pretty sure it wouldn't happen to her now. Betty was easy to be with, and Edith's mother was sure she'd be easy to live with. Again, people would draw nasty conclusions, and they'd have to weather those.

"They might not. They might think you're just good friends. Which is what you are," Edith said.

"I hope so. But if not, too bad."

"What about the house?"

"He can have it. I never liked it all that much. He was the one who chose it, way back when. I had nothing to say about it."

Edith asked if she would file for divorce. Her mother said she would. Then Edith asked what it was about her father's illness that brought her decision to the fore.

"Because I've been waiting on him all our married life, and now, with the condition he's in, I could go on doing so for years. And I don't care to."

Doreen finished in the sick room and bustled up the hall carrying a bundle of sheets. Then she was in the kitchen, putting a pan on the stove. Her mother said Doreen thought it her mission to get some soup into Edith's father every day, no matter what.

"I don't know how she does it, but he eats it. Whether she flatters or threatens him I couldn't say."

"And what does she do after he's been fed?"

"She'll read to him until he drifts off. She leaves when the night nurse comes between ten and eleven."

Her mother said she'd been taking most of her meals over at Betty's, and Edith was welcome to join them.

"Yes, I would like to do that."

"I'll give her a ring and let her know."

Edith went into the powder room to freshen up. She splashed water on her face and examined her reflection in the glass of the medicine cabinet over the sink. She looked pale. Her face seemed taut as if it were being pulled by an invisible string somewhere in her head.

Edith drove to Betty's. Her mother didn't feel up to it because of the scotch she'd had. Edith had had just as much but didn't think it worth mentioning. It felt strange to be behind the wheel after so many years. Her mother told her the way. They passed Walter's parents' house, and Edith asked her mother if she'd seen them.

"No. We fell out of touch."

"Are you sorry?"

"I always liked Louise. Walter Senior I could never stand."

Betty lived on the other side of the university, in the last house on a cul-de-sac surrounded by stately elms. A new Buick sat in the driveway. Given how successful her books were, Edith wondered why she didn't own a Cadillac. The same modesty was reflected inside. The furniture was solid and comfortable, but nothing fancy. Betty herself was dressed in a simple brown-and-white dress. She was a tall, slender woman. Her gray hair was pinned up in a bun on the top of her head. The smell of roasted chicken reminded Edith how little she'd eaten all day.

"I'm so sorry about your father," Betty said and gave Edith a gentle squeeze. She led them into the dining room where the small table was set with good china and lit candles. She said dinner wasn't quite ready, but she had just opened a bottle of lovely French wine if they cared to sample it?

They sat. Edith realized both her mother and Betty were watching her. Surely not because they wanted her approval? Or maybe just her blessing for what they were about to undertake. But Betty wanted to talk about Edith and the bookstore she'd bought.

"It's doing all right. I think we'll clear a profit for the first month. Not a big one, mind you. I think the Square is still getting used to me," Edith said.

"And what about your partners?" Betty asked.

Edith described Mary and Henry, calling them true British bluebloods. Henry was everything you'd imagine an English lord to be, shy and unassuming. Mary, on the other hand, was much more outgoing.

Betty asked about Walter and his law career. Edith said it seemed to be going swimmingly.

"He's not wild about my working at the store. He says it interferes with my other duties," Edith said. She wondered how much longer it would be before the food was ready.

"And yet you persist," Betty said.

"Yes."

Edith said it was the thrill of a lifetime to discover who she really was. She had a million questions about her life as an author, though thought now probably wasn't the time, under the circumstances.

"After dinner, then," Betty said. She excused herself to get the chicken out of the oven and to check on the potatoes and spinach. Edith leaned back in her chair. She'd been so well raised that sitting upright was an instinct, one she now happily abandoned.

She told her mother she thought she'd be happy here, and later, when things were truly settled, she and Betty should come out to visit them.

"Won't Walter disapprove?" her mother asked.

Edith didn't know and didn't care.

chapter fourteen

Edith stepped off the train in Boston two days later. She hadn't gone into her father's room again. Most of the time she was at Betty's with her mother. She liked talking to Betty a lot. She described her struggle to get published way back when, and said not enough writers starting out had the necessary persistence to make it. She wanted to try her hand at serious fiction and give mysteries a rest. Edith said from what she'd read, her novels were quite literary, which made them serious. How did she invent her plots? Betty said just by watching people and trying to figure out what they wanted most. They also talked about how to make the house comfortable for a second person. Edith's mother would have her own room, of course, but it was small. Edith said she'd read in a magazine the right wallpaper would make it feel bigger. Her mother said once Edith had a house of her own, she would no doubt enjoy decorating it.

At home, Edith was restless. At the store, she was more focused but still uneasy. Walter was glad to have her back and took her out for dinner the first night. He was genuinely sorry to hear how different her father now was. She was tempted to tell him about Betty and her mother and didn't. She wanted nothing to distract him from the attention he showered her with, which lasted all of a day. Then it was business as usual, with him occupied with school and thoughts of the future, leaving her to struggle with a growing sense of dread.

During her time away clerical work had piled up, mostly bills and unanswered letters from publishers. Why hadn't Mary seen to them? Mary, it turned out, had barely been in. The two college girls and Patricia had been making do without her.

Edith closed the office door and went through the stack of envelopes. All were typed, except one, addressed to her personally, in an uneven script. It was from Clara Levy.

Dear Miss Sloan,

I cannot tell you how delighted I was to receive your kind offer to read at The Turned Page. I am quite familiar with the bookstore. Mr. Samson and I have known one another for a long time. I was sorry to learn he is in ill health, a condition which sadly comes to us all.

It is for this reason I write to you now. I am not a young woman. Oh, that I were! I have been told by my doctor to limit my activities. This means I spend much time seated before my window, penning poems, and watching students on the street below. There goes the Future, I say aloud, though the only one around to take note is my cat, and he has learned to ignore my vague pronouncements.

But I digress. (This is the privilege of one approaching advanced age.) I wonder if you would like to visit me in my home? I would be pleased to receive you next Thursday, if convenient. Around three o'clock. I will offer you tea. Perhaps you would care to bring a friend. The more the merrier, I always say. If you agree, please write and let me know.

Yours,

Clara Ruth Levy

She sounded delightful, Edith thought. Of course, she'd go. She wondered about inviting Mary, then quickly recalled her thinly veiled anti-Semitic remarks. Walter? Certainly not. Patricia? Perhaps, but then the conversation would veer toward Mr. Samson since Miss Levy would be sure to want to know in great detail how he was faring. One of the college girls? She saw enough of those out her window, from the sound of it.

What about Henry? He was a perfect choice. Cultured, urbane. But maybe he thought the way Mary did. She'd have to ask him directly if that were the case. Under no circumstances would she subject Miss Levy to any of that nonsense.

She called their apartment. Henry answered on the first ring.

"It's Edith."

"My dear. What a pleasant surprise! Walter said you'd gone away again. Something about an illness in the family."

"Yes. My father. I'm back now. Obviously."

She got right to the point. She was going to meet a local poet, a lovely-sounding Jewish lady. Would he care to come, too? Unless he had any problem with that.

"What sort of problem?" he asked.

"An anti-Semitic sort of problem."

"Certainly not. Why do you ask?"

Edith hesitated. "Never mind."

"Did Mary say something?"

"Well, she thought I shouldn't agree to let her come and read, but I did anyway."

"Good for you!"

"She can't, though. She was overly optimistic when she made the request, and her doctor forbids it. But she invited me to tea."

"And you would like me to escort you."

"Yes, if you're free."

"What day does she want us?"

"Next Thursday."

"That'll be fine. On Thursdays I only have class in the morning," he said.

"How are they going? Your classes, I mean."

"Quite well. Though I don't know if I'll continue next year."

"Why not?"

He said nothing. Then, "I may wish to pursue other opportunities."

"I see."

He was quiet again.

"I'm sorry Mary hasn't been at the store as often as she should. I'm afraid she's letting you down. She's grown quite fond of riding, it seems, though I should say her passion has been rekindled. She was always a keen horsewoman," he said.

"Yes."

The office door opened, and Patricia leaned her head inside. She withdrew when she saw Edith was on the phone.

Henry asked where Miss Levy lived. Edith said on the Square someplace. They could walk. They could meet at the store and go from there.

"Splendid!" he said.

Edith appreciated his enthusiasm. They said goodbye.

Before she answered Miss Levy, she opened the other envelopes. Two were past due notices for books purchased before Edith came on board; one was an overdue electric bill, and two others were from publishers announcing new titles. She returned to the past due amounts, did a quick tally, opened the checkbook in the desk, and was shocked to see one hundred and twenty-five dollars had been withdrawn in cash from the account. Mary had written the check. But why? She and Henry were loaded. It had to be for the doctor who took care of the baby she didn't want to have. Of course, she wouldn't have asked Henry for the money, at least not told him directly what it was for, but couldn't she have made up a story? Some long-lost relative in the old country suddenly surfaced without a penny?

Because of Henry's deposit after the store first opened, there was enough to settle all bills and pay salaries and rent for the next two months. Receipts weren't exactly robust, but they were coming in steadily. They would be fine if there were no more emergency reductions in cash flow. Edith would have to keep Mary away from the checkbook. She would take it home with her whenever she left for the day. If Mary ever asked why, Edith would be blunt.

Patricia leaned her head in again and said someone was asking to see her.

Edith went out to discover Babs, who'd come with her husband to their get-together. She wore a nicely tailored coat with a faux fur collar. She was standing before a display of children's books. Maybe she was expecting.

Edith came up and said hello. For a moment Babs didn't seem to recognize her, then a steely smile settled on her face.

"Edie, how nice!" she said.

Edie? She thought back. Had Walter introduced her that way or called her that at the party?

"What brings you by?" Edith asked.

"I wonder if you'd like to have lunch with me."

"It's only a little after ten."

"Is it? Well, how about a cup of coffee, then?"

"Well, I don't know."

"Please. It's important." Babs' voice was gently urgent. Edith asked if she knew Devlin's, one street over.

"Yes, of course."

"All right. You go ahead. I'll be right behind."

Edith found Patricia and said she had to go out. Patricia nodded. She seemed down. Edith asked if everything were all right. She said Mr. Samson had had another bad night, according to his landlady, who spent a lot of time helping out. Edith said she was sorry to hear that and asked if there were anything she could do.

"You've helped a lot, just by taking this place off our hands," Patricia said, though she didn't sound grateful, just worn out. Edith asked if she needed some time off, with pay, of course. Patricia said no, she would rather stay busy.

The sky had cleared, and the light was brilliant. Edith felt a surge of joy. It would be a good spring, she decided. A happy spring. She'd become more like Walter and focus on the future. Her father's illness had begun to free her. She would be who she was always meant to be, and if she didn't have a clear vision of that person yet, she would, before too long.

Devlin's was a college haunt full of students bent over books, a cup at one elbow, and an ashtray at the other. The warmth from the radiators fogged the windows. Babs was seated at the back. When Edith had finally managed to wend her way through the closely packed tables and people looking for a place to sit, she was met by a steaming cup of coffee Babs had ordered on her behalf. There was a small silver pitcher of cream and a bowl with cubed sugar.

"I didn't know how you take it," Babs said. Her coat was draped over the back of her chair. Her sweater was a pretty plum shade.

Edith's eye was drawn to the brooch in the shape of a bumble bee that sat just below the collar.

Babs seemed uneasy. She talked about the weather, saying that as a girl from Philadelphia she should be used to rotten winters, but somehow in New England they were that much worse. Then she asked how Edith liked working in a bookstore.

"I'm the owner. Well, one of them," Edith said. She dropped two cubes of sugar into her coffee. Then she pulled out her pack of cigarettes. She offered one to Babs, who helped herself. Edith lit hers first, then extended the lighter across the table to Babs.

"Really? That's marvelous. How do you balance the demands of being in business with your duties as a housewife?"

"I have a small staff of people to help me."

"How very enterprising."

Her admiration seemed genuine. Edith asked how she'd been, and how . . . here she paused because she couldn't remember her husband's name.

"Andy," Babs said.

"Yes, Andy."

"Oh, we're just fine. Andy's fretting about midterms, poor kid."

"Does he have a job lined up?"

"Actually, that's what I wanted to talk to you about."

"Me? Why?"

Babs said Andy has been hired by the same firm as Walter. In fact, they'd gone to that reception recently, only Edith hadn't been there. Edith had forgotten about the reception. Walter hadn't said anything about how it went. Edith said her father was ill, and she'd gone back to Illinois for a few days.

"Oh, I'm sorry. I hope he's better now," Babs said.

The last letter from Edith's mother, which she'd gotten just yesterday, said there had been no change. She hadn't told him yet she was moving out. It seemed as if she might be having second thoughts, though she didn't hint at this.

"It will be a while, I'm afraid," Edith said. She smoked her cigarette.

Edith said it was great Walter and Andy would be in the same firm. Did Babs happen to know Charles Blackman? Apparently, he'd been offered a position there, too.

Babs stared at the table, then stubbed out her cigarette in the plastic ashtray.

"Well, here's the thing," she said. Edith waited for her to continue. She drank her coffee, aware a feeling was rising in her chest, not fear exactly, just a sense of being overly alert.

"It seems that Andy's gotten the idea Walt has a bit of a crush on me. It's nonsense, of course. I mean, how could he, when he's got you? And I'm not just handing out empty praise here, my dear. Everyone knows you're quite lovely."

"Why does Andy think that?"

"Because last summer, when you were . . . away, we had Walt over, and of course we all drank too much, and well, to be blunt, Walt made a pass at me."

"Last summer?"

"I know. You'd think Andy would have had time to get over it by now. I mean, these things happen, even with the most faithful of married men."

"And you haven't been able to persuade Andy that it was just a harmless flirtation."

"That's right."

"And what do you want me to do?"

"Ask Walt to talk to Andy."

"Why hasn't Andy brought this up himself?"

"You know how men are."

"I have some idea."

Babs smiled. Edith didn't. She recalled the party at their place, and Walter dancing with Babs while she and Andy talked in the kitchen. Andy seemed unhappy that night, she thought because he didn't care much for law school, but now she thought it was because Babs, whom he'd termed *lively*, or something to that effect, was, in fact, a dangerous flirt. Edith wondered if she had made the pass, not Walter, and in any case, what exactly had that pass consisted of.

They finished their coffee. Edith promised to see what she could do. She was uncomfortable when Babs shook her hand goodbye.

The minute Walter walked through the door, Edith asked him what the hell happened last summer with Babs. He dropped his briefcase on the floor where he always put it.

"What kind of a crazy question is that?" he asked.

She told him about having seen Babs that morning, that Andy had been suspicious for months, and needed reassuring. Walter removed his coat, hung it on the rack in the hall, and stayed there a moment before returning to the living room where Edith was pouring herself a second scotch. She didn't offer him one. He asked her to sit, so she did. He sat down, too.

His face changed, as he sat there with her. It grew still and somber, and the light in his gray eyes became brighter and more tightly focused. She found it hard to breathe.

"It wasn't my idea," Walter said. "I want to make that clear."

"What wasn't?"

"She'd had a lot to drink that night."

"I gather that."

"We all did. Andy turned in early."

"And?"

"Babs and I made love. On the couch."

"Oh, my god!"

He hung his head. "I never wanted you to know. I never wanted to hurt you."

"She said you made a pass at her."

"It's a little more complicated than that."

"Well, clearly!"

"No, I mean, more complicated on her end, I mean."

"Walter, did you get her pregnant?"

"What? Of course not! She'd look like a whale by now if that were true."

Not necessarily, Edith thought.

"Then what do you mean?" she asked.

"She has feelings for me."

"Do you mean . . . Babs is *in love* with you?"

Walter looked at his hands, held loosely in his lap.

"So she says," he said.

"Are you seeing her?"

"No. Not since that night."

Walter watched her closely. Her face was hot, and her heart thudded stupidly. Walter and Babs? Was it possible? And did they only sleep together once? That would have been enough for Babs to see what a terrible lover Walter was.

Walter leaned toward her and took her hand. He said he was sorrier than she'd ever know; he didn't know what made him do it, except when she was gone, he'd been so lonely, so unbearably lonely.

"Are you saying this is my fault?" Edith asked.

"Of course not. I'm just sure if you'd been here, it would never have crossed my mind."

"You've never thought once about sleeping with another woman?"

He didn't answer. Then he said, "Thinking about it and doing it are two different things."

"Indeed, they are. And when I went to see my father the week before last, did you sleep with someone then?"

"Of course not!"

"Don't raise your voice. You're the one at fault here. I should be yelling at you."

"Yell then, if you want."

"I don't want."

He dropped her hand. Tears formed in his eyes. Hers remained dry. She sipped her drink and tried to digest the fact she wasn't jealous, just surprised; not hurt, just . . . curious, more than anything.

"So, what do we do now?" she asked.

"Either you can forgive me, or you can't."

"And if I can't?"

"I guess we'll have to decide if we can still live together."

"Oh, Walter, what the hell were you thinking?"

She reminded him he'd been so eager to cement his reputation as a bright young law student with a wonderful future that he axed her plans to get her doctorate. And then what does he do? Have an affair with the wife of a colleague. That didn't exactly show good judgment, now did it?

"Please, Edie! Can't you see how hard this is on me?" he said.

"On you? When I'm the wronged party?"

She was about to roll out the incredible harm he'd done to her ego, their marriage, their future, but stopped herself. She wasn't exactly innocent herself, was she?

If she were to confess in a spirit of honesty, and shared acceptance of their faults, he'd be shocked, enraged, accusatory. She'd get a lecture about how *her* cheating was worse than *his* cheating, it was more damaging to the social fabric or something like that. A man is expected to cheat at least once in his married life; a woman, never.

Her entire life had been lived by a set of rules men didn't have to follow. And it would never change. She'd always be in second place. She put her glass on the table, and a moment later discovered she was crying.

Walter took her in his arms. She didn't resist. He told her she was the only woman in the world for him; Babs was nothing—meant nothing; all that mattered was the future, their future, and the life they would make together for themselves and their children.

She leaned into him. She was worn out and needed the warm bulk of his body to comfort her. Then she pulled away.

"Did you like it better with her than you do with me?" she asked.

The color rose in his face.

"How can you ask such a thing?" he asked.

"It's a simple question."

"No."

"No, what? You didn't prefer her to me, or it's not a simple question?"

"Edie, listen to me. I barely remember that night. It was all so jumbled and rushed. To be honest, I'm not sure we actually achieved anything."

"So, maybe it was just a case of heavy petting."

"That's what I thought at first."

"What changed your mind?"

"Babs."

"I thought you haven't seen her since."

"She rang up the next day."

"What did she say?"

"That she was mad for me but had made a terrible mistake and made me promise it would never happen again."

Was she really in love with him? Edith supposed it was possible. She would never say Walter wasn't charming. But if you were in love with a married man, you'd want more than anything to keep his wife in the dark. She'd have made her plea to reassure Andy directly to Walter, in that case. Babs *wanted* Edith to know what had happened between them. Was she flaunting her powers of attraction, or trying to show Edith what kind of man she was married to, and warn her what she might be in for down the road?

Babs said they'd just flirted, and Walter made a pass. Walter said they'd slept together, and Babs was in love with him. One of them was lying. If Edith had to bet money, it was Walter.

But why would he want her to think he'd been unfaithful when he hadn't? Why drop such a damaging thing on her? Because he wanted to open the door on the possibility he might be unfaithful again if she didn't keep him happy. To establish himself as a man who would yield to temptation, if she left him alone too long.

He got up and poured himself a drink. He lifted the decanter to ask if she wanted another. She shook her head.

"Andy never said a thing to you about any of this?" Edith asked.

"Not a peep."

"Will you talk to him?"

"I suppose I'll have to."

"Are you going to tell him you had sex with his wife?"

"No, I don't think I can say that."

"Then what *will* you say?"

"That I'm no good at holding my liquor and it won't happen again. Then we'll shake hands, and that will be that."

He sat down next to her. He looked calm, in possession of himself.

"Believe me when I say I'm truly ashamed," he said.

"Good."

He nodded and tasted his drink.

"Can you forgive me?" he asked.

"I don't know."

"Please try. I love you so much."

She let him kiss her. And then she let him take her to bed. Afterward, she thought about his gamble. Some wives—most wives— would have thrown him out. Maybe he wouldn't have cared if she had. Maybe, after knowing her for almost ten years—four of them as her husband— he was less committed to her than she always assumed. Or for him, commitment was a practical thing, like showing up for dinner and paying the bills.

So, what did love mean to him? How could she possibly know, when she couldn't say what it meant to her?

chapter fifteen

The snow turned to sleet just after lunch and fell through the afternoon. Henry arrived at the store promptly at three-thirty to find Edith behind the cash register, ringing up a book for a young man wearing a beret. He bought a volume of new poems by William Carlos Williams and asked Edith if she'd read it yet. She said she hadn't. He said she really must, he was a marvelous poet.

"I'm a poet, too, though not nearly as good as he," the man said.

"Ah." Edith wrapped the book in plain brown paper and tied it with string. She handed it to him.

"There's a lecture on him next week on campus. You should come with me," he said. Edith stared at him. He looked younger than she was. His brown eyes were merry.

"Should I, now?" she asked.

"Absolutely."

"I'm married."

He shrugged and grinned at her. She told him he'd better be on his way. He brought his finger to the edge of his beret in a parting gesture.

Henry approached after he'd gone. He had his hat in his hands. He looked marvelous in his gray overcoat and deep red scarf.

"Had quite a bit of cheek, that one," he said.

"Yes."

Henry looked around the room. Edith said Mary wasn't there. In fact, she hadn't been in for ten days.

"I'm so sorry. I guess her interest was just a flash in the pan," Henry said.

"It's all right. We're managing."

Edith feared for a moment Henry would ask to see the ledgers and checkbook and wished she'd thought of that when she suggested they meet there. The bank statements were sent to the store, not to his home, and if he insisted on reviewing those, he'd see the withdrawal Mary had made. Edith decided she wouldn't lie for her, but he asked only if she were ready to go. Edith summoned Patricia and said she was leaving for the day.

They walked quickly against the sleet. Edith slipped on the sidewalk, and Henry offered her his arm. She took it. Miss Levy's building was a charming brownstone with carved vines and flowers over the doorway. The stone steps were iced and treacherous, and they took their time climbing them.

The heat in the foyer was fierce, so they removed their coats at once. Henry took Edith's. With his free hand, he brushed tiny pieces of ice from the top of her green velvet hat. She said it was a silly thing to wear in that kind of weather.

"It looks charming on you, though."

"Thank you."

He looked her over. She was wearing a new dress, knit polyester with velvet at the neck and cuffs. She'd taken care to get the seams in her stockings straight. She did her nails the evening before. Walter was at the library, or so he said. Since his confession about Babs, she had trouble believing him.

Miss Levy lived on the third floor. Edith thought the climb must be awfully hard for an old lady to manage. Edith knocked, and after a long moment, the sound of someone approaching the door could be heard. Then a cat meowed and was told to wait a minute. The speaker had a high, wobbly voice.

Four locks were slid before the door opened. Edith had expected Miss Levy to be small, but she was much taller than Edith was. Her hair wasn't gray, but black, and recently dyed, judging from the faint staining around the hairline. Edith gave their names, and Miss Levy welcomed them inside. A gray-and-white striped cat was at her feet, looking at them curiously. Miss Levy told Henry to drop their coats on the chair in the hall, then led them into the living room. She walked with a cane, and their progress was slow. Miss Levy talked the whole time about the weather and how awful it must be for people who had to be out and about in it.

The living room had one large bay window, in front of which was a desk where Miss Levy must write the poems she referred to in her letter. There was a fireplace with a fire going; a small sofa and one chair; and a wooden table on which a tray with a teapot and cups had been set. Miss Levy asked them to sit, and Edith offered to pour.

The minute Miss Levy sat in the chair, which was near the fire, the cat jumped in her lap.

"This is Edgar," Miss Levy said.

"After Poe?" Henry asked.

"Yes! How clever of you."

"Are you fond of American Gothic literature?" Edith asked and handed her a teacup with the requested slice of lemon on the side.

"Not particularly. But I read everything, as one must."

Edith asked how Henry would like his. He said with cream and no sugar. She prepared his cup and gave it to him. She took her own with lemon and two lumps of sugar. Henry sipped his and complimented Miss Levy. He said it tasted like Darjeeling.

"Right you are. I never thought I'd find myself serving tea to an Englishman."

Edith asked her to talk about her poetry if she didn't mind. Miss Levy held her cup in one hand and petted the cat with the other. Then she put the cup in the saucer on the small table by her chair. Edith admired her heavy silver bracelets, and the colorful shawl draped around her shoulders. Her face was pale and creased, yet her eyes were full of life.

She said she'd never been interested in poetry as a girl. She wanted to be a doctor. Well, that was sixty years ago, when women graced salons and presided over dinner tables, and certainly didn't study medicine. Her father was more broad-minded than her mother. Her mother groomed her for marriage; her father sent her to college.

"Really, where?" Henry asked.

"Radcliffe. Just around the corner, more or less."

"And what did you study?"

"Mathematics."

"My father is a professor of Mathematics. Well, before he had a stroke," Edith said.

"I'm sorry to hear that. About his stroke, not his profession," Miss Levy said. The cat jumped out of her lap onto the floor and stared lovingly at Henry. Henry patted the space on the sofa between him and Edith, and the cat jumped up, purring.

"I'm afraid you'll leave here covered in cat hair," Miss Levy said.

"My man works wonders with a clothes brush," Henry said.

"He'll be busy for days." Miss Levy laughed heartily, then coughed for a long moment. "I beg your pardon," she said, resting her hand on her chest.

She continued. She was engaged to be married before college ended but found she couldn't go through with it. She'd observed her mother's life closely for years. There were five children in the family, Miss Levy was the eldest, and her mother worked around the clock keeping them fed, clean, behaving properly, and delivering her daily lectures about the path to a useful life. Miss Levy didn't care to be useful the way a woman was supposed to be—having a horde of children and growing old before her time.

"How did you live?" Edith asked.

"These are modern times so I will be frank. I became what's known as a kept woman."

Henry lowered his cup. His eyes twinkled with amusement.

"You don't believe me, Mr. McCormick?" Miss Levy asked. "Keep in mind, I was once beautiful. And I knew my own mind. Some men find that very attractive. In my case, more than one did."

Miss Levy said after she broke off her engagement, she went to work as a secretary in a law firm. That was in 1891. She was twenty years old. The typewriter freed her. It brought independence. If the attentions of one employer were unwelcome and couldn't be discouraged, she moved on. The men she worked for were always married, and usually unhappy. One fell for her and paid for a nice apartment. She didn't have to work. She saved money and began writing poetry. When he died suddenly, she went back to work for a while and then another man became interested, and so on.

"I was kind to them. And they were kind to me," she said.

Time passed, the First World War came, she was middle-aged, still attractive, but not drawing the eye quite the way she used to. That's when she met the love of her life, Arnold Stein.

"A nice Jewish boy, my mother would have said."

Arnold was a painter—and a good one. They went to New York and lived together. It was possible to do that, in some circles, and not have to pretend you were married. They made a beautiful life. After decades of fumbling, her poems took on substance and began to be published. But Arnold's work wasn't as successful, and it bothered him.

"He saw me as a competitor, not a friend, not a lover. It was painful," Miss Levy said. She asked Edith to please pour her another cup of tea. Edith did. She asked Henry if he cared for more. He didn't.

She and Arnold parted. She never got over it. She returned to Boston, resumed work as a secretary, and never became romantically involved again.

They sat, watching the fire. The sleet beat against the glass. Edith asked her about *Holocaust*, her recently published volume. Miss Levy said she became interested in how the world came to blame the Jews for the war, even after it was made known what had happened to them in the Nazi concentration camps. Destruction of any kind begins with blame, she felt, and this is what she tried to probe in her work.

"Not hatred? I would have thought that was the source of all evil in the world," Henry said.

"Hatred needs a tool. The tool is blame."

Miss Levy asked Edith to take the book on the table by the tea tray. It was bound in red leather with silver embossed lettering. The title and Miss Levy's name were on the spine and cover. Inside the first few pages were blank and then the first poem appeared.

"There's no publisher listed," Edith said.

"That's because I published it myself."

"Really?"

"Indeed."

"But why?"

"Why not?"

She explained as she got older, she didn't care to wait on the decisions of other people.

"Who published your other books?" Edith asked.

"This is the first."

Edith flipped through the pages. The paper was thick and of good quality. She asked who put the volume together for her. Miss Levy said an old friend, with a particular interest in bookbinding.

Edith came to one poem that caught her eye. It was called "Silence."

"This one looks interesting," Edith said.

"Which?"

Edith showed her the page, and Miss Levy asked if she would read it aloud. Edith said she'd love to.

Old words, new words
Greater worlds, lesser worlds
Flags furled, flags unfurled
In the ward
Running toward
The one who knits,
Refuses to purl
Row by row

Backside, frontside
All the same
Except to her
Semantic, romantic
Antics enacted
Hearts redacted
Given the smack
Better keep quiet
Can't cause a riot
By breathing words
That mustn't be heard
All those twisty devil-angel words

"After blame comes censorship," Miss Levy said.

"And after censorship?" Edith asked.

"Death."

Miss Levy coughed and brought her hand again to her chest.

Edith asked her if she thought poetry were always political.

"It might not have been, once, but now, certainly."

"What about love as a poetic topic?" Henry asked.

"Love is the most political problem we have."

Miss Levy apologized for ever thinking she was up to reading in public. Her doctor had chided her for the very idea.

"He's a bad-tempered old Jew, like me," she said.

Edith laughed. Miss Levy asked her about The Turned Page, how she'd come to buy it, and what it was like, being in charge of such a wonderful place.

Edith said it was Henry's wife who'd suggested it, and Henry had graciously made it all possible.

"You're passionate about books," Miss Levy said to him.

"Yes."

"And do you help at the store?"

"No. I'm a student. Studying Shakespeare and other English masters."

"You've come a long way to connect with your countrymen."

"Yes."

Miss Levy waited for him to continue. He didn't. She asked Edith if she were married, and if so, what her husband did. Edith answered.

"I've always heard law is a sturdy profession," Miss Levy said.

Her voice had grown hoarse, and Edith glanced at Henry to suggest they should be going. Edith promised to stay in touch, and Miss Levy asked her to come again when she felt a bit stronger.

The weather hadn't lifted, and Henry suggested they go have a drink somewhere.

"After all that tea?" Edith asked.

"Naturally."

Edith didn't want to look for a bar. She didn't want to bring him back to her place, either, because Walter was probably there. Thursday, he ended early. She mentioned this and Henry said they could go to his apartment. Mary was sure to be out.

"Riding, in this weather?" Edith asked.

"It's in an indoor ring. She's friends with the man who runs it. His daughter is fascinated with Mary. Mary's teaching her to ride."

Edith thought the daughter of a man who ran a horse stable would have been born in the saddle, as it were, but kept that to herself.

They hailed a cab and were grateful when one arrived quickly. They talked about Miss Levy on the way over. Edith asked Henry if he thought she'd really lived as she described. He said it was entirely possible. It was probably more commonplace than people assumed.

"Did you ever . . . provide support for someone you were . . ." she said.

"Sleeping with? Yes, once."

"That was good of you."

"She was in dire shape, financially speaking. She'd lost her husband in the war. Well, actually, they'd never married, and so she wasn't eligible to receive the benefits she would have, as a widow."

"This was recent, then?"

"Two, maybe three years ago. We parted as friends."

Edith wondered how that could have been possible. That would be like her and Philip being friends.

Edith asked if he'd cared for her very much.

"Yes, I did."

"And she returned your affection?"

"Not entirely. Not the way I hoped. Too much went out of her when the man she'd been in love with died. She wasn't looking to start over with someone else."

"Were you?"

Henry didn't answer, and Edith wondered if she'd gone too far. It seemed impossible to, given the nature of their conversation.

They arrived at Henry's building and rushed in against the cold. At the apartment, Alistair was there immediately to take their coats. Henry told him they'd be in his study. Then he asked if Lady Mary had rung. Alistair said she hadn't. Edith couldn't read Henry's expression.

The study was a wonderful room with the same fine view of the river the living room enjoyed. Henry's desk was cluttered with books; there were shelves on three walls, also full of books; a sofa sat before the fire that was going robustly; next to the fireplace was a wheeled cart with crystal decanters and glasses.

"Would you care for sherry?" Henry asked.

"Yes."

"Dry?"

"Yes."

He poured out two glasses, then joined her on the sofa. They sat in silence, enjoying the dancing flames and the pleasure of being inside. Edith's mind wandered back to Miss Levy and the poem she asked her to read aloud. She admired its energy. All good writing should have that inner drive, she thought. What lay below the words was as important as the words themselves, the subtext and the text working together to take you someplace else—or to confirm you understood the place you were in.

"What did you mean the other day, about maybe not continuing with school?" Edith asked.

"Oh, I shall finish out the year, I expect. But after that, I don't know."

He put his glass on the table in front of the sofa. He said his life was in a strange place. It was changing in ways he hadn't seen at first, but now had a better grasp on.

"Meaning?" Edith asked.

"Meaning Mary has informed me she intends to return to England."

"What? Why?"

"She wants to be with her brother."

"More than she wants to be with you?"

"Yes."

Henry said she hadn't wanted to come to America at all. He thought it would be a fresh start for them, but the problems they had at home followed them across the Atlantic.

"What problems?" Edith asked.

"We want different things, I suppose."

Henry said they got along fine, but affability wasn't enough to hold a marriage together.

"You're talking about sex."

"I'm afraid I am."

Edith gazed at the amber liquid in her glass. It was a lovely color. She thought about having complete control over the store, which she did then anyway, but it would become official once Mary left.

Henry asked what she was thinking about. She told him.

"You've a highly practical mind," he said.

"I don't know about that."

"Tell me why you gave up your academic career."

"Walter wanted me to."

She filled him in, describing as fairly as she could Walter's concern for his own professional future, and how conservative law firms view the wives of the men they hire.

"So, you gave up what you wanted so he could have what he wanted," Henry said. He offered her another glass of sherry, and she accepted.

Edith said she wasn't sure she really wanted it. She'd lost interest. Or rather, she didn't have enough passion for it to overcome Walter's reluctance. She hadn't been willing to fight for it, so it seemed only fair she give it up.

"Why should you have been put to the test like that, just because you were married?" Henry asked.

"I never looked at it that way before."

Henry stared at the fire. He said noble ambitions should never be thwarted, and he hoped she would discover her creative expression in the store.

A moment later she found his hand in hers. She squeezed it. Without letting go, she told him about Walter and Babs. Henry leaned back and regarded the beamed ceiling. He asked if she believed it. She said she didn't know. He said usually, a man denied any involvement with another woman and didn't make up a story about something that didn't happen. Edith shared her theory—Walter was putting her on notice not to leave him alone again. She realized she needed to explain the real reason she'd gone to New York the summer before and said Walter's aunt hadn't been ill at all.

"You left him," Henry said.

"I did."

"But you came back."

"Yes."

"Why?"

"Well, I think I got scared."

"Of what?"

She told him about Philip, then said she hoped she could trust him with what she'd perhaps unwisely shared.

"Of course you can," Henry said.

"You didn't know you were making an illicit offer to a woman who has a history of behaving illicitly."

"It wouldn't have mattered."

Edith said she should be getting home. She stood up and asked if Mary knew when she'd be leaving.

"No, not yet."

"She might change her mind."

"Oh, I don't think she will."

Henry walked her to the door, helped her into her coat even though Alistair was on hand, then kissed her lightly on the cheek as if she were a sister or an aunt. His eyes were kind, and she liked looking at them. She asked him to stay in touch. He promised to.

chapter sixteen

Edith woke from another uneasy sleep to find the sky reluctantly taking on light. The telephone was ringing. She was out of bed by the third ring and answered on the fourth.

"Edie, this is Mama. Papa died early this morning."

Edith sat down on the couch.

"Edie?"

"I'm here."

Her mother sounded calm, and Edith wondered if the shock just hadn't hit her yet. She was talking about a funeral and said Edith didn't have to come. She'd done her duty, after all, by coming out before.

"Where are you?" Edith asked.

"At the house. They're taking him away now."

"Oh, my god."

"Betty's with me. It's all right."

Then she said she was going to sell the house and share the proceeds with Edith.

"Don't do that. You'll need that money," Edith said.

"Your father was squirreling it away for years. I only found out the other day, when I finally went through his things."

Her mother said he had accumulated close to nine thousand dollars.

"What in the world was he planning to do with it?" Edith asked.

"Who knows? He never had any pipe dreams, as far as I know."

Maybe he was saving it to start a new life somewhere—one without Edith's mother. Well, too bad about that now, Edith thought.

Her mother didn't know how long the house would take to sell, but she was going to get it listed right away. If there were anything in it, some piece or other Edith was particularly attached to, she should let her know. Otherwise, the furniture would be part of the sale, after personal items were removed, of course.

"It's all in terrible shape, but someone might want it," her mother said.

Edith thought back to the single bed she'd had as a girl and slept in through college. It was odd to think of someone else using it. But why not? It was just a place to lie down in at the end of the day.

She asked what the house might go for.

"Betty thinks around eighteen thousand."

Walter came out of the bedroom and asked who the hell she was talking to at that hour. Edith waved him away. He went into the kitchen and was noisy filling the coffee pot. Then he said he couldn't get the burner lit and asked if she'd told the landlord the stove wasn't working right again.

Edith said she had to go. She promised to write soon.

"Give Betty my love," she said. They hung up.

Edith went into the kitchen, where Walter had managed to light the stove after all.

"What's wrong with you, bothering me like that when I'm on the telephone?" she asked.

"Gosh, Edie, I'm sorry, but it's so early! You know I don't do well first thing in the morning."

She told him to sit down, and she'd fix his breakfast. He asked if she could go down and get the newspaper, first.

She did. When she opened the door to the porch where the paper was left each day, the air felt surprisingly warm. This was a classic New England spring thaw that would be followed by another deep freeze.

She climbed the three flights back up slowly. She lived in a world her father wasn't in. It felt awfully strange, though he hadn't been in her world for a while.

Walter had poured them each a cup of coffee and set out the skillet, the carton of eggs, and a package of bacon.

She put the paper on the table and sat down.

"My father's dead," she said.

"What?"

She said nothing. He stared at her, then rushed around to her side of the table and put his hand on her arm.

"Don't be silly, Walter, I'm not going all to pieces, if that's what you're worried about," she said.

He poured her a glass of water and told her to drink it. She took the glass from his hand, put it on the table, and lit herself a cigarette. She leaned her head back and blew smoke toward the ceiling. She'd never noticed the large water stain up there, but of course, it had to have been there all along.

"This place is a dump, Walter. I'll be glad to move," she said.

"Edie."

"I'm all right."

"What happened?"

"To Papa? He died. How, or exactly why, I don't know. Does it matter?"

"No, I suppose not. But I am sorry."

"Thank you." She smoked for a few moments. "You liked him, didn't you?"

"Well, sure."

"Why?"

"Edie, what a question!" Walter looked at the skillet on the stove as if he wished breakfast were underway.

"It's a fair question. I mean, why does one person like another person? Why, for instance, do you like me?"

Walter sat down. His face was heavy and tired. He'd had a lot to drink with friends the evening before. Another visit to a tavern before coming home.

"Because you're fun. Smart. Pretty. You keep me on track," he said.

"Oh, Walter. Can't you be more original?"

"Well, what do you want me to say, for Heaven's sake? It's six o'clock in the morning."

She hadn't realized the time. She got up and made breakfast. He ate happily; she ate nothing. She offered him her plate. He shook his head.

He asked if she were going back for the funeral. He could come, too, if she liked.

"I'm not going back, no. There's no point," she said.

"What about paying your last respects?"

"I paid that son of a bitch enough. Every day of my life."

"You shouldn't say such things."

"Walter, you should stop talking now."

Irritation flashed in his eyes. There was something else there, too. Fear?

She put out her cigarette and said her father was a monster to her. And to her mother. And no one ever knew. They never said a thing.

"I don't know why we kept quiet. I guess we just got used to the idea that his precious reputation was terribly important," Edith said.

"Lots of families have problems."

"Did your father beat you?"

"No, of course not."

"Insult you?"

"Sure, but nothing terrible."

"Does he respect you?"

"I don't know. Probably not."

"My father made me feel like dirt."

"I'm sure you're exaggerating."

"I'm sure I'm not."

"You're upset, naturally."

"I'm not upset at all."

"You are. I can tell."

He was quiet for a moment. Then he said there was another mock trial scheduled and this time he was playing the role of the judge. He could use a little more time to prepare.

"Can you help me?" he asked. She looked at him skeptically. Then she asked what she had to do. He went into the other room and took some papers out of his briefcase. He gave them to her. It was essentially a script, where she, as the attorney for the plaintiff, was presenting facts in a breach of contract case.

She spoke her lines. Walter forgot what she said half the time and asked her to repeat herself. When she pointed it out, he said he wasn't used to getting up so early, and he wished the phone hadn't woken him up.

She put the papers down on the table and said she was going to see if she could get more sleep. He followed her into the bedroom and lay down with her. When he put his hand on her stomach, she pushed it away.

"Come on," he said.

"Please leave me alone."

He took a shower, got dressed, and said he was going to go over to campus and review his notes in the library. She said nothing.

"I'm sorry about your father," he said.

"Thanks."

"I'll try to get home early."

"Okay."

He blew her a kiss.

As soon as the door closed behind him, she wept. Not for her father, surely. For herself? And the mess her life had become?

She didn't know how long she'd been sleeping, but the light in the room had risen a lot. The clock said it was past eleven. She was due at the store. Why hadn't Patricia called her? Then she remembered Patricia was now taking Thursdays off.

She put on a pair of wool slacks, not caring what the customers might think. She hoped there wouldn't be many today, in any case. She wanted to be left alone to read in the comfort of the office, a log burning gaily in the fireplace. She was deep into Virginia Woolf's *To the Lighthouse*. When she finished it, she was going to dive back into poetry, starting with everything by Emily Dickinson. Then it would be Browning, Alfred Lord Tennyson, and a bit of Lord Byron. She would borrow the books from the store, take care with them, and then mark fifty cents or a dollar off the price. People didn't seem to care if a book weren't brand new. A man who'd picked a used copy of *Walden* for his wife said, "The more hands, the better." Edith liked that. Books should be held and caressed lovingly.

When she got to the store, the door was unlocked, and the lights were on. Mary was in the office drinking tea. She hadn't been in for weeks. She'd called Edith the week before at home to tell her she was going back to England for a little while to see about her brother. Edith had sounded surprised and then turned sympathetic. "You're very devoted to him, it's clear," she'd said in her most soothing tone.

Mary lowered her cup as Edith came into the office.

"I came to say goodbye," Mary said.

"I thought you weren't leaving until next week."

"The steamship line called. They had a cancellation. All the first-class staterooms had been taken, but now they have one for me if I can sail on Saturday."

"You'll have to take the train to New York tomorrow, then. I was hoping to have you and Henry over for a drink before you left."

"How thoughtful! But I'm afraid there just isn't time."

"That's a shame."

Mary was looking at her in a way that made Edith uncomfortable. Could she hear the lie behind her words?

Edith sat behind the desk, grateful Mary had left it unoccupied. She wondered if she'd written herself another check. She pulled open the drawer the checkbook was in and casually flipped through it. There was nothing amiss.

"I'm sorry I haven't been more help around here. I think the steam went out of me after . . . well, you know," Mary said.

"Yes, of course."

"All I seemed to have a taste for was riding. I find it a very pleasant escape."

"You'll take it up again, once you're home?"

"I hope to."

Mary sounded wistful, but her face was hard. She opened and closed her left hand over and over, maybe as a way to calm herself. Then she lit a cigarette. Again, Edith admired her elegant holder. She saw Mary would have felt very out of place in Boston, despite a certain set that was monied and long-established. She was an aristocrat in a way an American could never be. Henry seemed to have adapted, but maybe he was simply a stronger person. Or perhaps it was the city itself—being in a city—that was hard for her. Mary might be longing for the gentle countryside and a slower pace.

"I hope you'll look after Henry while I'm gone," Mary said. "He's fond of you and Walter."

"We're fond of him, too."

Mary said nothing. Edith cast about for something to say. She could tell her about going to visit Miss Levy, but she'd have to say Henry had come, too, and that would be awkward.

"My father died," she said.

"Oh, Edith, I'm so terribly sorry!"

"Thank you."

"Was it sudden?"

"He'd had a stroke. They thought he'd recover. I don't know the details, but obviously, it took him, in the end."

"Should you be here? I mean, shouldn't you be home?"

"There's nothing I can do there. I'd rather be working."

"I suppose it helps to keep one's mind off things."

Mary offered to make her a cup of tea. Edith said that sounded lovely. Mary went into the tiny adjacent bathroom and filled the kettle from the sink. She put the kettle on the hot plate and asked Edith which blend she wanted.

"What did you have?"

"Darjeeling."

"Perfect."

Mary removed a pretty lace-trimmed handkerchief from her handbag and patted her face. Edith asked if she were feeling all right.

"Oh, I have these little moments. They pass quickly enough," Mary said.

"I'm sure that's only natural."

Mary put her handkerchief away. She studied Edith closely, as if she'd just noticed she wasn't wearing lipstick or powder, and her hair hadn't been washed.

"Please forgive my asking, but have you and Walter discussed starting a family?" Mary asked.

"A bit. He's quite keen."

"Men usually are. The burden is hardly on them."

"Only the financial burden."

Mary looked vague as if worrying about money were an alien concept, which Edith supposed to her it was.

"Managing a store would be difficult with a child unless of course, one had a nanny," Mary said.

Edith laughed. "I can't see Walter ever consenting to hire a nanny."

"I can't imagine why. People do it all the time, don't they?"

"Not people I know."

"Ah, well."

Mary looked sad and a bit lost as she gazed around the room. Maybe she was trying to fix it in her memory, but Edith thought something else was probably on her mind.

"I must be on my way. Please write to me and give me all the news," Mary said and stood. Edith stood too. She came out from behind the desk and shook Mary's hand. She was not the kind of person one embraced.

When Mary had gone, Edith turned off the hot plate. She didn't want any tea. She sat, feeling worn out. She thought about her father, soon to be in the ground, and her childhood home, occupied by strangers. But then her mother would still be around, in Betty's snug, happy house. Her thoughts turned again to the money her mother had promised her when the house sold. She wondered if she should tell Walter about her mother's offer. He was odd about money. He talked as if it didn't matter, and he didn't care about it, when in fact he cared deeply. She managed their checking account, but he looked at it every month, sometimes more often if he wanted to buy something. When they were first married and she was still working, she had her own account. He made her give it up. He didn't like the idea of her having money he didn't know about. She said lots of husbands had money of their own they didn't make specific to their wives, but he ignored her.

A shipment of books arrived with the noon post, a box of *The Crooked House* by Agatha Christie. She thought about Betty, writing her mystery novels under a pseudonym. Why hadn't she used her own name? Did she feel like a different person when she took up her pen? Or was she ashamed of the name someone else had given her?

Edith unpacked the books. It was a small shipment, only eight copies. She'd been ordering fewer books at a time because she didn't want to have too much inventory sitting in the basement. The storage shelves hadn't been installed. She'd promised Henry she was going to get a man out to take measurements, but she hadn't done it yet. She looked through the telephone book and found a local contractor. She called, his wife answered, and Edith asked for an appointment to be set. The wife said he could come on Tuesday of the following week. Edith gave her name, address, and the phone number of the store. Then she made a note in her appointment diary.

She went into the store and wandered around. Eloise and Isabelle had been doing a reasonably good job keeping the place tidy. Edith remembered Eloise had said she would be leaving at the end of the month. She was getting married in June and needed time to prepare. Should she be replaced? Couldn't Edith, Patricia, and Isabelle manage? But then, Isabelle probably wouldn't stay on during the summer. Edith needed to find out her plans.

Over the next few hours, Edith stayed in the office and read. She got up when the bell rang. Only three customers came in—an elderly gentleman asking if she had anything on stained glass windows (she did); a middle-aged lady looking for a new cookbook (the only one available was on French cuisine); and a teenage boy offering to sell her a stack of used comic books. Edith said she had no use for comic books. The boy looked stricken, said he'd been all over the Square that morning, and he just had to sell them.

"What do you need the money for?" Edith asked.

"I want to buy a record."

"What record?"

"A new recording of Beethoven's Seventh. For my mother. She hasn't been very well, and it's her favorite."

Edith figured his story was a lie, but it was an inventive one.

"What do you want for your collection?" she asked.

"Three bucks."

"You'll never get rich that way."

She took the money from the cash register, wrote a note with the sum, and put the paper in the till as a reminder to pay herself back. She gave the boy the money, and he handed her the stack of magazines which he'd thoughtfully wrapped in brown paper and secured with twine.

His face lit up.

"You're a peach, lady," he said and left. Edith put the bundle on a shelf behind the counter and went back to her reading.

Isabelle arrived first, as she usually did. She was glum. She'd gotten a poor grade on a paper she'd written on the Continental Congress. Edith sympathized, though she'd never gotten a poor grade on anything. Eloise swept in a moment later, babbling about a man who was standing on the corner, singing Irish folk songs.

"In this cold? He must be quite dedicated," Edith said. She told them she'd left their paychecks on the desk in the office, and they could help themselves to tea as always if they liked.

"Can't stand the stuff," Isabelle said. She ran her fingers through her curly hair.

"How do you feel about comic books?" Edith asked and explained about the stack she'd gotten from the boy.

"Love 'em," said Eloise. "Though my mother thinks they're common."

"Well, take a look, help yourself to anything."

Edith left the store, and though she didn't pass the corner where the man was singing, she could hear his lovely tenor as she went. She didn't know the name of the song, but it filled her with a bittersweet emotion she put down to a delayed reaction to the news her mother had given her that morning. But that wasn't it, was it? She felt no grief for her father. She probably stopped grieving for him years before.

At home, she was met by a stunning bouquet of long-stemmed roses in a crystal vase, and Walter, lounging with a legal textbook in his lap on the couch and a drink in his hand. He stood up when she came and embraced her warmly. She asked what he was doing home so early, and he said the professor had had to cancel class because his sister was ill. He looked her over.

"You went out, dressed like that?" he asked.

"I see women in slacks all the time."

"Not a lawyer's wife."

"No one knows I'm a lawyer's wife."

He looked down at her skeptically.

"Thank you for the flowers. They smell wonderful," she said.

"Oh, they're not from me. Henry sent them."

"Why?"

"I assume because of your father."

"Mary must have told him. She came to the store to say goodbye."

She sat down and asked him to pour her a drink, though it was still early. If he were having one, why shouldn't she?

He gave her the glass and asked how she was feeling. She said she felt numb. He thought that was to be expected. He'd written his parents that morning while he was on campus, letting them know. He wasn't sure Edith's mother would think to contact them, though he supposed the notice would be in the paper. He thought they would want to attend the funeral if Edith's mother didn't mind.

"I can't imagine she would."

"Are you sure you don't want to go?"

"Yes."

"Good. Because we've been invited to a party."

"What? Where?"

"At Andy and Babs' place."

"Walter, I don't think that's a good idea."

"Nonsense. Water under the bridge. Besides, they have good news."

"Oh, what?"

"Andy didn't say. Maybe about his job offer, though everyone already knows about that. I bet she's expecting."

Edith nodded. She asked when the party was. Walter said on Saturday.

"I don't think I'll be much fun. Why don't you go without me?" Edith asked.

"Oh, come now. It will be good for you to get out. Besides, Henry will be there."

"Henry? Is he friends with them?"

"No, but as I was chatting with Andy, he was walking on the quad and stopped to say hello. When I introduced them, Andy mentioned the party, and said he should come along."

"How generous."

"I thought so."

Edith closed her eyes for a moment. She felt woozy from the drink. She realized she'd forgotten to eat lunch again. She tried to think of what was in the refrigerator she could turn into dinner. Nothing came to mind.

She opened her eyes. Walter was watching her closely, the way he always used to, but with less warmth in his eyes. She wondered if he knew about Henry's attraction to her. Maybe he'd guessed it, after all. But that probably wasn't it. He was probably thinking of their recent conversation and his admission of something that never took place.

"Walter, tell me, did you talk to Andy? About what was worrying him?" Edith asked.

"Sure. I told you so."

"Did you? I don't remember."

"Why else would he invite me, if I hadn't?"

"I don't know."

"Oh, Edie, what am I going to do with you?"

His voice was teasing, but his expression was hard. What wasn't he telling her? She was too exhausted to try and find out. She asked him if he'd mind going down to the deli in a bit and picking up a couple of sandwiches for dinner. He said he had to get back to studying.

"Please," she said.

"Oh, all right. You do look a bit peaked."

She went to lie down. She fell asleep quickly, and when she woke, it was morning.

<h1 style="text-align:center">chapter seventeen</h1>

On the day of the party, Edith found three letters in her mail slot. One was from Kathleen addressed to her and not Walter; another was from her mother; the third was from Aunt Margaret.

From Kathleen:

> *Dear Edie,*
>
> *I heard it first from Pop, then later the same day from the darling boy. Can't tell you how sorry I am. I know you two didn't get along all the time—fathers can be difficult, and believe me, I know so first-hand, but he was your father, after all. Remember him the way he was, and always cherish his good points.*

She went on to talk about the miserable Chicago winter at some length. The heat had gone out in her building for most of a day, sending her—at the building's expense—to a suite at the Drake. She also said she and Dennis had set the date for May 5th. The wedding would be in Urbana because Dennis only had his mother to invite. She lived in Skokie. Kathleen wanted her and Walter to take the train out. How did Edith feel about being her matron of honor?

From Aunt Margaret:

Dear Child,

I heard from my hard-hearted brother that your father passed recently. I say "hard-hearted" because he relayed the news unsympathetically, as he does everything in this world. No matter. I suspect they share some long-standing professional rivalry, though I can't imagine why. Well, perhaps Philosophy and Mathematics are more closely allied than one knows.

She said she wished her well, would love to hear from her, and from Walter, too, who hadn't dropped her a line in well over a year. She hoped his studies were going well. And she'd heard Edith was working in a bookstore. She thought that marvelous!

From her mother:

Dearest Edie:

The house has been listed. The junkman had quite a time with the mess in the attic. I saved anything I thought you might want one day, mostly photographs of you as a child. Betty's been a brick, as usual. I've got most of my stuff over at her place already. The funeral was yesterday. Walt's parents came. They were kind but brief. I hope you are very well. I miss you. Write to me when you can. All my love.

Patricia called up from the bookstore to let her know another box of books had arrived, and she was unpacking them. Edith asked what had come in.

"*A Rage to Live; A Good Man is Hard to Find,* and *The Sheltering Sky.*"

"Wonderful."

Patricia also said the censors had come by looking for copies of *1984*. Edith knew they'd be around before too long. Patricia had warned her. That's why they kept banned titles behind the counter.

"What did you tell them?" Edith asked.

"That we didn't carry it."

Edith asked what they were like. Patricia said they were two clean-cut young men. One talked, the other stayed quiet and kept looking around the store.

"Sounds creepy," Edith said.

"Oh, they were all right. I was pleasant, motherly. I offered them tea!"

"You didn't! Did they accept?"

"No, thank goodness!"

Edith told her to have a good afternoon, and she'd see her on Monday.

Walter wanted to know who'd been on the phone. She told him. He grunted and returned to his book. Then he asked her to make him a sandwich. She offered ham and cheese, his favorite. He thought that sounded swell. She put it together for him. Sunlight washed across the counter where she worked. She took Walter his sandwich and told him about Kathleen's letter.

"Are you sure it wasn't addressed to me?" he asked, taking a big bite. Edith showed him the envelope.

"What does she have to say?"

"Offering condolences. She and Dennis are getting married in May."

"Marvy!"

Edith hated it when he spoke with his mouth full. She wondered if he did that at the law firm reception she missed when she went to see her father. Maybe Babs kept her eye on him just to keep Andy from looking bad since they were friends and going to work together. Edith didn't like thinking about Babs, which was awkward, given they were due at her place in a couple of hours.

Edith put on the dress she'd bought for their anniversary. She wore rhinestone earrings and a rhinestone brooch. She took time with her makeup. She applied liquid eyeliner and then lengthened her lashes with heavy mascara. She'd been saving some deep red lipstick she bought herself on a whim a few weeks ago. She spread it on very carefully and checked her teeth.

Walter couldn't decide which tie to wear, so Edith picked one out for him. He said it wasn't dressy enough, so she chose another. Then he said his shoes needed to be shined. She offered to do that for him and worried she might dirty her dress. He put on another pair that looked better. She pointed out he was wearing one brown sock and one black one. He said that was her doing. He wished she were still doing the laundry and not sending it out.

"But you were the one who suggested I send it out it when I said I was always so pressed for time."

"Well from now on check it when it comes back."

"Don't speak to me in that tone."

"What's the matter with you anyway? You don't have to be nervous. It's just a simple cocktail party."

Edith went to sit down on the bed until she calmed. Walter waited for her in the living room. When she didn't move, he came to find her. He had her coat over his arm. He helped her into it and said this time next year she'd be wearing a new one, possibly a fur.

"I don't need a fur coat," she said.

"Every woman needs a fur coat."

"Your mother seems to do fine without one."

"I don't mean a woman like her."

Edith didn't pursue it.

Andy and Babs lived in a small, charming house in North Cambridge. Edith wondered how they could afford it and assumed Babs' parents made it possible. Of course, Andy's folks could be well-off, too, but Babs always projected an air of affluence Andy didn't have. Unlike Walter, he didn't seem to think money was all that important. The furniture was new and comfortable. Babs had a passion for pewter bowls and pitchers, which Edith suspected she'd developed living in New England. She liked crystal, too, because there were several sets of heavy candlesticks set out on the mantelpiece, the table where trays of hors d'oeuvres were set up, and the top of the upright piano in the living room. Edith found the effect fussy. Walter admired them and told Babs she had great taste.

Babs had on a red dress with a plunging neckline that made Edith's dress look dowdy and old. She'd had her nails done, too, in the same shade as her dress. She hugged Walter warmly and told him he looked in the pink. Andy stood by her, smiling. There was something odd about him, Edith thought.

Clara and Joe-Joe were there. Edith asked Clara how her baby was doing. Clara said she'd had a heck of a hard time finding a sitter, and frankly was nervous about leaving them alone. Joe-Joe told Edith Clara was just being a mother hen. It was good to get her out of the house so she could enjoy herself.

Luann and Steven Blake arrived next. Luann apologized for being late and blamed it on the train. They *should* have taken a taxi, but *someone* didn't want to spend the money. Steven said no one was interested in hearing about that, and she'd feel better with a drink in her, at which point Andy appeared and said he'd make her whatever she liked. His speech was slightly slurred, and he gave off a smell of liquor. Steven shook Andy's hand and said it looked like he'd started early.

Edith wandered into the kitchen. Henry stood at the counter, mixing a pitcher of martinis.

"Oh, hello," Edith said.

"Well, hello there! They put me to work the moment I arrived. Nice friends, you've got."

"Not my friends. Walter's."

"You know I was joking."

"Of course."

Henry wore a pale gray suit with a red striped tie. His cufflinks were shaped like horseshoes. Edith assumed they were real gold. He looked well. She asked after Mary.

"She docks on Thursday. I imagine she'll cable me then," he said. He lined up a row of glasses and filled one almost to the brim. Then he dropped in two green olives. Andy came into the kitchen and asked if the martinis were ready because Luann wanted one. Henry handed him the glass he'd just filled. Andy walked away with it, trying not to let it slosh and spill. Henry asked Edith what he could fix for her. She said scotch would be fine. Henry poured her out a small glass.

Edith looked into the living room to see Babs and Walter standing close together, talking. Babs smiled and brushed something off of Walter's lapel. Walter put his mouth close to her ear, said something, then reclaimed a polite distance between them. Babs laughed quietly, and Walter beamed down at her. Andy approached and slipped his arm through Babs'. Babs looked at him with annoyance. Walter turned away and began a conversation with Steven.

Edith saw Henry watching her. He asked if she were all right. She said she had a bad feeling.

"About what?" Henry asked. She brought her hand to her forehead. She sipped her drink. Her eyes brimmed with tears. Henry handed her his handkerchief. It had the most lovely smell—clean and slightly citrussy.

Babs sauntered into the kitchen and asked Henry if he could make up a couple of old fashioneds.

"Of course. Won't take me a moment," he said.

"Where did you learn how to mix drinks?" Babs asked.

"From my father's butler."

"Ah, how interesting."

Edith was aware Babs was staring at her. Edith complimented her on her dress.

"This old thing? It was in the back of my closet. I thought I should give it a good airing," Babs said. The doorbell rang and then there was the sound of voices raised in greeting.

"Here you go, two brand-new old fashioneds," Henry said. Babs took the glasses.

"Your husband is so funny, Edie, I've never known him to like an old fashioned, and now, out of the blue, he's just dying for one!" Babs said and left. Music played from the radio in the living room. A woman laughed. Edith heard Walter's voice, but not what he said.

"Won't you tell me what the trouble is?" Henry asked.

She leaned toward him and whispered "It wasn't a lie. They did have an affair. Probably still are, from the looks of it." Henry's expression was inscrutable, but some heat came into his eyes, and his lips drew tight.

"I should have sent you two dozen roses," he said.

"Oh, I'm sorry I didn't thank you before. That was very thoughtful."

"It was entirely my pleasure."

The music in the other room switched from classical to swing. Edith couldn't stand it and couldn't stand being there. She asked Henry if he could take her home.

"Of course," he said.

She went to find Walter. He was dancing with Babs. Andy was on the sofa by himself, a drink in his hand. Luann and Steven were talking to the couple who had come in. Joe-Joe and Clara were standing at the window, looking out at something. No one said anything as she and Henry crossed the room. He took their coats from the closet, helped her with hers, then put his on.

On the street, away from the house, Edith broke down. Henry walked with his arm around her.

"I don't know why I should feel so bad," she said.

"Because it's a bad thing."

"I cheated on him, too."

"But you didn't tell him. You spared him that. And you didn't carry on with your lover right under his nose."

At the next intersection, he waved down a cab. Edith wondered if Walter had noticed her absence yet, and what he'd say when he got home. The thought of their apartment made her feel even worse, and she begged Henry to take her to his place.

"I was about to suggest that," he said.

They rode in silence. Snow fell. Edith shivered, though the cab was warm. She asked what the winters in England were like. He said it depended on where you were, of course. In the north, they could be hard, though not as hard as they were in Massachusetts.

She wondered how Walter and Babs carried it off. Where did they meet? Had they ever used their apartment? When Edith got into bed, was she lying on sheets they'd used? It wasn't a pleasant thought. What was she feeling, exactly? Not jealousy. Shock? That anyone would want to have sex with Walter when he was so . . . clumsy?

Maybe he wasn't clumsy with Babs. Maybe she brought out a better lover in him. If that were true, how had Edith failed? What made it possible for him to be a different person with Babs?

Idle speculation. She would never know for sure.

"I don't know what to do," she said.

"About Walter?"

"Obviously."

"I suppose the big question is whether you wish to remain married."

"I don't think I wanted to get married in the first place."

"To Walter?"

"To anyone."

She leaned back and closed her eyes, hoping the motion of the cab would lull and soothe her. It didn't.

What if she were wrong? But she had seen what she'd seen—two people who were intimate. It must have been obvious to everyone there.

"I'm just so embarrassed," Edith said.

"That's understandable."

They arrived at Henry's. Alistair was out. Henry said it was his afternoon off.

"He gets just the one?" Edith asked.

"And any time he asks me in advance. I'm pretty lenient."

Edith asked if there were enough to keep Alistair busy, with just Henry to tend to. Henry said Alistair was learning to cook and trying out a new dish almost daily. Besides that, there was keeping the place tidy, and typing Henry's papers for class. Alistair was an accomplished typist, which Henry hadn't known until recently.

"Who did your typing before?" Edith asked as she followed Henry into the living room.

"I did. Then Mary tried."

Henry offered Edith something to drink. She hadn't finished the scotch she'd started on before, so she said she'd like another. Henry poured two fingers of scotch into a crystal glass. He asked if she wanted it on the rocks this time.

"Please."

He dropped in two ice cubes he took from a covered bucket on the liquor cart. He gave her the glass.

"Thank you."

She held it and didn't drink.

"I was thinking. Why don't you stay here?" Henry asked.

"I'm afraid I don't understand."

"I mean, don't go home."

"You can't be serious."

One look at his face said he was. Edith dropped down on the sofa. He took the chair across from it.

"Henry, it's impossible," she said.

"Don't tell me you care what people might say."

"No, I don't care. But what about Walter?"

"I should think he'd be the least of your worries at this point."

"I can't just leave."

"You can't stay with him, under the circumstances."

 "You sound angry."

"I am."

"I'm sorry."

"Why?"

"Because you're friends."

Henry paused.

"Unless that's all over," Edith said.

"It very well may be. And that's a shame because I enjoyed his company. He's quite charming. Highly intelligent. We had some very good conversations about politics and the state of the world," he said.

She and Walter didn't talk about those things, though they had, once. Was that why he was attracted to Babs? She was up on current affairs? Edith realized she was going to look for reasons why Walter had fallen for her, though she'd probably never really know. All she *could* know was Babs made him feel something she didn't.

"It's odd," she said.

"What is?"

"I was just thinking about a party we had last fall. I was talking to Andy about how it all comes down to how something makes you feel," Edith said.

"I see."

"Well, there's a bit more to it than that, but I don't want to go into it now."

Henry said that was perfectly fine. They would have a lot of time to talk after she moved in.

"I haven't said I would," Edith said.

"Are you really going to go back to him?"

"I could live alone."

"Do you want to?"

"I don't know."

She never had lived alone. It didn't seem like such a terrible thing. Lots of people did it. But having someone to talk to was lovely. Someone you didn't have to go out and find.

"Where would you put me?" Edith asked. Henry got up and went over to the fireplace. He lit a match and stooped to bring it to some carefully rolled-up newspaper and kindling piled below two stout logs. He stood up and watched the flames take hold.

"One of the guest rooms has a lovely view of the courtyard. I think you'd be comfortable there," he said.

"What if Mary comes back?"

"She won't come back."

Edith went to him.

"Are you afraid of being lonely?" she asked.

"I'm always lonely. I don't look to you to cure that."

She asked him what caused this permanent loneliness. He said a sense of never quite belonging anywhere, of always having an empty space inside that nothing could fill.

"But surely, you're happy sometimes?" she asked.

"Often. You can be lonely and happy at the same time."

"Oh, I don't see how."

"When you accept loneliness and no longer fight it, the door opens for things that can bring you pleasure."

"You make me feel sad."

He put his arms around her. She held him back. Then she stepped away and returned to her place on the sofa. She said she was hungry. She'd eaten practically nothing all day. He offered to take her out somewhere. She asked what he had in the refrigerator.

"Let's go take a look," he said.

He led her by the hand into the kitchen. The refrigerator had a roasted chicken; a carton of eggs; several kinds of cheese, some sliced, some in a block; champagne; carrots; a nice cabbage; a head of lettuce; and some sliced roast beef. The bread box had a fresh loaf. The butter dish had a new stick. Alistair kept things in good shape. Edith offered to make them scrambled eggs. Henry said that sounded delightful. She told him to sit down at the kitchen table and keep her company. He did. Where might she find an apron? He said he had no idea. She opened a drawer, then another, and discovered one, freshly washed and ironed. She slipped it on. It came down to mid-calf. As she brought the ties around her back, he stood up, took them from her, and tied them himself.

"Thank you," she said. Rather than ask him where the skillet was, she looked through the cupboards and drawers until she found it. It was a nice kitchen. The cabinets were new. Everything was new. She mentioned this to Henry, and he said it had all been remodeled just before they moved in.

"That was lucky," she said.

"Not really. I'm the owner. I didn't see why we shouldn't make it nice."

"You own the apartment?"

"Of course."

"You say that as if it's normal. You forget, most people don't have your kind of money."

Henry shrugged. She cracked six eggs into a bowl. She sliced bread and put it in the toaster. A few minutes later, everything was ready. She found some silverware. It wasn't as nice as what they'd had at Thanksgiving. This must be the everyday set, but still, it was much nicer than what she and Walter used.

Henry said her eggs were delicious.

"Alistair always overcooks them. What's your secret?" he asked.

"I stir them constantly."

"Ah. Genius!"

"You're easy to please."

"Doesn't Walter like your cooking?"

"I don't know."

"I'm sorry. I shouldn't have brought him up."

Edith said he was likely to be a regular topic of conversation. Henry agreed. He put the dishes in the sink. Edith offered to wash them, and Henry told her not to be silly. Alistair would take care of them.

"I don't know how I'll like living with a butler," Edith said.

"I imagine you'll get used to it."

"Won't he disapprove of our arrangement?"

"Is there to be an arrangement, then?"

The telephone rang. Henry went on sitting until the third ring, then he stood up and went over to the wall and picked up the receiver. After he said, "Hello?" he was quiet while the caller talked for what felt like a long time, but probably it was less than a minute.

"It's Walter," Henry said. Edith went to the phone.

"Hello," she said.

"What the hell are you doing? Someone said you and Henry just left the party without telling anyone."

"You're having an affair with Babs and I'm not putting up with it."

"We went through all that!"

"Walter, stop. I saw how cozy you two were. The game's up."

"You're being hysterical. Calm down."

"I'm perfectly calm."

He wanted to know what she was doing at Henry's. She said she just had some eggs and toast. He demanded she come home at once. She said she wouldn't, and if he had any idea about showing up there in some caveman attempt to drag her off, he could forget it. Her voice had taken on an edge that brought Henry over to where she stood. He took the phone from her.

"Walter, be a good chap and let dear Edith have some time to clear her head. I'll take good care of her, I promise," he said.

Edith heard Walter's voice on the other end. He went on for a bit until Henry interrupted him and said, "Yes, I understand. Goodbye," and hung up.

They went back into the living room. Alistair had returned.

"Ah, please make up the south guest room. Mrs. Sloan will be staying with us for a little while," Henry told him.

"Very good Milord."

Alistair went down the hall where the bedrooms were. Edith sat down on the sofa and put her face in her hands. She felt hollow. Soon an awful feeling would rush in. It always did. She made herself focus on her breathing. She opened her eyes. Henry was sitting where he'd been before, watching her.

"We'll have to do something about getting your things out of your apartment," he said.

"I'll stay here tonight. Then I'll go home and decide what to do."

"As you wish."

"What did Walter say to you?"

"That you were out of your head, not seeing things clearly, running off half-cocked."

"Well, he's got his story all set, hasn't he? He'll be telling everyone the same thing before too long."

"I'm afraid that's probably true."

Alistair returned to say the room was in order. Henry thanked him. When he'd gone, he and Edith sat for a long time, not talking, watching the fire die down. Then she said she must sleep. Henry walked with her down the hall, opened the door, and kissed her on the cheek.

"Good night," he said.

"Good night. And thank you."

The bed was soft. She sank into it without removing her dress. She didn't drift off for a long time. The last thing she remembered was the small clock on the table by the bed chiming it was one in the morning.

chapter eighteen

Edith waited until she was certain Walter was at class before going home. As she unlocked the door, came in, and saw for sure he wasn't there, she was disappointed. He should have waited for her so he could plead his case, or beg forgiveness, anything to prove he cared about her feelings. Maybe he was ashamed to face her. Maybe he was with Babs, telling her the time had come to break it off, once and for all.

She packed a suitcase with as many clothes as she could stuff into it. The bed hadn't been made. The ashtray on the floor was full. Walter had had a bad night, too. Because he loved her and hated hurting her that way? Or because she'd thrown a wrench into his carefully laid plans? Her legs felt funny, and she sat down on the bed. The only thing that mattered was they couldn't go on living together.

She looked at her suitcase. Should she leave a note? The empty closet would tell him what he needed to know. She bent down to pick up the ashtray and put it in her lap. Then she lit a cigarette. She wanted to feel like she was escaping, not running away. Henry had told her over coffee he would agree to whatever she wanted. She trusted him completely without understanding exactly why. Probably because he didn't expect anything from her. He seemed like a man who had learned to get by without relying too much on other people.

The door opened and a moment later, Walter stood in the doorway to the bedroom. He hadn't shaved or showered. His clothes were wrinkled. She took in these details without looking at his eyes.

"You came back," he said.

"Not for long."

"You're leaving then?"

"Why shouldn't I?"

He sat down next to her, causing the old springs to creak. He said nothing was going on between him and Babs.

"Walter. I'm not stupid. It's so obvious you're involved. Why do you deny it?"

He nodded helplessly. "I never wanted it to be like this," he said.

"Like what? My figuring it out? Or getting involved with her in the first place?"

"Both, I guess."

"You *guess*?"

"It all just got so out of control."

She looked into his bloodshot eyes. She said it didn't matter, they couldn't possibly go on living together. He nodded miserably. She said she'd be in touch when she had organized herself, and she could be reached at Henry's.

"Are you sleeping with him?" Walter asked.

"No."

He looked at his hands. There was an ink stain on the middle finger of his right hand. What had he been writing? Something to her, or to Babs?

She put out her cigarette and handed him the ashtray. She stood up.

"You won't tell anyone, will you?" he asked.

"Tell what?"

"That we're having problems."

"Stop worrying about how things look and start thinking about how they *are*."

She left the apartment and went down to the sidewalk. The suitcase wasn't hard to carry. She got on the train, even though Henry had given her money for a cab. She'd told him to keep it. Staying with him was one thing, but she didn't want him to support her financially. She thought of the check she'd have soon when the sale of her old home was final. Her mother should know about her change in status and where to send her letters from now on. What would she tell Kathleen? Would she still attend her wedding? How was that going to play out?

She didn't want to think about that. The future was an abstract concept. What mattered was now.

Henry said she looked as if things hadn't gone well. She said Walter crept in at the last moment, and she'd had no choice but to speak with him. Henry said it wouldn't be the last time. These things took a while to resolve.

"You mean, divorce?" she asked.

"That's how Americans end their marriages. In England, we tend to separate."

"If you have money, you mean. I'm sure less well-off people in your country head to court just as we do."

"Let's not quarrel."

"We're not. I'm just tired and angry."

"It's normal you should feel that way."

They were in his study where he'd been scratching out a term paper. She walked around and looked at all the beautifully bound books on the shelves. She wanted to spend hours in that room and that brought to mind the bookstore. Not having to wait on Walter would free her. No more watching the clock and thinking about getting dinner on the table. The idea was startling.

"I just realized I'll have more time to devote to the store," she said.

"I suspect that's true."

"I want authors to come and read, whether they're published or not."

"I should think published would be better. Then, you could carry and sell their books."

She said in any case, she hadn't been approached by anyone besides Miss Levy, but there must be a way to reach out to local writers. Henry suggested a simple notice in the store window. Had she thought about how many people the store could accommodate? Would she serve refreshments? As with anything, the devil was in the details.

He lit himself a cigarette. The cigarette case was exquisite, with an inlay of lapis and turquoise. When he saw Edith looking at it, he said an uncle had gotten it in India during the First World War. She asked if she could hold it for a moment. He gave it to her. It fit perfectly in the palm of her hand. She returned it to him.

"What about a small press?" she asked.

"You want to become a publisher?"

"Maybe."

"Tricky business, I imagine."

"Well, I'm no doubt getting ahead of myself. First things first."

"And what are those?"

"Henry, you ask a lot of questions."

"Do I?"

She smiled at him. He smiled back.

She thought of how bad Walter looked. Where had he been, anyway? He had no idea how to take care of himself. He always sought out other people to help him. Maybe he was aware he wasn't a capable person in certain ways and was simply being practical. Desperation informed so much of what he did, she realized. He'd always been like that. What was he so deeply afraid of?

"Tell me something," she said.

"Of course."

"What's expected of a man, generally, I mean?"

"I'm not sure I understand."

"What is a man expected to do in life? To be?"

Henry leaned back in his chair and regarded her across the room. The morning light improved him, she thought. He seemed both relaxed and alert. Was it due to her presence, Mary's absence, or both?

Men are supposed to succeed, he said. To carry on whatever tradition they'd been born into. To do their duty, not complain, and take it on the chin.

"Are you ever afraid?" she asked.

"Yes."

"Of what?"

"Oh, I don't know, really. Not living life to the fullest, I'd say. Missing out on something important."

"What's important?"

"Edith, you ask a lot of questions."

She continued to stroll along the shelves. She took down a small book whose leather was worn. The gilt lettering had faded. It was a first edition of a collection of poems by Percy Shelley.

"This must have set you back a pretty penny," she said.

"Which?"

She brought the book to him. He said it had belonged to his father, who had quite an extensive collection.

"And you came by this how?" Edith asked.

"Well, the fact of the matter is, I stole it."

"Oh, stop."

"It's true. He didn't know I'd taken it."

"Did he ever discover the loss?"

"He did. He wasn't a bit pleased. But he was glad it stayed in the family."

"Do you get along, you and your father?"

Here Henry's mood altered. He said his father wanted certain things from him he found hard to give. It was assumed he'd go into business of some kind and not just live idly. Henry had no interest in business. After the war and his work in intelligence, he wanted rewarding pursuits. He was expected to fill his older brother's shoes after he died, to help his father's ambitions, and he didn't care to. He wanted to live his own life.

"Your brother died in the war?" Edith asked.

"Oh, no. He died years before from scarlet fever. He was only eleven at the time. I was nine."

"I'm sorry."

"Thank you."

Henry's father had invested in housing and automobiles during the war and made a filthy bundle. Henry didn't have the slightest interest in helping him make more, and his grandmother's legacy let him break with tradition.

"Is that why you came here? To get away?" Edith asked.

"Partly. Mary and I weren't very happy there, and I hoped a new place would give us a new start."

"But it didn't."

"No."

Edith hoped he didn't think she was prying, but why had he strayed from his marriage? Was it just because of what failed to happen in the bedroom?

"No. Mary isn't a warm person," he said.

"I thought English women weren't supposed to be warm."

"Perhaps the word I should have used is *loving*."

"She didn't love you?"

"I don't think she knows how to love anyone."

"Not even her own brother?"

"She hates her brother."

That was another complicated wrinkle in their lives, he said. George, despite his injuries, became an instant hero. Mary felt overshadowed. Then she was supposed to take care of him, even after she married because she had no children of her own.

"She's not really going back to England to help him, then, is she?" Edith asked.

"No."

"To do what, then?"

"Make her own life, I suppose. One that doesn't involve romantic demands."

Edith said that didn't sound like much of a life to her. Henry held out his hand. She went to him and took it. He brought her hand to his lips, kissed it, and let go.

"You're silly," she said.

"No doubt."

"But sweet."

"Do you really think so?"

"Well, yes. And I hope I'm right."

Edith wandered over to the window and looked out. She asked if Walter spoke of her much during their weekly lunches.

"Quite a bit," Henry said.

"Must have been awfully dull."

"On the contrary. I came to see how unhappy you both were."

"Please explain."

He said Walter was worried she wasn't content in their marriage. Oh, he never came out and said so, but he referred to a worrisome restlessness, irritability, and a nagging sense he'd disappointed her deeply.

"I thought only women talked about their marriages," Edith said.

"We go about it a bit more obliquely."

Henry said Walter thought she had deep issues with her father, and these lay at the heart of her reluctance to be a wife.

"How Freudian," she said.

"Did you have issues with your father?"

"Other than his being a monster and making me and mother miserable? Not at all."

"You don't have to go into that if you don't want to."

"Some other time. Right now, I should probably go and unpack."

"I should think Alistair took care of that for you."

"Well, bless Alistair."

Her clothes were hung in the closet. Her slips, stockings, nightgowns, and panties were folded neatly in the dresser drawers. She didn't like the idea of Alistair handling her things like that, but then she supposed he was used to it. He'd put her toothbrush in the bathroom, and thoughtfully donated a new tube of toothpaste, along with a bar of soap. The towels that hung on the racks were soft and thick. The writing desk in the corner had been stocked with a small stack of good-quality stationery, envelopes, and even a sheet of stamps. There was a lovely, red-lacquered fountain pen, too. Alistair thought of everything, didn't he?

Edith sat and wrote a letter to her mother in which she said she'd left Walter and thought the break was permanent. She stopped for a moment to reflect on her mother's letters to her the summer before, urging her to return to her marriage and cautioning her about life as a divorced woman. Given what she'd learned of her mother's own marriage, Edith was sure her mother was simply saying what she was supposed to say. While Edith understood that, she wished her mother had taken her side. It would have been impossible to do, with her father still in the world. Edith saw that now.

Next, she wrote to Kathleen, gave her the essential points, and said she didn't know if she'd be coming to her wedding. She wanted to but didn't want to cause any awkwardness. She stressed Walter had been having an affair with the wife of a fellow law student and this was why Edith had moved out. Again, she stopped, pen poised above the page. Should she tell Kathleen the truth about her own misdeeds?

What good would it do? She didn't want to alienate her. She was someone she wanted to stay close to as the years went by.

She didn't know which return address to put, so she used the store's. She stamped the envelopes. She would ask Alistair to mail them for her.

Henry knocked discreetly on her door, although it wasn't closed. He wanted to know if there were anything special she felt like doing.

"I'd like to go to bed and read all day."

"Why don't you, then? I can let you know when it's time for lunch."

"Why are you being so kind?"

"Because I like talking to you. It's not easy to find someone who can converse without passing judgment."

"True."

She went into his study and chose Wharton's *The Age of Innocence* from the shelf. For the next few hours she was lost in an earlier world, but one just as circumscribed as her own.

The days went by. Walter sent her a brief, miserable letter, addressed care of Henry, in which he said he couldn't live without her, but if her mind were made up, they should probably get serious about next steps. He asked if she wanted him to forward her mail. She replied he should send everything to the store.

A few days later she was surprised to receive a letter from Walter's father. She braced herself and tore open the envelope.

Edith:

I'm sorry things didn't work out between you two. Forgive my saying so, but I always felt you were too good for him. His mother and sister would call upon God himself to strike me dead, were they to know I'd written these words. I'm sure he will be all right, in time. I know you will be, too.

P.S. I was sorry to hear about your father.

The next was from her mother, who said she understood Edith's frame of mind and asked if there were anything she could do. She wanted to know about Henry, and what his presence in her life was likely to mean. She closed by saying the proceeds from the house would come next week. Did she want her to send the check to Edith's new address, or the bookstore? She sent her love and said she hoped they would see each other again very soon.

Edith realized a tear had rolled down her cheek, reading her mother's hand. They had always quietly understood each other. Maybe now, with so many obstacles out of the way, their relationship would be more open and happier.

She helped Patricia unpack and display several titles that had arrived over the weekend. They talked about the coming summer, though it was still two or three months off. Edith wanted to hire permanent sales help and not rely on the college girls.

"Permanent staff will cost more," Patricia said. She looked worn out again, and Edith asked how Mr. Samson was faring. The way Patricia shook her head in reply cast a grim mood. Then Edith said regarding new staff, she was soon to come into a bit of money, and more things would become possible. She mentioned the possibility of setting up a small publishing venture. Patricia thought that sounded wonderful.

Alone in the office, Edith combed through the ledger, looking closely again at all the costs the store incurred. She reflected on the sum she was to receive and decided to ask Henry to sell her the store outright. Mary would have to agree, but she'd leave that to Henry.

Walter wasn't an obstacle because his name had never gone on the documents. He stopped asking about it. His affair with Babs no doubt distracted him. It was a surprise he was managing to get up, go to class, and complete his assignments.

Edith thought of Andy. How was he faring through all this? She looked up his number in the telephone book and dialed it. If Babs answered, she'd hang up. Andy answered. She identified herself.

"Mrs. Sloan, what a pleasure," he said.

"Please, call me Edith."

"Edith."

"I know this may sound odd, and I hope you'll forgive my being so open with personal news, but I wanted to let you know that I've left Walter."

"I see."

"On account of, well, you know."

"Babs."

"Yes."

"I take it you were aware of the situation."

"I had my suspicions."

They paused. Edith begged for his patience once again as she asked what his plans were.

"You mean, will I ask her for a divorce?" he asked.

"Yes."

"She's already asked me for one. She and Walter have been talking, apparently."

"Do you think she wants to marry him?"

"I honestly couldn't say. We don't talk much these days. We're in separate rooms. Have been for a while."

"I'm sorry."

He said he was glad Edith called and hoped she would stay in touch. Then he had to go and hung up.

A dismal wave of panic washed through her. Was her marriage really over? Wanting something and having it stare you in the face were different things. She told herself it would just take getting used to, the idea of being a single woman again.

Henry wasn't in when she returned. Alistair said he was still on campus. He asked if Edith cared for a drink, and she said not at the moment. Then she said if he ever needed any help in the kitchen, to let her know. He thanked her, but she could tell he was mildly offended by her offer. Her clothes had come back from Henry's dry cleaner and were hung up for her. There was another letter from Walter, saying if she had no objection, he wanted to terminate the lease on their apartment a couple of months early if he could get the landlady to agree. He saw no reason not to look for a place closer to his new job once he graduated. He said it looked as if she'd taken her things, but what about the books? He'd like some of them, of course, but if there were any she was particularly keen to keep, she should let him know. His business-like tone depressed her. At the end he wrote, *I miss you terribly. Babs thinks I'm being a huge sap,* and she felt even worse.

She lay down and continued to read *The Age of Innocence*, but the longing of Newland Archer for Countess Olenska pulled her down, especially when she realized his wife, May, most certainly knew of or at least suspected his infatuation.

It was almost six when she heard Henry return. She went down the hall to speak to him. Alistair was hanging up his coat. Henry didn't have the briefcase he usually took to campus. Edith asked where he'd been, and he ushered her into the living room.

"I had a drink with Walter. Actually, several," Henry said.

"Oh, dear."

"It was my idea. I thought we should be frank with each other."

"And what did this frankness entail?"

"I told him you were welcome to stay here as long as you pleased, and we were not romantically involved."

"And?"

"He didn't believe me."

"Oh, who cares what he believes?"

"Are you sure you feel that way?"

"Sometimes. When I don't feel awful."

Henry wandered over to the liquor cart, and just stood staring at it. Edith said she wouldn't mind a sherry if it weren't too much trouble. He got it for her.

"Henry, you're out of sorts. Was it just seeing Walter?" Edith asked.

"I'm not sure, to tell you the truth."

"Do you regret inviting me to stay?"

"Not in the least."

"Then, what? Are you missing Mary?"

"I do miss her, but not inordinately."

Edith sipped her drink. As before, she found it delicious and calming. When Henry finally sat down, Edith asked if school were troubling him.

"I think I'm tired of winter," he said.

"I understand. It's a dreadful season."

He watched her hold her drink. She said she was thinking of buying the bookstore from him and making herself the sole owner.

"How?" he asked. She explained about the money coming to her. She hoped to look into establishing the press after that. There was much research to be done on that score. It felt a bit daunting, to be honest.

"I'm sure you're up to the task," Henry said.

Edith put her glass on the table and leaned back. She was exhausted. She thought about Walter's letter and the cooler tone he took. He was moving forward faster than she was. But then, he'd had a head start.

"My dear, I didn't mean to make you sad. Please don't cry," Henry said.

"It's all my fault."

"Don't be ridiculous."

"No, I mean it. If I had loved him the way he needed to be loved, this would never have happened."

"You can't know that for sure."

She cried for a little longer. Then she wiped her nose with the tissue she had shoved just inside the sleeve of her dress. What drove her mad, she said, was wondering if he knew she had been unfaithful to him, first. When someone felt justified in doing wrong, it was easier.

"Do you speak from experience?" Henry asked.

"I suppose I do. The first time I cheated on Walter was because he didn't want to go to bed with me before we got married. I was still a virgin, and the thought of still being one at my wedding was just too awful. And I liked him, Reynolds, the man I got involved with. Only he turned out to be married, too."

"Infidelity everywhere."

"Yes."

She talked about Philip, and how it had been sudden and crazy. They were drunk and lost themselves in the moment. There were times afterward when she thought of calling him and begging him to continue the affair, even though the logistics were almost insurmountable.

"But reason prevailed," Henry said.

She nodded.

She said she'd been thinking a lot about her father, too, and wondered if his cruelty to her had ruined her as a woman. Maybe Walter had touched on something important there. Maybe she was incapable of being faithful. Maybe sex was too important.

"Sex can never be too important," Henry said.

Edith was surprised to find herself blushing.

"Oh, Henry, you're a rare bird," she said.

She begged his understanding in what she was going to say next. Walter was a dud in bed. An absolute dud. She didn't understand how Babs could stand it unless of course, he was more skilled with her. Maybe she inspired him in some way Edith hadn't.

"That's something you'll never know," Henry said.

"Then why is it great with one person and terrible with another?"

"Magic, for want of a better word."

Edith said she was tired and might just skip dinner. Henry urged her to try to eat something later. He'd check in, but if she preferred, he'd leave her alone.

She went to her room, closed the door, undressed, and took a long shower. She toweled her hair until it was just damp. She put on her bathrobe and sat at the vanity, considering her reflection. If only she could see behind her own eyes and untangle her own peculiar truth. She lay on the bed and hoped to fall asleep. She didn't. Her thoughts were everywhere but slowed after a time. Her new press would publish only poetry, at least to begin. She'd not served that art by giving up her studies. Maybe now, she could.

She enjoyed how quiet the apartment was. The old place in Cambridge was often assaulted by street noise. Walter always said it made him feel alive and full of memories of Washington. Edith didn't care for city life much. She wondered if one day Henry might be tempted to buy in the country.

Was she really doing this, assuming there was a future with a nice man who'd given her a place to stay? Not just that, one who'd been open with her in ways Walter never was. If things didn't work out, and they very well might not, especially if she didn't grow to love him, honesty would be important. So would kindness.

She got up, opened her door just enough so he'd know she was awake, lay back down, and picked up her book.

THE END

about the author

Anne Leigh Parrish lives in a forest in the South Sound Region of Washington State. She is the author of the *moon won't be dared*; *a winter night*; *what nell dreams*; *maggie's ruse*; *the amendment*; *women within*; *by the wayside*; *what is found, what is lost*; *our love could light the world*; and *all the roads that lead from home*. Find her online at anneleighparrish.com.

about the press

Unsolicited Press is rebellious, much like the city it calls home: Portland, Oregon. Founded in 2012, the press supports emerging and award-winning writers by publishing a variety of literary and experimental books of poetry, creative nonfiction, fiction, and everything in between.

Learn more at unsolicitedpress.com. Find us on twitter and instagram: @unsolicitedp